MYSTERIOUS WAYS

LAKE CHELAN BOOK 6

SHIRLEY PENICK

MYSTERIOUS WAYS

Copyright 2019 by Shirley Penick

All rights reserved. No part of this work may be reproduced in any fashion without the express written consent of the copyright holder.

MYSTERIOUS WAYS is a work of fiction. All characters and events portrayed herein are fictitious and are not based on any real persons living or dead.

Photography by Reggie Deanching of RPlusM Photo

Cover Models: Kristen Hope Mazzola and Bryan Snell

Back cover photo by Tim and Diane Penick

Editing by Carol Tietsworth

Formatting by Cora Cade

CONTACT

Contact me:
www.shirleypenick.com

www.facebook.com/ShirleyPenickAuthor

To sign up for Shirley's New Release Newsletter, send email to shirleypenick@outlook.com, subject newsletter.

To my brother Tim and his wife Diane. You have both been a great support and have encouraged me, so much, in my writing journey.

Answering questions of all kinds about firefighting, cattle ranching, lawyers, and many more than I can remember. You've driven me all over the mountains of Colorado whenever I come to visit and have given me some excellent pictures to use in promotion.

Last, but not least, the antics of your kids have given me much fodder to fill my books. Ha. Thanks so much for your love and support. Love you!

CHAPTER 1

Scott Davidson finished putting in the last screw on the new announcements board the council had purchased for the church. He personally thought it was a waste of time and money, but someone in the congregation had asked a board member to bring it before the group to vote on. He'd not even heard the idea until it was brought up in the meeting. That had irritated him, the fact that they'd gone around him. But people—even church members—could be sneaky and devious. Just because a person came to church every Sunday did not make them perfect. He was a prime example. He had enough of his own failings, and he was the pastor for goodness sake.

He slipped the electric screwdriver back into the tool belt and climbed down off the ladder, when the door burst open and a young woman rushed inside. She stopped for just a moment as her eyes adjusted and a zing of attraction hit Scott, stopping his breath and flooding his body with desire. She was only about five feet tall with long nearly black hair, that she had jacked up into a pony tail. Her brown eyes sparkled as she saw him, and she jolted a second before smiling tentatively at him. She had a wide mouth that was made for kissing and… *whoa, reign it in home boy, do not go down that path.*

She looked around the church foyer and then back at him. "Can you tell me where to find the pastor of this church?"

He cleared his throat to give him a second longer to regain his composure. "That would be me, Scott Davidson, at your service. How can I help you?" He held out his hand to shake hers.

She frowned, but shook his hand. "You're the pastor? Aren't you a little young for that?"

Her handshake sent a bolt of electricity shooting through his body, short-circuiting his brain. He couldn't even remember what she'd said to him. *Fuck* he was standing there like a moron, lusting after this woman, and swearing. He cleared his throat again. "Sorry, got some dust from hanging the board." And now he was lying. *Great, batting a thousand, Davidson, get it together.*

She stood there looking at him skeptically. So, he said, "Yes, I'm the pastor, my dad retired a few years ago and I took over for him. I was a late in life child, he was ready to retire, so I stepped in at a younger age than normal." Now he was babbling. *Dear God, just strike me down, please.*

God didn't strike him down, which meant he had to deal with it. "So, what can I do for you?"

She folded her arms and didn't say anything for a moment as though weighing her options. Then she breathed out a huge sigh and her shoulders drooped. "I need to talk to someone. And since you're a pastor you have to keep our discussion confidential, right?"

That snapped him out of the craziness, this woman needed his help, not his lust. "As long as no one is suicidal, or a child is in danger. I'm a mandatory reporter in some cases. Pretty much anything else is confidential, yes."

She looked around the room again. "Do you have an office or something?"

Well hell, he was still being clueless. Normally he would not meet alone with a person of the opposite sex. But he didn't have any choice today, there was no one else in the church, since it was a day the church was normally closed. He'd come in on his day off only to hang the cork board. But he wasn't going to send her away when she needed his help. "Of course, come with me."

She pointed to the ladder and drill laying on the floor. "Do you need to take care of that, first?"

Scott shook his head. "Nope, it'll be fine right where it is. Follow me."

As they walked to his office, he gave himself a stern talking to. She needed help and he needed to get his head straight and give her the ear she asked for, no more craziness.

NICOLE ROMAN FOLLOWED the man who said he was the pastor at the church. He sure didn't look like any pastor she'd ever seen. With his piercing gray-blue eyes, dark hair cut close and a trimmed beard, he was a handsome man. He was easily a foot taller than her own five-foot-one stature, and he looked damn good in his jeans and tool belt.

His handshake had been firm and warm, but it had sent little tremors through her body and she had to wonder what that was about. She'd never had that happen before. As she followed him down a hall, she got a whiff of him. It was a pleasant scent of soap, and man.

On one hand she was disappointed he was a pastor,

someone to hook up with for a couple of days might relieve some of the stress she was under. It had been a nightmarish few months. On the other hand, if she didn't talk to someone about what she was going through, she might explode.

He seemed like a nice enough guy and had said he would keep what she had to say confidential. Even if he did blab, this town was so tiny the news wouldn't go far.

She remembered a vacation here a dozen years ago. There hadn't been much to do, then. Now, the town had an amusement park, and the city park had been updated with a climbing tower that looked like a dragon. And most of the shop owners were dressed in costumes. She had no idea why. If she was here long enough, she would find out what was going on.

The pastor—did he say his name was Scott?—opened a door and ushered her into a room. It looked like a typical office, there were some diplomas on the wall that did—in fact—pronounce Scott Davidson was a pastor. Well, that was good. There were also pictures of family members and friends. She walked over to a set of framed pictures depicting a fishing boat. She found him on it along with other people. They seemed to be having a great time.

He walked over to her and pointed to some of the other people naming names and saying they'd had a competition and their team had lost.

She turned her head. "You wouldn't have lost if I'd been on the team."

A slow grin slid across his face. "You're a fisherman? Uh, fisherwoman?"

"I am and if I do say so myself, I'm damn good at it. Oh, sorry for the language, darn good at it."

His smile grew. It was a killer and did things to her insides she didn't want to think about. "I've heard the word before. Even used it here and there, and not only in a sermon."

She cleared her throat and moved down the line of pictures and away from the hot man. But the rest of the pictures didn't interest her, so she turned toward his desk to take a seat in a visitor's chair.

He followed suit and sat in his office chair, dropping the tool belt on the floor next to his desk. Then he looked around kind of lost and asked, "Would you like a bottle of water or a soda or something? I don't have any coffee on, I bought one on the way in from the bakery."

"No, I'm fine. So, you said as long as someone wasn't suicidal or hurting children you could keep this discussion confidential."

"I can. As long as no one is in danger."

Not exactly the same thing. But as far as she knew no one had been harmed, at least so far. "Can you just listen to start with, and ask questions at the end?"

"Yes, I can do that. Can I take notes, in case I need to remember something?"

She thought that would be all right. So, she nodded.

He drew a steno pad over and picked up a pen. "Can we start with your name? Sorry I know that's a question, but it's hard not to wonder."

Nicole puffed out an exasperated breath, she hadn't realized she'd never introduced herself. "Of course. Silly of me not to remember to introduce myself. My name is Nicole, Nicole Roman."

"Nice to meet you. Nicole. I'm ready when you are."

She took a deep breath. She wasn't ready, not in the least, but she needed advice and maybe even help, so she didn't have a choice. Her brother, her sweet brother, needed help and she was the only one who knew him well enough to get him that help.

"It all started when my parents died nine months ago.

They were in a car accident, another driver fell asleep at the wheel and swerved into my parent's lane. They were killed instantly in a head-on collision."

Pastor Davidson was immediately sympathetic. "I'm so sorry."

She held up a hand. "Thanks, but that's just the beginning. Or maybe it's the middle. Anyway, I'm okay, it's been hard for me without them, but I'm dealing. My brother, on the other hand, is not."

Pastor Scott sat back in his chair and made a go on motion with his hand.

"My brother Kent is a few years younger than I am, five in fact. He's always had some issues, but my mom and dad got him help when he was little, and they kept him steady. He had a good job, a girlfriend and was doing really well, until they died. Then he kind of lost it."

Nicole squirmed in her chair. She wanted to talk about it, but then again to admit what was going on, would be to put her brother on the radar. He was a good man and had been a sweet boy, they'd been close growing up, despite the age difference. She had to remember that he needed help and he wasn't going to get it unless they could find him.

"He tried to maintain for a while, but he couldn't fight it without my parents. He fought with his girlfriend and quit his job. Kent left town and I wondered if I should go after him. I didn't right away, but after I got wind of the second incident, I didn't have a choice."

So cold, she felt so cold and alone. Wrapping her arms around herself she squeezed her arms to give herself the strength to go on. "I quit my job and have been trying to catch up with Kent for the last eight months. He seems to be getting worse. I need help finding him to get him back into counseling."

Scott asked, "How can I help?"

"I think he's here, in Chedwick. It looks like he's visiting all the vacation spots we went to as children. We came here about ten years ago, it was one of the last family vacations I went with them on, where we were all together. I started working in the summers after that."

"Why do you think he's here?"

"He's going in the order of our vacations on this side of the country. I'm worried when he leaves here, he'll go to the east coast, from the vacations on that side of the country. Mom kept a scrap book that he seems to be following."

"But that still doesn't say why he might be here and why you're so worried about it."

She had to finish. He needed to know. She had to stop Kent. This small town might be her only hope to find him. It wasn't big enough to hide in and she'd seen police when she'd gotten off the ferry. They'd been checking on the people leaving, so there was a good chance he was still here.

She gripped the arms of the chair. "Kent is a pyromaniac."

Pastor Scott sat forward in his chair, his eyes boring into hers, but he waited for her to finish.

She continued in a low voice. "I think, no, I know he's been starting fires in the vacation places. I'm fairly certain he started the one you had last week. I was on my way after the house fire you had at the beginning of the summer. But I kept running out of money and had to stop to work long enough for gas and food. I blew through all my savings almost immediately. And I wasn't as concerned about the house fire, mostly because a house fire isn't his normal thing. He primarily sets deserted buildings on fire. So, I didn't think it was him. But I didn't hear of anything else, and this was the next vacation place we came to, so I kept coming this way."

Shock covered Scott's face, but then he frowned. His voice was stern and cold when he said, "You think your brother is the one that started the two fires we've had this summer?"

He looked furious, but she nodded. "I need to find him and get him into counseling."

Scott muttered something that sounded like, "Or into jail."

Fear drenched her. She pleaded with him. "Can you help me? He needs help, not jail. But regardless, he needs to be stopped before someone gets hurt."

Pastor Scott ran his hands over his head through his hair. She watched him battle what he wanted to do versus what she'd asked him. A shrill tone sounded from a radio in the corner which startled her. A voice started speaking. "Trash fire in the city park. Caller reports it is contained to one barrel."

Nicole gasped. Oh no, it couldn't be, please let it not be true. "You're a firefighter?"

He nodded, and her stomach sank. She'd just ratted out her brother to a firefighter. No, no, no, this was horrible. She jumped to her feet, but the man was quick. He came around the desk and took her arms.

"Nicole, wait. I'm not going to say anything. At least not yet. Let's talk this through. No one wants to harm your brother, but you're right. He has to be stopped."

She didn't know what to do. She wanted to run but looking into his eyes she just felt like she had to trust him, that she *could* trust him. Nicole decided she would give him a few more minutes, so she sat back down.

This time Scott sat next to her in the other visitor's chair. So, he could keep her from running? Probably. "Has he set two fires in any of the other locations?"

Nicole shook her head slowly. "No, he's only ever set one. At least I've never heard of a second one. He used to set fires to relieve stress. He's never hurt anyone with his fires. I was thinking that maybe when the first fire turned out to nearly hurt those people, that had caused more stress, so he stayed to complete his mission by finding something truly abandoned. I don't have any hard evidence, I simply know in my heart it's him."

Scott nodded. "That makes sense. Although it could mean he's escalating to multiple buildings. How long has he used fire in this way?"

"He started when he was really little, five or six. When my parents found out, they all went to counseling for years. When he hit his mid to late teens it seemed like the threat was over and he'd learned better coping skills. But those skills involved talking things over with mom and dad. When they died, he obviously couldn't transfer that to me or his girlfriend."

"And you think he started using fire again."

CHAPTER 2

Scott didn't know what to say or do. He wanted to help this woman and see her brother get the help he needed. He also wanted to call both the police and the head fire department personnel and give them the information. Both options fought, as he tried to determine which was right and best.

Could he convince her that letting the authorities know would be a good thing? If there were enough people with a description looking for this Kent guy, they would probably find him. That really would be best, but would she trust them? If he could explain everything the right way, the town would back him up. Good people lived here.

She didn't know that, though. It was his job to convince her. He prayed for guidance.

"You've taken on a lot of responsibility in trying to track down your brother. I would be happy to help."

Her shoulders relaxed, and a relieved smile lifted her lips. She was so beautiful he was stunned for a moment. He gave himself a mental shake. He had to admire her courage in seeking someone out to help her find her brother, it wouldn't be easy.

"You mentioned having to work on your way here. Do you have someplace to stay?"

The wariness was back in her eyes. "Not yet. I just got off the ferry, and saw the church, and came straight here."

"I hate to ask, but do you have money to rent a place?"

"Maybe for one night. I need to find work while I look for my brother."

She was in quite the predicament, he wondered what her skills were. Her stomach rumbled and he was feeling kind of hungry too. He should have Maureen order them some lunch, except Maureen wasn't out there at her desk and she wasn't coming back. She'd run off with some guy to Jamaica or Hawaii or somewhere. He was still in shock. Hey, wait a minute, maybe Nicole could take the job at least while she was still here in town.

"My secretary-slash-admin just left last week. Do you think you could take over for her for a while? Basically, it's just taking care of me, making coffee, ordering lunch, plus answering the phones, typing up the Sunday bulletin and sending any emails I need sent to the board of directors or whoever."

"What happened to the secretary?"

Scott shrugged, "She ran off with some tourist to Jamaica or Hawaii or Cabo, I don't know where exactly. I was too surprised to listen properly"

Nicole's eyebrows had climbed toward her hairline. "She ran off with a tourist? How long had she worked here?"

"Since before I was born. I'm pretty lost without her, she knew where everything was and everyone's contact information. I know nothing."

"So, she wasn't some young kid."

Not even close, she was old enough to know better. He

didn't want to be judgmental, but he thought it was the stupidest thing ever. The guy had only been in town a couple of weeks. How could anyone know they were in love after two weeks? "Nope, she will be sixty-eight next month."

A bright smile lit Nicole's face. "Wow, that's kind of cool. I mean to up and take off with some guy at that age. How old was he?"

"In his seventies, I think. She said it was her last chance for love and to see the world, and she was taking it." He felt like rolling his eyes at the foolishness of it all, but to each his own. It was Maureen's life not his and he did wish her every happiness.

"Good for her."

"Yeah, I guess, but I still need help. Even if you can only do it for a while. Maybe you could find out everything I need to know and help me get it together. And perhaps get us some lunch?"

Nicole laughed. "I suppose I can do that. I don't imagine you know where any of the hiring information is kept."

"Nope, the only things I have are her keys and the passwords for the computer and the answering service."

"Do you have anything in this town that delivers food? I could get started if I don't have to leave to feed you."

"The pizza shop delivers during the day in the summer. Only at night during the school year."

She shook her head. "Welcome to Mayberry."

Scott grinned, handed her the keys, the paper with the passwords on it, and twenty-five dollars. "I like meat, veggies are okay as long as the meat overpowers them. There might be a menu in her desk."

"Or online?"

"Sure… maybe… I have no idea. I usually just go there when I want food."

"Okay Andy, I'll get you some lunch."

He laughed at her teasing him, it felt good. She went out the door to take up residence in Maureen's desk. He still needed to decide what to do about bringing in the authorities to find her brother. But first he needed to eat, he didn't think well on an empty stomach and they could talk more over the meal.

~

NICOLE UNLOCKED the desk and booted up the computer. Coming into the church had been a good idea. She'd enlisted help to find her brother and she had gotten a job. Nicole had no idea what he was paying, but lunch was a great start.

She'd had a muffin early this morning before she got on the ferry. Leaving her car in Chelan and riding the passenger ferry was a lot cheaper than using the barge to get her car here. When her family had come ten years ago, they had been surprised to find that the ferry didn't take cars, only passengers.

The towns up-lake were small enough to walk to see everything or there was some public transportation to get people to their hotels. The ferry had not changed in the ten years, it was still only a passenger ferry. It was very odd to her to see lots of people walking on the ferry to spend the day traversing the lake.

Nicole didn't really like leaving everything she had with her in Chelan. But she thought she could go get it in a few days or at least after her first paycheck. She'd stuffed some of her clothes and a few toiletries into a backpack to bring along with her.

She still needed to find somewhere to sleep. But first she needed to get pizza to feed the hunky pastor, with the sexy eyes. She did indeed find a menu in the desk drawer, so she dialed the number.

"Pat's Pizza Palace, what kind of pie would you like today?"

Nicole realized she didn't even know the address of the church. "Hi um, I'm the new admin at the church."

"Well isn't that a quick answer to prayer? We all love Pastor Scott and he gives a great sermon. He's a good firefighter too and a cutie, but that man couldn't find his way out of a room with no windows and only one door. What's your name, girlfriend?"

"Um, Nicole. I don't know how long I'll be in town. But I'll be helping out for now."

"Good to meet you Nicole, I'm Sylvia and even if you've only got five minutes to spare it will be good for Scott."

"Seriously? He's that bad?" Nicole had thought maybe he was being kind in offering her the job, not believing he needed a keeper.

"Yes, yes he is. But he's as nice as can be, just hopelessly disorganized. I'm guessing you called to get some food in the man? Maureen always ordered a meat-lovers, with black olives and green peppers to get a couple of vegetables into him."

Nicole chuckled. "That sounds perfect. Can I also get a mixed green salad with ranch dressing? I would like a few more veggies."

"Sure thing, we'll send a little extra in case you can poke a couple of forks of it into Scott."

Nicole glanced back at Scott's door. "I don't know if I have much influence in that area, but I can try."

"Good for you. Are you going to be staying in the rectory? I think Maureen left it mostly tidy. Even with her running off to Tahiti, she didn't want to leave a mess for the next person."

The rectory? She didn't know anything about that. "We haven't talked about housing yet."

"That's because he'll never think about it. You bring it up. Tell him it's part of the salary and don't take one cent under twenty-five dollars an hour. The church can afford it. I'm on the governing board, so I know."

"Wow. Thanks so much, Sylvia." Nicole didn't know whether to be charmed by Sylvia deciding everything, or horrified. Was this part of the small-town lifestyle? It was a little freaky, but she had no intention of biting the hand that fed her.

"You're welcome, I'll get that pizza out to you soon. Call me if anything else comes up."

As Nicole hung up the phone, she marveled at all that had happened today. Twenty-five dollars an hour was a great wage for someone walking in off the streets and for a church. Having the rectory to sleep in would help too. Now if she could just find her brother and get him some assistance.

She unlocked the computer and there in the middle of the screen was a document that was titled "Everything you need to know to keep Scott organized" she smiled as she clicked it open.

Her smile grew wider as she read through it. Maureen had everything very well documented, an idiot could follow her instructions and keep the church running and Scott organized.

The very last line of the document had her laughing out loud, it read "Now I know that this file is simple enough for a child to follow and keep Scott and the church out of trouble, but don't let on that it's easy. I've worked for years to make both Scott, and his father, think I was slaving away. Don't blow it! You'll still earn your money, but not because of stress. Good luck and God bless. Maureen Black."

She printed out a copy to take and read over again tonight. A teenaged boy walked into the office carrying a large pizza box and a huge container of salad. There were several ranch packages, peppers, cheese, paper plates, napkins, and plastic-ware that were piled up on top of the salad.

The kid put the food down on the desk. "Sylvia said to tell you she would put the food on the church's tab."

Nicole took the five-dollar bill and handed it to the kid. "Well, here's your tip then. Tell Sylvia thanks."

"Thanks for the tip. Have a great day."

As the teenager left Nicole realized she *was* having a great day. Well, maybe not all the way to great but certainly better. The best day she'd had in nine months. She pushed the intercom button, *seriously an intercom in this day and age? Can we say Dark Ages*? When Scott answered she asked him where he wanted his lunch, he said he'd be right out.

She didn't think she'd even closed down the intercom before he was at her desk. He lifted the food and said, "Follow me."

They ended up in an eating area off what looked like a commercial kitchen. He set the food down on a table and walked over to one of the soda machines along one wall.

He put money in the machine and took out a cola. "What can I get for you? We have pretty much everything from bottled water, to juice of all kinds, to soda."

She looked over and saw he wasn't kidding. "Just water for me."

He shook his head but put the money in for a bottle of water. When he put it down in front of her, he said, "That's kind of boring."

She shrugged. "Maybe so, but it sounds good with the pizza."

"Suit yourself." He sat down next to her and took a couple of pieces of pizza. She put some salad on a plate and nudged it towards him.

He grimaced but didn't complain. Then he bowed his

head and said a quick prayer, which kind of shocked her. Even though she knew he was a pastor, he just didn't really act like one. Not that she knew what a pastor acted like, but still, shouldn't he have some kind of holy vibe going?

After the prayer, he took a huge bite of pizza, chewed maybe twice and washed it down with a guzzle of soda. The man had a body like a Greek god and ate like a nine-year-old. How could that be sexy? She had no idea, but it was.

~

NICOLE WAS LOOKING at him like he was a Neanderthal. He swallowed the salad he'd eaten, just for her, and asked, "What's wrong?"

She ducked her head. "Nothing's wrong. I was just, um, thinking, um… oh, Sylvia at the pizza place put the food on the church's tab. Here's your twenty back." Nicole fished the money out of her pocket and laid it on the table.

Scott didn't care about the money and still wondered what she'd been thinking, her cheeks had turned pink, so he knew there was more to it than the payment method for the pizza. He just waited.

"Sylvia also mentioned that maybe I could stay in the rectory."

"Of course, you can. Ever since our family outgrew the place when I was a kid, Maureen has lived there. Her husband died about the same time, so she was on her own and it all worked out perfectly. I have my own place, so I don't need it. I'll take you there after we eat."

"Great! That will be handy to work and live at the same location."

"Did you bring a car with you?"

She shook her head. "No, I left it in Chelan. I wanted to

get here as quick as I could, and I didn't have the money to get it on the barge."

Scott frowned. "Well, let's get that taken care of." He pulled out his phone and scrolled through his contacts. He told his buddy at the ferry landing what he wanted. Within a few seconds, it was all arranged. He'd had work not to roll his eyes at the girly hybrid she drove. They didn't even sell cars like that here in the mountains, clearly, she was a city girl. He had to concede that with her driving all over, it would have saved her a lot of money on gas.

He pushed end and looked up. "They'll come by and get your keys in a little while. The ferry will give them to the barge operator, and he will bring your car over on the trip tomorrow."

Nicole was clearly shocked at what had happened, but he didn't know why exactly, so he just started eating again.

Finally, she must have figured it out. "I'm confused. You can't function or run the church without an admin. You don't even know where she went when she left. And you clearly aren't really even interested in changing that. But within seconds you have my car all arranged, and it will be here tomorrow. What gives?"

He shrugged one shoulder. "I have lots of contacts that can do things for me. I only have to call them to make the arrangements. I'm not actually doing anything, really."

She shook her head at him and took another bite of pizza.

He decided maybe to continue this subject into her problem. "You know while you were getting us this fine lunch it did occur to me that we could maybe get some help to find your brother."

She stiffened, but he went on. "We've got a close-knit town and we all work together well. I was thinking that if we talked to a few key people and explained the situation that maybe we could join forces and find him. You know the police have the road and the ferry monitored. But if they had a picture or description of him, we might find him quicker."

"I want to get him help, but the police will want to arrest him."

"The police mostly want to stop him. Whether that's in jail or in counseling and monitored, they don't much care. None of us want to see him hurt anyone. At this point, all he's done is burn down abandoned buildings and one house. It might end up being a jail sentence, but it also might be exactly what you're looking for. If he escalates and hurts someone, it's jail for sure."

Her eyes were shuttered, and her body was rigid. He didn't want her to run off, so he decided to let her think about it.

"You just think about it. I'm not going to do or say anything." *Yet.* Changing the subject, he said, "So did Sylvia tell you how much I was paying you?"

He got a tiny smile out of her. "She did, she said no less than twenty-five dollars an hour."

He huffed, but a grin slid over his face when he said, "Highway robbery. But what Sylvia says, goes."

"I noticed she was very decisive and authoritative about it."

Shaking his head, he said, "Yes, she is, and she'd been bossing me around since I was in diapers. It's very hard to be an authority figure with people who wiped my butt when I was little."

That got a chuckle out of her and he felt like he'd won the lottery, this woman needed to smile, maybe even laugh. She'd had a rotten year. He was determined to help her, with the police or not. She needed a reason to smile, he wanted to assist her with that.

CHAPTER 3

Now that Nicole had eaten, and gotten a few things squared away in her life, she was starting to feel lethargic. She was feeling relaxed for the first time in what seemed like forever. Maybe she would even be able to sleep tonight without waking up every few hours worried about her brother and where she was going to get the money to continue tracking him.

Nicole still needed to think about Scott's suggestion to bring in the local authorities, but right this minute her brain had turned to mush. She tried to stifle a yawn but didn't manage to succeed.

Scott apparently noticed her fatigue. He stood and said, "If you're finished eating let me show you the rectory and you can use the afternoon to settle in. You can start work tomorrow." He shoved the twenty back towards her. "Keep that and use it for anything you might need."

She looked at it longingly, but pushed it back. "Oh, I couldn't..."

"Sure you can, if I'm paying you twenty-five dollars an hour that's less than an hour's pay and I know you spent that much time getting into the computer and ordering the pizza. In fact, take the leftovers with you. I've got my dart tournament tonight and will eat at the bar." He shut the containers and stacked them, putting the twenty on the top under the salad dressing pouches.

"You're in a dart tournament at a bar?" This man seemed the direct opposite of any and all ideas she had about pastors. She didn't think pastors normally hung out in bars.

"Yes, you might notice I don't fit the stereotype for preachers, which suits me just fine."

She stood to follow him. "I did notice, you seem like just a normal guy."

"Thank you. I try to be a normal guy, whose job is being a pastor. I'm not perfect, nor do I come close. I'm just like everyone else."

Nicole didn't agree with that statement. He was a whole lot sexier than most men she'd met. *Was that an inappropriate thought to have about a man of God?* It didn't really matter if it was, because the thought was firmly entrenched in her brain and had no intention of leaving. She hadn't seen any pictures of a wife or kids in his office, but she still wondered if he was married. She casually looked at his left hand, which was holding the pizza box. *Hmm, no wedding ring.* Which didn't always mean anything, there were lots of married men out there not wearing a ring.

"Let me grab my purse and backpack."

He waited until she got back with her things and then turned toward the door. "Come with me."

She gathered up the trash and dumped it in the can, and followed him out the door and down the hall. He turned to the left and went out a door at the back of the church. There was a black SUV in a tiny parking lot. On the other side of the parking lot sat a cute little cottage that was made of stone and had to be at least a hundred years old.

He walked up to the back door which led out into the parking lot. There was a long sidewalk leading from the street to the front door. She hadn't even noticed the little house when she'd hurried into the church. The church steeple had been visible from the ferry landing and as soon as she'd seen it, she'd decided to go straight there to get some guidance. It hadn't been a long walk, only a few blocks. But she'd not been looking around as she'd walked, she'd been totally focused on the church.

He stopped and said, "Did you bring the keys Maureen left?"

She fished them out of her pocket. "Yes."

"It's the green one, I think."

Nicole took the green one and tried it in the door, which swung open easily. The air was only a tiny bit stale. "When did you say Maureen left?"

"Last week. Thank God you came along when you did, so I didn't have to go it too long alone."

She rolled her eyes. "I think you could manage on your own, at least after a while."

"I don't really want to manage on my own." He gave a half shrug.

Men. She walked into the cottage which opened into the kitchen. Scott set the food down on the small table near the wall and turned on the lights. She looked around the space. It was a compact kitchen with all the normal appliances. It had a homey feel, but the colors and décor were somewhat dated. Not that she was complaining. There was a four-burner gas stove, a microwave and a coffee pot, that's all she needed to survive.

Scott led the way into the hall and turned left into the main room of the house. It was a long skinny room with a fireplace on one end and windows on both sides of the front door. They had what she thought people called Priscilla curtains on the windows. They were nearly sheer and draped picturesquely over the windows leaving a small bottom area open to the glass in the middle.

The furniture was comfortable looking but not new. It was clean and only a little worn. There were actual doilies on the tables which made her grin. She didn't think anyone used doilies anymore.

Scott rubbed the back of his neck. "It's a little old-fashioned."

"It's charming. Not exactly how I might decorate, but that doesn't make it bad."

He turned and led her down the hall to the master bedroom, which was across from the kitchen. It wasn't a large room, but it had a bed, a dresser, a couple of bedside tables and a walk-in closet. She set her backpack down on the bed which had a handmade quilt covering it and followed him back into the hall.

He pointed to a room with a twin-sized bed crammed into it. "Spare room." Then the bathroom in the middle and a small laundry room on the other side of the hall. "Bathroom, laundry."

"I think there are towels and stuff left, obviously sheets are on the beds. And since it's only been a few days since she left there shouldn't be any spiders or anything. It's a well-made house and we've made sure it's been kept that way."

She would be very cozy here. The house felt friendly and welcoming.

"I don't know about dishes and stuff like that, but I don't think Maureen took a lot with her since she and her new man plan to 'See the world'." He looked pained as he said that, and it made her laugh.

"Good for Maureen and her new honey. It's never too late to travel."

"Right. Anyway, I'll let you settle in. Give me your car

keys so I can give them to whomever it is that comes to get them. I won't bother you anymore tonight. Come in when you feel like it tomorrow. I can stop by the bakery in the morning to get coffee."

She fished her keys out of her purse and handed them to Scott.

He stuffed them in a pocket. "You've got food for tonight. But I'll have to walk you through how to get more tomorrow. It's not an easy process here. We've got just a few things at the little convenience store-slash-tourist trap. The rest have to come by ferry from Chelan. I'll bring some pastries from the bakery in the morning to share. And call me if you need anything else."

"I don't have your number."

"Oh right. Give me your phone I'll program it in." He handed her his phone after he'd unlocked the screen. "You do the same."

When he took his phone back, he took a picture of her and attached it to the profile, so she did the same. Now she had a picture of her hottie new boss. Maybe she should text it to her friends back home. No, not yet, maybe in a few days.

Scott looked around then nodded. "Okay, then I think you're set. For now, anyway. Let me know if you have any questions or issues."

Then he walked out the door without looking back. She watched him go across the lot and back into the church. What a strange day this was turning out to be. When she'd left her home and job so many months ago, she would have never guessed at this turn of events.

Back then she'd thought it might take a month or two at the most to catch up with her brother. She'd quit her job because it was a mediocre one, with no advancement in the near future, and she'd been thinking about finding something new anyway.

Her friends were scattered across the country or busy with their families. A few were party animals, but that had never appealed to her. Denver was large enough that she'd probably want to move to wherever her new job would be, so there was no sense in keeping her ratty apartment. She'd still never even considered being gone this long or travelling this far. It was only a two-day drive, but following her brother's meandering path had taken her all over the western half of the country.

She went about putting things away and investigating her new domain. There was food in the freezer. Some microwaveable dinners, frozen orange juice, bread, coffee (yay), and toaster waffles. The fridge had eggs, butter, condiments, a couple of potatoes, and now half a container of salad and a few pieces of pizza.

Nicole opened each of the cupboards. They were all full. Dishes, canned food, baking ingredients, baking pans, small appliances, and pretty much anything you would ever want in a kitchen, filled the shelves.

Well, she sure as heck wasn't going to starve. She looked carefully through everything and made a list of the things she would need to buy when she and Scott talked tomorrow. It wasn't going to be a lot. Just some produce, and maybe a few dairy products.

Nicole investigated the rest of the house and realized she had everything she could possibly want or need. Maureen clearly had left everything except her clothes and personal mementos.

She unpacked the few clothes she had in her backpack and laid down on the bed to rest for a few minutes.

SCOTT WENT BACK to his office wondering if what he'd just

done was the right thing to do. He hadn't really thought about it much, he'd just gone with his gut feelings. Which usually didn't steer him too far wrong. But he didn't know her from a hot rock, but what if she wasn't who she claimed to be, and was here for nefarious reasons?

He shook his head at the stupidity of that idea. Right. Come all the way to the edge of nowhere, to a place that had literally two ways in or out of it, the single road that was mostly a goat trail and the ferry. He supposed a person could also hike in or take the seaplane that only ran in the summer, but still. It was one of the remotest places in North America.

Not exactly a hotbed for criminal activity.

He could do a google search on her name and see if it came up with anything. It would simply be due diligence on his part. So, he did. The only thing that came up was a college graduation and a couple of addresses. Not much to see. Until the search popped up a couple of newspaper articles about fishing tournaments in California. She was mentioned in both of them and was even in one picture with a bunch of older men. The names of two of the older men had her same last name, he wondered if they were her dad and an uncle.

Scott decided he better get back to working at his job and not thinking about his lovely new secretary. He hoped she would be comfortable in the rectory. He still needed to convince her to let him bring in others to help her find her brother.

Maybe he could talk to his dad about it and see if he had any recommendations, his dad knew far more about keeping the lives of others to himself. Surely, he'd been up against something similar in his day and could help his son through the minefield Scott was currently in.

Scott called his father to see if he had some time to stop by this afternoon for a few minutes and was relieved when he said he'd be there in an hour. During that hour Scott remembered to clean up his carpentry mess from the foyer, draft an email to his church board that he would have Nicole send out tomorrow, and make some notes about what he wanted to talk to his dad about.

Scott stood to greet his dad when he walked in. His father, John Davidson, was in good shape for a man in his mid-sixties, which boded well for Scott himself in his later years. John could still be working, but he'd turned over nearly everything to his son a few years ago. Scott was glad his dad still did the couples counseling, since Scott had yet to marry, and didn't know much about that kind of relationship.

Scott gave his dad a hug. "Thanks for coming, dad."

"Anytime, son. Let's sit on the couches instead of at the desk." John motioned toward the seating area. He set his coffee mug on the table and took a seat on the couch. This late in the day, the coffee would be decaf, or his dad wouldn't be able to sleep.

Scott grabbed the notepad and a pen and sat in one of the chairs. "So, I need some advice. I had someone come into the church today and asked if she could speak to me on a confidential level. I told her the standard. That I could keep whatever she said confidential unless it was child abuse or a suicide issue."

"Or that the person was intending harm to others like a suicide bomber or crazy person with a gun."

"Exactly, and while it isn't any of those specific scenarios, it is possible, that if the person escalates, they could cause harm to others. Not necessarily because they want to, but possibly unknowingly or because of the nature of their actions."

John nodded and took a sip of his coffee. "That makes it a bit of a sticky wicket doesn't it?"

Scott tapped his pen on the notebook he held. "I did ask her to think it over carefully because if we brought the authorities in to help, we might be able to find the person she's worried about quicker."

"What did she say to that?"

"She tensed when I first suggested it, but then said she would think about that. She's not from here so she doesn't know how we operate. I tried to affirm that we didn't want any harm to come to the person and that we were a close-knit town and had each other's back."

"So, someone from out of town." John sat back and made the humming noise he normally did when he was thinking.

"Oh, and I hired her to be my assistant while she's in town."

John chuckled. "Of course, you did. You know you really could handle things on your own."

Scott wasn't completely convinced of that, but he nodded. "I suppose I could learn. But she needs a job and a place to stay while she's here. She's been trying to catch up with this person for a while and has run low on funds."

"So, you set her up in the rectory and gave her a job."

It wasn't a question, but he answered anyway. "Yeah, I did. She called and got us a pizza and Sylvia ratted me out."

His dad chuckled. "Now that doesn't surprise me in the least. What's her name?"

"Nicole. Nicole Roman."

"Is she pretty? How old is she?"

Scott swallowed. "She's about my age, maybe a couple years younger. And yes, she is pretty. But we've kind of gotten off track here."

John lifted one eyebrow. "I think you've handled it the best way you can. Continue to try to get her to let you bring in the cops and whoever the other authorities are. Since you didn't say the police, I have to assume there are other authorities to bring in. Trust your gut and if you feel like you can't wait for her permission then call them in anyway. You don't want someone's life in danger. If it comes to that, a life trumps a promise of silence. But try to convince her to change her mind, so you don't have to break your promise."

"I will. Thanks, dad. That is exactly what I needed to hear."

"Glad I could be of service. Now I'm going to mosey on home, your mother had something that smelled delicious in the crock pot. You'll be at Greg's tonight throwing pointy objects around, correct?"

Scott grinned. "Yep, there's a dart out there with my name on it."

"Have fun and try not to get one stuck in someone's arm."

"Dad, that was over twenty years ago, you need to let it go."

John chuckled as he walked out the door. Scott thought he heard him mutter, "Never."

In Scott's opinion, fathers were both the best, and worst person to have around. They helped when a guy needed it but made sure to keep him humble at the same time. Not that a little humility was a bad thing but having old mistakes perpetually right in front of his eyes was not always pleasant.

CHAPTER 4

Nicole slept great in the cozy cottage, for the first time in months. She had a really good feeling about this town and finding her brother. She'd even thought about letting Scott bring in the authorities. Not today maybe, she wanted a chance to look around some first, and that would be easier with her car.

She wanted to get to her new job and find out when Scott thought her car would be here. She was pretty certain he'd said today, but her head had been kind of spinning with all the changes that had happened yesterday. She went from being alone, homeless and broke, to having a partner, job and a cottage to sleep in.

It was practically a miracle and she'd had darn few of those in the last few months. So, she would rejoice in this one and hope it boded well toward finding her brother. But she needed to get a move on if she was going to get to her new job at a reasonable hour.

She started the water running in the shower and it ran clean, so it hadn't had time to build up rust in the pipes. The shower head had good pressure and the water was nice and hot like she liked it. She had some mini bottles of shampoo from the last hotel she'd stayed in. That would be something she could order from Chelan.

Although she didn't have much money on her, so she'd have to be careful how she spent what she did have. She wondered what getting her car here was going to cost. Scott said it was taken care of, but he couldn't mean it was free. The barge had to charge for transportation and some kind of fee for the labor of finding and driving her car to the barge landing. She didn't think it was the same spot as the ferry, but she didn't know for sure.

She'd been in a hurry to get to Chedwick to catch her brother and hadn't looked all that carefully. But she would just have to cross that bridge when she came to it, maybe she could get a small advance on her salary to buy a few groceries and pay for her car. She didn't like this feeling of uncertainty.

She'd been living like this for almost nine months and she was darn tired of it. If she could just find her brother before he did something even more stupid or got someone hurt, then she could relax and decide what she wanted to do with her life.

But first she had to find her brother.

That wasn't going to happen with her sitting in her cozy cottage. She put her coffee cup and the plate she'd eaten her toaster waffles on in the sink and ran hot water over them. She would wash them when she had more than one plate, one fork and one coffee cup.

She checked her appearance. She didn't have any professional clothes in her backpack, but the jeans were clean, and the sweater didn't look rumpled, which was one of the beauties of a sweater. She dabbed on a little eye makeup and some lipstick and grabbed up her purse, which felt heavy with all the keys from the church in it.

This was a trusting town to give some new girl they'd never met before, and who had a pyromaniac brother who'd burned at least two buildings in their town, the full set of keys to the church. It seemed a little crazy to her. But since she was the beneficiary of the trust, she wasn't going to complain.

She might suggest to pastor Scott that he be a little more cautious in the future. Maybe she could stay around long enough to hire her replacement. She'd quit her job and given up her apartment when she went to follow her brother, because she couldn't afford to keep either, if she was gone too long. She'd been really glad that she'd taken those precautions, when what she thought would only be a few weeks turned into a month and then six months.

Here it was nearly nine months later, and she still hadn't caught up with him. But she had real hope this time. She just had to catch him. If the police could just keep him in town, she was certain she could track him down.

Maybe she should give them a copy of the picture she had of him, so they knew who to look for. She'd be very angry if he slipped through her fingers again this time.

She shook her head, she'd already decided to give herself today to look around, before she went to the authorities.

The black SUV was in the parking lot when she went out and locked the cottage door. Obviously, Scott was already there. So, she hurried into the building, and dropped her purse next to her desk. *Yay, her desk.* Then she proceeded to Scott's door and knocked softly.

She heard him call out a welcome, so she went in and almost stumbled at the beauty of the man seated behind the desk. He had reading glasses on and it made him look nerdy and sexy at the same time. Lust shot through her and she had to force her feet to keep moving forward.

"I brought you coffee and some rolls."

"Oh, I forgot you were planning to do that. I found coffee and toaster waffles in the freezer. I'll take the coffee but not the rolls."

He grinned and pulled the box toward himself. "More for me."

She looked at him and didn't see an ounce of fat, only muscles, lots of muscles could be seen under his shirt. It made her wonder how he could eat like that and still look like he did. Men, it seemed, got all the advantages in that department. It really wasn't fair, but she would happily ogle him as he stuffed a huge chunk of cinnamon roll in his mouth. He moaned his delight and that sent her thoughts straight to the gutter, not just ogling now, her imagination took her on a road straight to nakedness.

He interrupted her fantasies of having him naked in the cottage bed. "How did you sleep?"

It took her a full minute to get her mind and body out of the fantasy, so she could answer his question. "I slept the best I have in months. The cottage is cozy and very welcoming. I felt like I could finally relax. I feel very good about the chances of finding my brother here."

"Glad to hear it. Did you give any more thought to bringing in the authorities?"

"I did. I want to look around a bit tonight after I get my car. If I don't find him, we can bring in the authorities tomorrow."

He nodded, and she could tell he was disappointed not to bring them in right away, but he didn't fight her on taking one more day.

"What time do you think my car will be here?"

"Probably around one. I'll take you over to the landing dock to pick it up."

She looked out the window at the lovely day. "I can walk."

"No need. We can run by Amber's on the way and grab a sandwich for lunch and then pick up your car."

"All right. What do you want me to do this morning?"

"I wrote out an email that I need sent to the board about the corkboard I was putting up when you got here yesterday. If you could type it up and clean up the grammar, then send it out. I'm certain Maureen had a mailing list for everyone. I stopped and picked up the mail too. If you could open those, throw away the junk and distill it down to what I really need to look at, that would be awesome."

That sounded easy enough. "I can do that."

"Great, I need an hour undisturbed this morning to work on my sermon."

"So, keep everyone from bothering you?"

He grinned. "It's not like you'll need to fight them off or anything. Just letting you know I won't be bothering you for an hour."

"Oh, okay. I won't bother you either, then." She took the pages he held out to her, and the nearly foot high stack of mail, and went to her desk. *Her desk, yay!*

When she started looking at what he'd given her, she wasn't sure she could keep her word on what she'd just promised him. His handwriting was atrocious. She might need his help to decipher it.

She decided to start with the mail. Most if it was the typical crap that everyone got, flyers with coupons and special deals. Offers for credit cards. Fliers about sales and politicians. When she put all that into the recycling, she had a much smaller pile of what she considered "real" mail. She wasn't sure if he wanted her to open those, but it seemed to her like that's what he'd said so she opened them. A couple of them had checks, a few were bills, several were prayer requests, some anonymous and some not.

The last handful were from people in town giving him

suggestions for sermons or complaining about a recent one. She thought that was kind of bold and pushy. He was the pastor after all, why did these people think he should preach what they thought, and the complaining really irritated her. She'd never heard him preach so maybe they were correct, but the whining seemed to be about stupid things.

She looked back over the list of directives Maureen had left for her. She'd described the process for the checks and the bills, so Nicole followed those instructions and had the checks ready for Scott to sign so she could mail the bills. And the deposit slip was ready for the bank.

Maureen had said to give Scott the prayer requests and throw the sermon critiques and suggestions into the trash without letting Scott see them. Nicole thought that was kind of underhanded. But as she continued to read, Maureen explained herself.

Someone named Mrs. Tisdale always whined about silly things. Nicole noticed the whining notes were from a Ruth Tisdale, so she did throw those in the trash.

Vernon Whittaker gave the sermon suggestions wanting Scott to emphasize that the beliefs of today were wrong, and people needed to be preached to in a hellfire and damnation sort of way. Nicole found those suggestions and slipped them into the trash.

The last instructions were about some guy Maureen called Old Man Peterson. Who she said had been angry for over thirty years, ever since Scott's father had been put in as the preacher in town. Old Man Peterson had thought he should be the pastor, so he picked apart the message every week. Nicole saw the last one with a list of complaints and corrections was indeed from someone named Peterson, so she tossed that one too.

She agreed that the constant complainers were not worth Scott's time.

She finished reading the file from Maureen, trying to delay deciphering Scott's handwriting. At the end of the document Maureen mentioned Scott's handwriting and that she had saved a sample of his writing and what she had interpreted it to be after working for Scott and Pastor John for so many years. So, Nicole opened up the scanned doc of hieroglyphics and the letter it had turned into. She studied it line by line and finally started to see the pattern forming.

After studying the two for a few more minutes she decided to try with the new one Scott had sent. So, she opened a fresh email and clicked on Scott's email. She would type it up and send it to him for approval. She worked slowly and painstakingly through the scribbles until she had an email that mostly made sense. She sent it to Scott and looked at the clock, it had been an hour and fifteen minutes since she'd left his office, so she wondered if it was all right if she went in to have him sign the checks.

When her email pinged with a note from Scott, who had fixed a couple of places in what she had sent him, and he congratulated her on reading his doctor's handwriting, she decided he was finished with his hour of quiet.

Before she could gather up the checkbook and the deposit he walked out of his office. "I figured you would need me to sign checks."

"I was just about to come to you."

"No need for you to always be running after me. I have feet and can walk out here."

He leaned over her desk and scanned the checks and bills and signed his name to the checks. Then he glanced at the deposit slip and nodded and took up the prayer requests.

After he straightened, he glanced into her trash can and smiled. "I see Maureen left you instructions on dealing with the sermon critics."

"She did. Even before I read her instructions, I was miffed at those people for bossing you around."

He laughed, and her heart skittered at the sound. It was a deep-throated full-bodied laugh full of amusement. "You don't need to worry about me. I developed a thick skin at a young age. It's not easy being the PK, preacher's kid, other kids in school like to torment the 'goody two shoes' and the adults think we should have some kind of perfection down, that none of us have. A lot of bad kids are PK's that are sick of being restrained by everyone. My dad always talked things through with me, so that I knew he understood and expected me to do dumb stuff sometimes, like every other kid on the planet. But I still grew a thick skin early."

"Good to know. I can't imagine having everyone in town expecting me to behave a certain way."

"Oh, it wasn't everyone in town, just a few busy bodies. But the worst part is that 'the certain way' differs with each person. So even if I could please one of them the rest would expect something different." He shook his head and a wry smile curled the corners of his lips.

She tried not to stare at those lips because she wanted very much to give him a soft kiss to show him that she didn't judge him, or the little boy he'd been. But she didn't really even know him, so why she was thinking about kissing him was just plain insanity.

She shook herself internally and started putting the checks in the envelopes to mail, but her hands were shaking from where her mind had gone. She folded her hands, so he wouldn't notice. Then she asked if there was something else, that he wanted her to do this morning.

When he didn't answer she looked up and saw that he was staring at her in an odd way that made her stomach flutter. She whispered, "Scott?"

He shook all over like a dog and then straightened and said, "Sorry, just wool-gathering."

She chuckled at the old-fashioned term. "So, anything else you want me to do this morning?"

He looked around like something was going to jump out at him wanting attention. But nothing did, so he turned back to her and shrugged. "I can't think of anything right now."

"Okay… maybe I'll look through the computer at some of the documents that are in here, so I can get a feel for what kinds of things Maureen did."

"That's a great idea," he said a little too enthusiastically, and she realized that Maureen had probably kept herself busy a lot more often, than when Scott actually gave her work to do. Well, Nicole could certainly look through the computer to see what was there. Maybe familiarize herself with any programs that were on it, that she'd never worked with.

"I'll do that, then."

"Excellent, we'll leave here about eleven-thirty to go get lunch before the barge arrives. I can show you where the bank and post office are too, so you can mail the bills and deposit the checks."

"Sounds like a plan." She breathed a sigh of relief when he went back into his office. She felt awkward around him, from both not knowing what to expect and the sheer hotness factor. He seemed a little awkward around her too, but she didn't know why exactly. Maybe it was just because she was new in town and he didn't quite know what to do with her. Obviously, Maureen had been the secretary for so long that he didn't have to give her any directions. In fact, Nicole wondered if Maureen hadn't directed him more often than not.

Nicole went back to the computer, she sent the email to the governing board, after correcting it. Then decided to look at the calendar, that might give her a feel for the flow of the days. She clicked it open and saw several entries, some appointments for Scott.

A cleaning crew came in once a week on Saturday, Nicole wondered if they had keys to the building or if someone had to be on hand to let them in. Not that it would be hard, since she wasn't twenty feet away, except she planned to spend her days off looking for her brother. There was also a flower delivery on Saturday, she assumed those were for the sanctuary. Maybe Saturday was not going to be her day off.

Someone named Samantha brought rolls and donuts before church. Nicole wondered if she needed to make coffee before that. She went back to the document Maureen had left her and noticed for the first time that some of the pages had days of the week in the header. She hadn't noticed the header before.

As she looked more carefully at the file, she realized there was a day by day list of things to do. With nothing on Monday and Tuesday. Those must be her days off.

Today was Wednesday so she looked carefully at the list for Wednesday, sure enough mail was on the list and an email to the board of directors every other week. The rest of the list was things like ordering supplies, which referenced a supplies file. She looked around on the computer and found a spread sheet with a list of supplies. Nicole printed out a copy and then took her keys and went in search of where things might be stored. As she checked the bathrooms and found a storage closet, she tallied up what was available. There was also a storage area off the kitchen, so she checked that, too. As far as she could tell the only thing they really needed were some Zip Lock bags and tissues.

She still didn't know how to order things, so she went to Scott's office and knocked on the door. He called out for her to enter so she took her paper and went in. "I found a list of daily chores Maureen left and Wednesday is ordering day. There are a couple of items to order, but I don't know how."

"Oh, right. I was going to show you how to order things from the Safeway in Chelan. I knew there was something I was forgetting. Let's do that real quick before lunch."

They sat together, and he walked her through how to order on the church's account. Then they set her up a profile, so she could order her personal things. Sitting that close to him, working together on a computer was kind of intimate feeling.

Maybe she'd just lost her mind. Or maybe it was because she'd been chasing her brother for so long, she hadn't had any time to spend with a man and she needed to get laid. She kind of doubted the hottie pastor would give her a roll in the hay, so she would have to find someone else.

Scott interrupted her thoughts to explain that if they got the orders in before noon then the virtual shoppers could pick it early enough in the morning to get it on the next day's ferry. If they didn't, it would take two days.

It all seemed very straight forward to her other than the delay. But with the town being so remote she decided one or two days was still good. She thanked Scott and went back to her desk to order the things she needed. Out of the danger zone, her body and mind cooled down, so she could think to order what she needed. She only had a couple hundred dollars in the bank, but it looked like she could order a minimum of fifty dollars' worth. She clicked through the pages representing aisles and ended up with an order of about seventy-five dollars. Not too bad and she thought it would keep her in groceries until she got paid.

When she'd finished with all the ordering, she felt like she was making some progress. She looked back at the Wednesday list and didn't see anything specific other than checking to make sure the flowers weren't making a mess in the sanctuary. She got up and went toward the large hall, flipping through the keys until she found the right one. Each key was a different color or had one of those plastic things that went around the key head in even more color combinations. She realized once she knew which ones went to which doors it would be easy to keep them straight.

She opened the doors and went inside. A sense of peace filled her, and she decided that Scott was a preacher who spoke on God's love, not hell fire and damnation. She would have been surprised otherwise, he was too nice of a guy to yell at people. She'd been to a church that did a lot of yelling in her younger years, and she'd turned her back on church when they'd said that only people that went to their church were going to escape hell. Her parents hadn't attended that yelling church for long either, it just didn't fit who they were. She'd stopped going altogether when she'd gotten older, she'd had a job on Sundays, so it wasn't practical, plus she'd never really gotten much out of going.

Maybe she would sit in on a service of Scott's and see what he had to say. He hadn't made it a part of her employment duties, which had relieved her at the time, but she was curious enough to want to hear what he had to say.

Nicole went to the front and found the flowers, they looked okay to her, she checked to see if they had enough water and they did. She thought she'd seen some kind of meeting on Thursday nights in here, so she left them for that. She wondered again if it was her job to let all these different people in. She decided to ask Scott during lunch.

She looked around, as long as she was in here, to see if anything needed straightening, but it was surprisingly tidy. Since she knew the cleaning crew came on Saturday, she wondered who had cleaned up after the Sunday service. There was a baby grand piano, a guitar and a set of drums she itched to play.

Instead she took a few minutes to think about her brother and the help he needed and the help she needed to find him. And although it wasn't exactly a prayer, she felt an assurance that both she and her brother would finally get the help she wanted.

When she walked out of the room she almost bumped into Scott. Nicole was startled and for some reason felt like a kid who'd been caught with his hand in the cookie jar, so she quickly said, "I was checking the flowers to make sure they're okay to leave in there a few more days."

"Thanks for checking that. I appreciate it. I don't often think of the flowers. I know people like to see them." He shrugged and then looked away for a moment before turning back to her. "Don't feel nervous about going into anywhere, I gave you those keys, so you have access to all parts of the building. I'm not going to think it's odd to find you anywhere. Nowhere is off limits. Okay?"

"Thanks, it was very peaceful in there. I took my time."

He chuckled, "That's kind of the point of the room. Feel free to take your time in there whenever you want."

"Thanks, but you're not paying me to dawdle."

"Sometimes we need a few minutes to rest and think and pray. I get paid to do that every day, so you're good. Ready for lunch?"

"Speaking of lunch, I found a bag of cat food in the kitchen. Do you have a cat? Or did Maureen?"

Scott's ears turned pink. "No. I don't, but I do sometimes leave food out for the strays or probably in reality, someone's house cat that comes to mooch a second breakfast."

She laughed at his chagrin being caught feeding a stray cat. "Well, do we need to set out some food now?"

His ears stayed pink. "I did it this morning."

"In that case I will leave the feeding of the cats in your capable hands."

~

SCOTT KNEW Nicole was teasing him and he had to admit he kind of enjoyed it. Maureen had never asked when the bag of cat food appeared in the kitchen, so he'd never had to admit he put food out for the random cats that appeared. He knew both Maureen and his father had caught on, that he was doing it, but no one had ever asked him outright.

He decided that being teased was a whole lot better than lusting after this woman. Never in his life had he battled with this level of attraction, which, if he was honest, had made him a little cocky in the area of fighting lust. He'd certainly felt lust before but had easily brushed it aside. When people had talked about fighting lustful feelings he'd been surprised by their vehemence and had eventually decided he was just stronger than they were.

Nope, nada, not even close, he'd simply never met a woman he'd been that attracted to. He felt like he should go back and apologize to all the people he'd thought weak. Not that he'd let on he felt that way about them, but he knew he had thought it and that was what mattered. Of course, he wasn't going to say anything because that would make the other person feel bad, but these feeling sure put him in his place. And he didn't like it one bit.

Naturally, he never liked it when God showed him his proud and cocky attitude. There had been plenty of times it had happened. This was just the most recent. And he knew these feelings were not going to go away any time soon. When it was time for him to learn a lesson, it was long and brutal.

They stopped at the bank and the post office, and on the way to the restaurant he introduced Nicole to everyone, saying she was his new admin. Everybody was nice and friendly as he expected they would be.

Scott noticed as they drove to the different locations Nicole was diligently scanning in all directions. He figured that she was looking for her brother. He stopped by city hall to pick up a map. There were touristy maps at nearly every store. But he knew that the government building had one that was more a street map rather than a tourist trap type.

She looked surprised when he pulled up, so he said, "I thought you could use a real map of the city and surrounding areas. Those tourist ones they have everywhere, are fine, if you're looking for the amusement park, shopping and food, but don't have any of the other streets or the access locations to the mountains, except for a few easy hiking trails."

"I did notice that the one I picked up at the landing didn't seem very detailed."

"It will help you with some areas, but a street map will give you a better understanding of the layout of the town and remote camping grounds. I'll be right back." Scott hopped out of the SUV and hustled into the courthouse. It only took him a couple of minutes to get both a city street map and a map of the national forest surrounding their town.

When he got back to the car, Nicole had the tourist map opened and she was studying it. She'd made little red x's where the church, post office, bank, and city hall were. She folded up that map and he handed her the two new ones.

Nicole unfolded the city map and grinned. "Thanks so much. This is a lot more detailed."

He nodded stupidly, because he felt like a deer in headlights caught in her smile. Fortunately, she was busy looking at the map and didn't notice. *Get it under control, Davidson, and stop acting like a jackass. Or a kid in love.* He started the car with jerky movements and headed toward Amber's.

While he drove, he tried to remember his training, he tried to remember his advice to others, and he tried quoting scripture, all to no avail. He was a basket case. A certifiable basket case.

They were quickly seated in the restaurant and both ordered the soup and salad bar, so they had food within seconds. Scott decided that maybe talking about her brother would cool down his ardor and also maybe help in her quest.

"So how do you think Kent is living? Do you think he's camping? Or is he getting jobs in the areas he stops at?"

"I can only guess. He did take some camping gear we had. A sleeping bag, small tent and lantern. So, he could be camping. Most of the other places he didn't stay as long. My guess is he went in stayed for a week or two, then started a fire and left. So, he could manage for a short time in the tent, maybe grab some food."

Scott nodded. "But he's been here all summer. Or at least most of it."

"That's what it looks like to me. So, I think he would need a more stable environment. Maybe he did get a job somewhere."

"What kind of job did he have in your home town?"

"He's pretty handy and can work just about anywhere. I've thought about possibilities. He wouldn't want a job that would leave people in the lurch when he left, so some kind of temporary job. Maybe seasonal. Since this is a tourist town, I imagine you've got a fair number of those."

Scott thumped a thumb on his knee in frustration, they *had* a lot of seasonal jobs. "We do, maybe the first place to start looking is the amusement park, they have the most seasonal jobs and also the resort hotel. The rest of the summer jobs are one or two people, so it would be a lot more obvious to work there, but the theme park and the resort would be easy to be just a number."

She tapped a finger on her chin. "That does make sense. When we came here, many years ago, neither one of those existed. We came to play on the lake and Chedwick had better prices than Chelan or Stehekin."

"Did he ever play the *Adventures with Tsilly* game?"

Nicole nodded. "We had the first two versions and yes, he did play them and enjoy them."

"In that case the park would be my first guess, because it's based on the game. Although the resort and a lot of other places in town do have costumes to go along with the game. It helped build tourism when we capitalized on the game's success as the birthplace of it."

"Very clever of you." She took a bite of salad and he tried not to stare at her while she ate.

"Yeah it was a good idea, and everyone went along with it. Or, those that didn't got on board quickly."

Nicole waved her fork at him. "I imagine they didn't want to miss out on profit."

"Yeah, some people didn't like the idea of costumes to go along with the monthly theme, but Barbara was patient with them to design costumes that would be practical." He chuckled. "It took her a couple of tries here at the restaurant and others that serve food. No flowing sleeves or dragging skirts. Things like that."

"Makes sense. But they do add a flare to the place and make it more immersive into the game atmosphere. You know my brother could hide easier in a costume. Does the theme park have full costumes for the lake monster or anything like that?"

Scott knew they did and that would be a clever way to hide. Of course, Kent would have to realize he needed to hide. The only person that would recognize him was his sister unless she turned him in. "Do you think he knows he should be hiding? Does he know you're following him?"

"Know, might be too strong of a word, but he might wonder if I'm following him. Unless he saw me, and I didn't see him." She sighed, and her hand flopped on the table in frustration. "I really have no idea what he thinks."

Scott took her hand to give her his strength. But that zing of attraction sped through his hand and up his arm to his whole body. He decided he had to ignore it, she needed his comfort not his lust.

He squeezed her hand. "I'm sure you'll find him. If not today maybe we can enlist some help. Maybe just a few people. Like the park owner, he's a firefighter. So is Amber's husband and if he ever came in to eat, she would have noticed and maybe remembered. Or if he went to the bar to eat, the owner of that is the assistant chief of the fire department. If we could let a few key people know it might help. Maybe not bring in the police yet, although if they had a picture or even a description, they could keep him from slipping through when the seasonal workers leave town in a couple of weeks."

Nicole put her fork down and pushed her food away, and he knew he'd distressed her. "No need to decide right now and I'm not trying to rush you. Just giving you some different scenarios to think about. I just don't want to see you miss him, when this is probably the most closed environment you're going to find."

"I know and I agree. I just hate feeling like I'm turning against him."

"You're not turning against him, you're trying to get him help."

She sighed. "You're right, but I still feel like a traitor."

"I understand, but sometimes love has to be strong to help the person who needs intervention."

"Yeah, I just never wanted it to be me. But he does need help before someone gets hurt. An innocent, or a firefighter, or even himself."

Scott rubbed his thumb over her knuckles. "You're doing the best for him."

She pulled her hand from his and took her salad back to finish it. Scott felt like a piece of him had gone missing, he'd been content with her hand in his.

[illegible] comb over [illegible]

[illegible]

[illegible] hand from his [illegible] back to [illegible] felt like a piece of him had gone [illegible] her head in her [illegible]

CHAPTER 5

Nicole started out by driving up and down the streets of the town. She kept her eyes open looking for her brother's car, even as her mind thought back to having lunch with the hot man and how her skin had tingled when he'd held her hand, rubbing his thumb over her knuckles. She'd liked the touch, maybe a little too much.

Being on the road for so long she was only now realizing she'd missed human contact. And being able to talk about her brother with someone was a huge relief, she hadn't known how bottled up she'd felt trying to keep it to herself.

When she didn't find her brother's car on any of the streets, she went to the amusement park and drove up and down through the parking lot. It wasn't there either, so she went and did the same in the resort parking lot, where she discovered there were two lots, one for guests and one for employees. She wondered if that was true at the amusement park, too.

She drove back to the amusement park looking for an employee lot, but if they had one it was well hidden. She decided to ask Scott if he knew where it was, but it was getting late, so she went back to the rectory. The salad she'd had for lunch had worn off and she knew she had cold pizza in the fridge of her temporary home. She felt so grateful for that small thing, having a house and food to go back too. It was a gift and Nicole was determined to be thankful for it, and not take it for granted, as she had her whole life.

As she munched on the salad and the reheated pizza, she thought more about bringing in other people to help search for Kent. The search this afternoon had been disappointing and fruitless, she knew that he could have been driving down the very street she'd just checked. It was a small town but there were still plenty of streets, she couldn't be on all of them at the same time. If people knew what he looked like and what kind of car he had, they could help her find him. Finding him was more important than anything, he had to be stopped before someone got hurt. If that happened his crime would skyrocket in seriousness and would end in significant jail time.

With each bite of food her determination grew, he had to be found, he had to be stopped, and he needed help. The sooner the better, which meant she would have to bring others into her search. Before she carried her dishes to the sink, she called Scott.

"Hi Nicole, how can I help you?"

His deep voice skittered through her, igniting nerve endings. She nearly forgot what she'd called him for, but her brother was more important than this infatuation she had for the preacher. She cleared her throat. "I want to tell the authorities, so we can work together to find my brother."

Scott sighed like he'd been holding his breath. "Excellent. I'll gather up some key individuals and... let's meet in the conference room at the church in half an hour. If you've got a picture of him, please bring it with you."

Nicole hung up from talking to Scott and her hands

started shaking. What if she'd just sealed her brother's fate? She didn't really know Scott from a hot rock, what if he wasn't the kindhearted man, she saw him as? What if he joined forces with the others and they just threw her brother in jail and didn't care about his fate?

Her hands were cold and shook as she carried the dishes to the sink. Nicole wanted to run but there was nowhere to go. She and her brother were trapped. Her only hope was that the people in this town were as nice as they had seemed so far.

SCOTT WAS SO RELIEVED Nicole had called him. He didn't want to go over her head, but he couldn't in good consciousness just let a known arsonist wander around their town willy-nilly, either. It helped that he'd been diagnosed as a pyromaniac as a child that would go to proving the motive was impulse control rather than premeditated vandalism.

Scott called Nolan on his private number rather than through dispatch. He wanted the meeting kept on the down low until the key players could determine the best plan for the situation. Next, he called Greg and Jeremy since they were the fire investigators on the department.

Scott decided one last person should be brought in and that was his father, who would be a good referee type. Scott knew he was clearly on Nicole's side, so he wouldn't be objective. His dad would be.

He didn't tell anyone what was going on just that they needed to meet him. When Greg pushed back, since it was a working night for him, he'd told him that this related to the fires. Since Greg was the assistant fire chief and had been first on scene at both fires, he immediately changed his tone and didn't question anything else, but said he would call in his backup.

It wasn't a particularly busy night at the bar, so Scott didn't feel bad about pulling Greg away, this was much more important than pouring beers and keeping a lid on the rowdies.

He parked in the back where he always parked and unlocked the door. Nicole wasn't there yet, and he hoped she hadn't changed her mind. He understood family solidarity and he knew she was pitting that against turning her brother into the authorities. He prayed and asked God to give her the strength to do what was right and best for all.

He turned on the lights in the upstairs conference room and started a pot of decaf coffee. He knew his dad would want some at the very least. He could grab some water bottles on his way back up after he opened the doors for his friends.

He unlocked the front door and went toward the fridge but stopped when he found Nicole in the printer room enlarging and making copies of a picture, he assumed was her brother.

"Hey."

She didn't look at him, just kept watching the pictures come out of the church's color printer.

He walked over and put one hand on her shoulder. "You okay?"

She sniffed, and he realized she was crying. He grabbed a handy box of tissues and handed it to her, glad that Maureen had put them in every room of the church because she said, "You just never know when someone will need a tissue."

Nicole muttered a thank you and then pulled out several tissues from the box and used them to mop her face and blow her nose. Dumping the used ones in the trash, before taking another handful to put in her pocket.

"I'm not going to say I know what you're going through because I don't. But can I say I'm sorry?"

She turned to him then and walked into his arms where he held her close for a few minutes, until he heard people coming in the door and tromping up the stairs. He took her shoulders and set her back from him a bit. "I'll go up and greet everyone. You take a minute and come up when you're ready."

She nodded and turned back to gather her pictures. Before he left the room, he saw her gather them to her chest as if giving them a hug, and it broke his heart, for her and what she was about to do.

He wondered if he should talk to his friends and give them a heads up, but he knew everyone joining them tonight would be professional and kind. He grabbed the water bottles and went up the stairs.

He greeted his friends and said, "My new admin is going to join us. She has some information that you all need to hear. Then we'll need to decide what to do with that information. I brought some water or there's coffee on, it's decaf."

Everyone took their preferred beverage and sat, he reserved a space by him for Nicole. She came in a moment later and although the tear tracks were gone, everyone in the room could recognize that she'd been crying. He saw looks of concern flit across each face and he relaxed knowing they would have compassion.

Nicole sat next to him and flashed him a look of gratitude, he assumed it was for him saving her a space near him. Her hands were shaking as she set her pictures upside down on the table in front of her.

He cleared his throat and did the introductions. "This is Nicole Roman, my new admin." He went around the room introducing each key player. "Nicole, his is my father, John Davidson. Our chief of police, Nolan Thompson. Our assistant fire chief, Greg Jones and the other fire investigator, Jeremy Scott."

Nicole smiled at each one until she got to Jeremy and her expression changed to wonder, "The children's book author, Jeremy Scott?"

Jeremy smiled but ducked his head. Scott knew fame would never sit easily on the man's shoulder's, he'd been a famous author for over a decade and he still thought it was a fluke. Amber had helped him with some of that when they'd fallen in love, but it was simply his personality. "Yes, ma'am."

"Oh, I just love the stories of the little boy and his imagination. They are so clever and exactly like what my brother and I played as children. My favorite game was camping under the kitchen table. His favorite was always the carpet being lava and trying to not step on it, so we didn't burn up."

A shadow crossed her face and Scott knew she was thinking about her brother's obsession with fire. Her shoulders slumped, and she somehow looked even smaller than her five-foot frame. She looked younger too and he wanted to hold her like he would a child and comfort her.

Jeremy clearly noticed too, because he simply said, "Thanks."

Jeremy's words broke the spell, however. She sat up straighter and squared her shoulders. Without preamble she started speaking. "My brother is the reason I came to your town. He's a pyromaniac and I think he started the fires you had here."

Everyone in the room went on full alert and he could tell they all wanted to start asking questions. But each stayed silent to let her tell her story in her own way. His father looked at him and raised one eyebrow and he nodded. Yes, this was the woman he'd talked to his dad about.

"Kent had an obsession with fire as a child and my parents learned when he was quite young that he needed help with it. They took him to a lot of counseling sessions and he eventually learned to control his impulses to start fires. He'd been fine ever since then and never again started fires to relieve stress. But my mom and dad were his touchstones, if you will, and he would go to them to deal with his stress. He graduated high school and college and had a good job, a girlfriend, and a good life."

Nicole swallowed, and Scott knew this was where the story turned. "Nine months ago, my parents died in a head-on collision." Nicole drew in a ragged breath. Everyone in the room could see where this story was going, Scott could have cut the tension in the room with a knife.

"As you can guess, Kent couldn't take the stress of their deaths. He told me he was going to go on a drive to see if he could find his way, again, maybe visit our family vacation spots. Unbeknownst to me he quit his job, moved out of his apartment, and broke up with his girlfriend. I finally realized what he'd done when his girlfriend called to tell me what she'd discovered. He hadn't told her he was giving up the apartment or quitting his job. But when she found out she called to see if I'd known. I'd thought he was going to be gone a couple of weeks."

Nicole shook her head like she'd been a fool.

Scott's dad said quietly, "You couldn't have known."

Nicole looked up and nodded. "You're right, I couldn't. He'd hid it from me, his girlfriend, his boss, and his landlord whom he'd told he was moving in with his girlfriend. Everyone got just a tiny bit of the story. Once I realized what he'd done I started paying attention to the news and especially stories of fires. It took me a while because the fires he was setting were in old abandoned buildings. But I eventually started seeing the pattern."

She looked from person to person and pulled out a map Scott had never seen. On it was two types of markings, black x's and red circles. In their town was a black x and two red circles.

He saw Nolan and Greg look carefully at the map and then they looked at each other and nodded.

Nicole pointed at the map. "The black x's are areas our family went on vacation. The red circles are places that have had a fire, or two, in the last nine months. The most recent was here in Chedwick. I think my brother is visiting locations that the family went on vacation and had a great deal of fun, but when the stress gets too strong at the thought of never seeing our parents again, he starts a fire to relieve it."

She sighed a huge sigh and then looked at Nolan. "When I got here, I noticed you had officers checking ID's at the dock. Scott told me you have men on the only road out of town, too. I think my brother might still be here and since this is such a remote location it might be the best place to capture him and get him the help he needs."

Her hands shook as she placed them on top of the pictures. "I know he's been committing crimes and he needs to pay, but he also needs counseling and a way to learn to handle his stress, now that my parents are gone. I want to give you the information to help me find him, but I also want you to promise me that he'll get help and not just be locked in a cage."

She looked at Nolan. "I love my brother, but he needs help."

The room was dead quiet as each man processed all she'd said. Nicole sat with her hands folded on top of the pictures of her brother waiting for them to speak. She looked calm, but the knuckles on her hands were stark white as she waited for their verdict.

After less than two minutes, which he was sure Nicole felt was like two hours, Nolan looked around the room. Scott could see the silent communication between men he'd known all his life, or for at least the last half-dozen years.

Finally, Nolan said, "We'll help you find him, and we'll make sure he has a good lawyer and we'll help testify to his need for help. That's about all we can do. We're not in charge of the laws, nor can we sway the judge, but to the best of our ability we'll do what we can to get your brother the help he needs."

CHAPTER 6

Nicole wished they could give her more assurance, but she knew it wasn't really in their power to do so. She relaxed slightly and was ready to speak when Nolan continued.

"There might be a way to teach your brother to use fire in a constructive way, rather than destructive."

She noticed the rest of the men in the room smile and wondered where this was going. She looked back to Nolan.

"My mother and I are both glass artists. We use fire to sculpt. In order to do that a person must learn the true properties of fire and how to respect it. Fire can burn and destroy, but it can also be used to create. If your brother is willing, he might be able to channel his stress into a constructive use of fire rather than destructive. Not to take fire away from him, but to teach him to use it for good."

Nicole just sat there staring at Nolan as her mind whirled with what he'd just said. She thought back to how her brother had enjoyed going to glass blowing shops and watching the glass blowers work. Her family had always thought that he'd been concentrating on the fire in the glory hole, but what if they were wrong? What if he'd been watching the transformation of a glob of glass into something beautiful?

"You mean like a glass blower?"

The rest of the guys laughed, but Nolan said, "Yes something like that, but on a slightly bigger scale."

Jeremy rolled his eyes. Greg smirked, and Scott's dad winked at her. Scott muttered, "I'll show you tomorrow."

With that idea percolating in her head Nicole felt the first hope for her brother that she'd had in nine months. "Would someone really teach him? Would the courts agree to that?"

Nolan looked at Greg who shrugged and said, "It's possible, especially if it was you, Nolan, and he had an ankle bracelet or something to keep him in town. I'll call some friends."

Nolan looked back at her and said, "We'll work on it. But first we have to find him and detain him."

She looked down at the pictures under her hands and then up with a smile on her face. "I can help with that."

The rest of the time was spent with the six of them coming up with a plan to find Kent. The men asked a lot of questions that she would never have thought to ask. She didn't know why they were asking some of them, but she decided they were the experts and answered every question to the best of her ability.

It was nearly midnight when they had all the information they needed and had come up with a definite plan of attack. They'd decided to alert the owners of large businesses where he would be just a number. Unless he'd gotten some form of fake ID it was possible, he was working under his real name and social security number. Unless he wasn't working at all, but then it would be likely he was camping and even that required ID if he was in any of the places that had showers and bathrooms.

When they finally broke up and went their separate ways, she had a good feeling about the future for both herself and her brother. She knew her parents would be proud of her, so she was happy with the choices she'd made to bring in the help of this small town's authorities.

Scott walked her over to the rectory. Not that she was afraid or needed his escort, but she was content with it. She kind of liked the fact that he'd stood by her. She also liked all the men he'd brought in to help, none of them seemed like jerks that would be mean or condemning. And they'd all treated her with respect and not like a criminal's sister.

SCOTT WAS PLEASED with how the evening had gone. He was thrilled with Nolan's idea to teach Kent glass sculpting. If they really could turn her brother into using his fascination with fire for something good, he couldn't see any reason why he would have to go to jail. Unless some hard ass in another state was going to force the issue. That was the only roadblock he could see, because her brother had taken his burning spree across state lines, he didn't know if that would make it a federal offense. He hoped not.

He stopped at the door as she unlocked the rectory. Scott wanted to go in with her to just chat for a while, but he knew it wasn't a good idea. She reached up and brushed a kiss to his cheek, said a quick thank you, and walked through the door, before he could get his mind to re-engage.

His skin tingled where her lips had brushed his cheek. He muttered, "You're welcome," and walked back to his SUV in a daze, or maybe it was a haze of lust. He wasn't quite sure. What he was sure of, was that woman packed a punch, and he needed to go home and take a cold shower.

When he got to the front of the building, he saw his

father's car was still in the parking lot, so he pulled up next to it with the two driver's doors face to face. He rolled down his window. "What's up dad?"

"Nothing much. I think you handled that situation very well."

"Thanks…"

"So, there seems to be some kind of something between you and the girl."

Sometimes Scott hated how observant his father was. This would be one of those times. "Dad…"

"Are you denying it?"

"No, but I don't want to talk about it either."

His dad chuckled. "I can understand that. But you're also an adult and you might want to think about the future and maybe finding a nice girl to settle down with."

"Dad she's been in town less than forty-eight hours."

"I'm aware, but sometimes, when it's right, it doesn't take any longer than that."

Scott sighed. "I'll keep that in mind."

"You do that. But son, don't let lust guide you, a relationship needs to be more than physical to make it in this world."

"I know dad, and I have to admit, this is the most powerful attraction I've ever had for a woman."

"I noticed that, Scott, which is why I'm sitting here waiting for you, instead of being at home in my bed with your mother. I know I'm your father, but I'm still a man and a pastor. Come talk to me, if you need to. Don't be a fool and try to handle it alone."

"Thanks, dad."

"Goodnight. son."

As his father drove away, Scott realized he did feel better and more in control after talking to him. Maybe his old man was on to something.

CHAPTER 7

The next morning Scott knew there was talk all around town as the plan to capture Kent went into effect. The officers at the dock now had a face and name to look for. They continued to stop everyone as they had been doing, because that gave them the ability to slow down the loading, so no one could sneak through.

The officers on the upper road and the forest rangers also had the information to help them track any movements. The forest rangers would be going back through the camping logs for the last three months to see if Kent had signed into any of the campgrounds.

Scott, Jeremy, and Greg were going around to the large business owners to check hiring records for the summer workers. Jeremy had gone to the resort, Greg had gone to the construction company, and Scott was going to the amusement park. After they hit the big employers if they didn't find him in those records, they each had a list of the smaller ones to visit.

Nicole had wanted to go with them, and they'd talked about it. On one hand she would spot her brother quicker than anyone else would, on the other hand if Kent saw her first, he might try to bolt. In the end they decided to see if they could find where he was and then bring her into a location to watch without being seen, if that was possible.

She'd reluctantly agreed and had gone in to open the church, there was supposed to be a delivery for the things she'd ordered yesterday. She was also supposed to get her groceries from Chelan today, so Scott knew it would be good for her to be at the church. But at the same time, he could understand her desire to continue to be active in finding her brother.

Scott parked and walked into the amusement park's office. He'd called Chris and told him he would be by and Chris said he'd be in the office. The office was housed in one of the mountains on the US geography ride. Nothing in the park looked like a plain building. Everything was built to look like part of the fantasy of the *Adventures with Tsilly* game. Even the roads, equipment and storage for the park were in a subterranean network. It was fascinating.

The door in the side of the mountain opened for him automatically, so clearly someone was watching for his approach. That he found interesting, but also a little creepy. Although it did indicate that if Kent worked here, he might be easy to find if everything in the park was monitored.

He went in the door to a bright and cheery office. It might be a room with no windows, but it was not in the least gloomy. Chris met him in the reception area before Scott could even say why he was there.

The men shook hands and Chris said, "Come on back to my domain. Would you like some coffee, or soda, or water?"

"Already had coffee on the way here. Some water might be good."

Chris stopped at some large refrigerators and grabbed two water bottles. Scott noticed just about every kind of soda and juice were in that cooler, including iced tea and a couple flavors of energy drinks.

"Wow, that's quite the drink assortment you've got, are they all free?"

"Yep, a caffeinated worker is a happy worker. That also goes for sugar and hydration. Just one of the perks of the job that doesn't cost a lot, but keeps the workers happy."

"Nice. We have some machines at the church, but the money goes to the ladies' group. They keep them stocked and take the proceeds to use for crafts, or supplies to make things for the senior center."

He followed Chris into an office that was also brightly lit and cheerful, and the two men sat on either side of the desk. "Sounds fair to me. Profit versus non-profit changes things. Plus, people are only at the church for a couple of hours not all day like they are here. But, I don't think you came to discuss the merit of soda machines."

Scott laughed. "No, I didn't. Two days ago, a young lady came to the church to ask for a confidential consultation. Fortunately, she changed her mind on the confidential part and has asked for help from the authorities. I brought in Nolan, Greg and Jeremy to meet with her last night."

Chris sat forward in his chair as the significance of who had been in the meeting registered. "The arsonist?"

Scott nodded, glad that he didn't have to explain every little thing to Chris. "Yes, but he's a pyromaniac and the woman's brother."

Chris frowned. "So, he's setting the fires for stress relief, not maliciousness."

"Exactly, he was diagnosed as a child and they got him help, he's been able to control it for fifteen or so years."

"What changed?"

"Their parents died in a head-on collision about nine months ago."

Chris grimaced. "That sucks. But why here?"

"It's one of the vacation places they came to as a family. He's been to a few others on his way here."

"Anyone hurt?"

"No. He's only burning deserted buildings."

Frowning, Chris said, "Well except for the Howe's. He's escalating."

Scott shook his head, hoping that wasn't the case, even though he was fearful that it was. "Nicole, his sister, thinks it was an accident. She thinks he probably thought it was deserted."

"Maybe but it was a house with furnishings and a for sale sign in the yard. That's not exactly deserted."

"Which is why she's asked for help. She wants him caught before it becomes more than a misdemeanor."

"Smart girl."

Smart and beautiful, but he didn't have the time or luxury to go there. "Anyway, she thinks that maybe he's still here since the police have been monitoring all the comings and goings of everyone. Nolan's got some people checking the records. But we thought to check for any seasonal workers."

Chris sat back in his chair. "So, that's why you're here. I hire a shit ton of them."

"You do, Jeremy went to the resort and Greg is checking the construction company. If we don't find him with the heavy hitters, we'll start on the smaller ones."

"All right then, let me call in Francine. I could poke around in the database for an hour, but she'll get the same accomplished in less than two minutes."

While Chris called in his admin, Scott looked around the office. There were pictures on the walls of the many stages of getting the park up and running. Some schematics also covered the space and Scott recognized the bones of several attractions. He liked the extra-large photograph of opening day at the park.

Scott chuckled when he saw that the nasty article that the reporter had written shortly before the grand opening was framed and had a place of honor on the wall. The article had pulled the town together to fight against the implication they were nothing but a bunch of hicks and could never pull off an amusement park of this magnitude. The article had also filled the hotels with people that came specifically because they always disagreed with the reporter. If he hated it, they knew they would love it and they'd flowed in from every corner of the country.

Francine walked into the office and over to Chris's desk. Chris stood so she could take a seat at his computer. "We need to run a search to see if someone is working here."

Francine asked, "Social security number or name?"

"Kent Roman, here's the social." Scott handed the woman the paper it was written down on.

She nodded and tapped some keys. "I've got a K. Allen Roman with that number."

Scott leaned forward. "Really? Do you have a photo for a work badge?"

"Of course." She clicked the mouse and the printer on Chris's desk spit out a color picture of the man they were looking for. He looked older and thinner than the picture Nicole had, but it was clearly him.

Chris asked, "Is he working today?"

Francine shook her head. "No, he's off today. Back on tomorrow."

Scott asked, "What's his job? What time does he come in? Do you have an address for him?"

Francine frowned at him. "He's in maintenance and he starts at nine. His address is confidential information, Scott. I would need a warrant."

Scott pulled out his phone and called Nolan who answered on the first ring. "I'm at Chris's he works at the park, but today is his day off. Anyway, could we get a search warrant today? To get his home address?"

Nolan said, "I'll call you back."

Chris shook his head, "Oh for Pete's sake. Thank you for your help, Francine. You can go now."

"Chris, he could sue us if we give out personal information."

Chris just stood there until she walked out the door. Then he rattled off the address in the file.

Scott started to write it down and then looked at Chris. "It's fake."

Chris winced. "Yeah, I guess whoever entered it into the system was a temp worker, too."

Scott wasn't happy about that development. "So, he's using his middle name and gave a fake address. Not real clever, but he is trying to hide, at least somewhat."

Scott's phone rang. Nolan. "Never mind, it's a fake address."

"Couldn't reach the judge, anyway, seems he's out fishing. Sometimes this one-horse town drives me a little nuts."

"I hear you, but sometimes it's a lot easier too. So, we need to regroup and decide what we want to do tomorrow when he comes back to work." He looked at Chris but said into the phone, here or at the church?

Chris mouthed, "Church."

Nolan answered in kind, "It would attract less attention for all of us to meet at the church. We don't want to freak out tourists, or alert anyone who Kent might have made friends with."

"Chris agrees with you, we'll head there directly. I'll call Jeremy."

"I've got Greg. I assume Nicole is at the church already."

"Yeah, see you in a few."

Scott texted Nicole.

Scott: Found job, his day off. We're on our way there, can you put on a pot of coffee?

Nicole: Yay! Will do.

NICOLE SET HER PHONE DOWN. They'd found her brother. Well they didn't exactly have him in hand, but he was still here, and they'd found his job. She wondered why they weren't going to get him at his house, but figured they had their reasons, and she'd find out when they got here.

She hurried to go start a fresh pot of coffee. Too bad she didn't have any rolls or sandwiches. *Silly girl, it's not a party.* If they wanted food, they could always get some, it was still early in the day, not quite lunch time. It hadn't taken long, at all, to find him. But maybe that was just luck on their part, or maybe it was simply small-town living. She'd never lived anywhere this tiny and remote, so she didn't know what to expect.

She was both excited and worried that they'd found him. She so wanted the best for him. But what if the judge didn't agree with her or one of the other states wanted him brought back to face charges in their state. It was scary to be at the mercy of others, but her brother had made poor choices and would have to face the consequences. Still she hoped for the best possible consequences.

Waiting the ten minutes it took them to get to the church seemed like an eternity. Nicole paced and looked out the window and paced some more. Finally, vehicles started showing up, she breathed a sigh of relief and at the same time tensed. She didn't know who was in which car, since the only car she'd seen was Scott's and he hadn't driven in yet.

But she was capable of playing the hostess, so that's what she did.

Greg and Jeremy arrived first, so she told them she'd made coffee if they wanted to grab some before going upstairs to the conference room.

Next came Scott's father, John, who patted her on the hand and told her everything was going to be just fine. For some odd reason she believed him and relaxed.

Nolan came in at the same time as someone she didn't know. Nolan said, "Nicole, this is Chris, my brother-in-law and also the owner of the Tsilly amusement park."

Nicole asked, "Is my brother working at the amusement park?"

Chris looked at Nolan who nodded and then Chris said, "Yes he has been, all summer in fact."

She repeated the information about the coffee and then stood there wondering what was taking Scott so long. She also thought about her brother being here all summer while she was driving all over trying to find him, and felt a flair of irritation.

It was the first time she'd actually thought about what all this was costing her, rather than simply trying to find her run-away brother. It didn't change how she felt too much, but it was a tiny shift in focus. Her secret fear was that if her brother went to jail, she would be all alone in the world, but spending her life chasing him across the country wasn't exactly what she had in mind either.

Nicole saw Scott's SUV come down the drive where he would go around the back to park, so she went up to the conference room to wait for him. The guys all had coffee and were sitting around the table, not saying a lot, just waiting. It was a little eerie.

Scott came in with a bakery box. "I figured a little something from Samantha's wouldn't go amiss as we work on plans."

The men all dove in like they hadn't eaten in a week. She waited until they'd sat back down before looking into the box to see if they'd left anything. But Scott clearly knew the men well, because the box was still half full. She saw a scone that looked tasty and took that. She didn't look at the guys like they'd been pigs, and rude not to let her go first. She was an independent woman, but she didn't mind a man being a gentleman either.

When she sat down with her coffee and scone, Greg apologized for being rude. The other's followed suit so she told them she was fine and perfectly happy with her scone.

Scott laughed. "It doesn't hurt them to remember to be polite, however. Maybe I need to preach about that on Sunday."

Jeremy groaned. "No please don't, none of us want to explain to our wives or girlfriends what put that particular bee in your bonnet."

Scott gave him a wicked look. "That's exactly why I should. Your female counterparts will be more than happy to take you to task. Plus, you listen to them better than you do me."

Nolan grimaced. "That's because they're meaner and have more pull."

Scott grinned and nodded.

Nicole started to feel sorry for the men but decided that maybe it would be good for them.

John said, "Enough silliness, let's get this meeting going. I take it that our young pyromaniac is working at the amusement park, since Chris has joined the group."

Chris shrugged then said, "He is and has been working there all summer, since shortly after the fire at the Howe's.

We looked at his supposed street address and it wasn't even a street name we had in town. So definitely bogus."

He rattled off the address and Nicole gasped.

Scott looked quickly to her and asked, "What is it?"

Nicole had to draw a deep breath and will her body to calm down enough to answer. "That's the street our parents died on and the house number is the date of their death."

Chris said, "Well, hell. I'm so sorry. Scott mentioned that your brother seems to be going a little crazy since your parents died. That address kind of confirms that idea."

Nicole nodded because tears had backed up in her throat and she couldn't speak for a moment. Scott took her hand which gave her strength. She swallowed and squeaked out, "He'd not had any trouble with fire in years, until their deaths."

Chris said, "I looked through his file and he seems to be a model employee, always on time, willing to stay late or take an extra shift. Works hard. Nothing to indicate any problems."

Nicole said quietly, "He saves his troubles for matches and kerosene."

That got everyone's attention. Jeremy asked, "Does he always use kerosene?"

"Yes, he always has. We had some camping equipment and some spilled on the ground when they were refilling a lantern. Just a tiny bit, so my dad put a match in it to burn it off the driveway where they were finished filling the lanterns. Kent was fascinated by the stuff from that day forward. He'd always liked watching the flames when we went camping, but once he saw the kerosene ignite, he was hooked. Were the fires here started with kerosene?"

Nolan nodded.

"I'd half hoped it wasn't him but, at the same time stopping him is more important. Plus, I would like to get back to my life."

She noticed Scott was looking intensely at her. He probably was worried about losing another secretary. So, she shrugged. "Not that I know what that might entail. I quit my job and moved out of my apartment. But not chasing my brother across the western half of the United States would be a good start."

Scott gave her a weak smile and turned toward the group. "So, let's get to the point of this meeting. How do we want to go about collecting Kent without trouble?"

As they talked about plans and who to bring on board and where would be the best place to catch him, Nicole thought about what her life might look like once her brother was caught and sentenced. She supposed that she might want to stick close to him even if it was to visit him in jail. She did not relish being alone. She had friends back in their home town, but her brother, well it was just different.

First things first, they had to catch him. Chris pulled out a picture of Kent, and Nicole couldn't believe how much he had changed. There was an exhaustion in his eyes and a sadness that hurt her heart. He was thinner and just flat out didn't look good.

She wondered if she'd changed as much as he had. Nicole didn't think so, but then again, she would have seen any changes as gradual, so it was possible.

She tuned back into the discussion. "I think I should be there. I might be the one that recognizes him first."

Nolan shook his head. "It could be dangerous."

Nicole rolled her eyes. "He's not vicious and he wouldn't hurt me. He's not been getting into fights, he's been burning abandoned buildings."

Jeremy said, "The Howe's house was not abandoned."

"I can't believe he knew they were living there. Didn't you say they'd been gone for a few weeks?"

Scott nodded. "Yes, they had been, but you still don't know if your brother has changed."

She held up the picture Chris had brought and pulled out the one she had and put them side by side. "He certainly has changed, he's exhausted and heartbroken. There is no violence in either picture."

The men couldn't argue with what was staring them in the face. "He needs to find hope and love again. I can give him that, at least. I know I can't save him from the consequences of his actions, but I can tell him I love him. Plus, I will recognize him quicker than anyone else does."

They finally relented and went about deciding where would be the best place for her to observe. All employees had to clock in, and they decided that the clock for his group would be the best place to wait. There was an observation room not far from it, that Nicole could be in to watch the door and alert the men when Kent drew near.

They decided on timelines and who else would be part of the operation. Nicole thought they were going a little overboard to capture her brother, but she didn't argue with them about it. They were going to let her be there and that's what mattered to her.

Scott said he would drive Nicole, so Kent didn't see her car with its out of state license plates in the parking lot.

CHAPTER 8

When all the plans were made, and the men started leaving, Nicole stayed seated thinking about all that had been discussed and what would happen tomorrow. Was it almost over? Or would the hardest part just be beginning? She didn't know. A numbness had crept over her as the plans had been made, she felt removed from her own body. Like she was somehow detached and watching from above. She hardly noticed when Scott came back in the room after walking his friends out.

He sat beside her and took her hand in both of his, they were so warm. "Are you all right?"

She slowly shook her head. "I don't know. I feel odd."

"That's not really a surprise. You've been following your brother for a long time, totally alone in your quest. To have it coming to an end with a group of people you don't know has got to be weird."

She nodded and finally looked at him. "It is. I just hope it works out for the best. I realized I'd never thought through what I would do when I found him. I'd never even considered having the police involved. But…"

"But you might not have been able to stop him by yourself."

She nodded as tears filled her eyes and her throat closed. "I'd hoped."

Scott rolled his chair closer to her, so he could put his arm around her. "Of course, you did. And it might have worked, too. But this way you know he'll get some help."

"I hope so. I can't give up on him. He's the only family I have left."

Scott's voice was rough when he said. "You won't need to give up on him. We'll make sure he gets the help he needs. Besides that, I can share my family with you."

What a sweet offer. "Your dad is nice."

"My mom is too, and she loves to fuss over people. I'll take you to meet her in a couple of days."

Nicole knew he meant after her brother was captured and things had settled down. Did she want to meet his mother? It seemed a little odd, at the same time it sounded kind of nice. She could use some fussing over. Her heart hurt, and she felt bruised inside. "That sounds good."

It also felt nice to have Scott's arm around her. She could feel him tracing circles on her arm, a soft movement, meant to soothe. It was working, too.

~

SCOTT DIDN'T KNOW what to do to help Nicole. She'd looked so lost when she'd said her brother was the only family she had left. His heart had broken for her then, he had his mom and dad, no siblings, but he felt like the whole town was his family.

He didn't think he would ever feel as alone and adrift as Nicole expressed, as long as he stayed in Chedwick. The tiny town he lived in made it feel like family. Irritating family sometimes, but still family. He couldn't imagine living in a huge metropolis where he didn't know most of the people. He'd gone to college in a larger town and wasn't a fan, fortunately the college campus had been like a small town inside the larger city.

He'd ventured out into that larger town during his six years of college and seminary, but he'd never found anything to recommend moving to somewhere like that, and had been perfectly happy to come back home.

"If you stay here long enough all the nosy people in town will become your family whether you want them to or not."

She looked up at him from where her head had been resting on his shoulder. "You mean like Sylvia at the pizza place."

He chuckled while he reigned in the desire to kiss her. "That's exactly what I mean. You'll have all kinds of people trying to run your life and tell you what to do. In fact, I'm a little surprised the Ladies Auxiliary hasn't been by to meet you yet."

"I've not been here three full days yet."

Scott drawled, "Which makes them about two and a half days late."

She laughed at his exaggeration, like he'd hoped, and he felt good that he'd helped her that tiny bit. He couldn't fix all her problems but making her laugh was a step in the right direction.

He heard someone call up the stairs, "Yoo hoo, is anyone here?" He recognized the voice of Mable Erickson. The Ladies Auxiliary had arrived.

"Yes, Mrs. Erickson, we'll be right down." He hollered and then whispered to Nicole. "And there they are, prepare yourself, the Ladies Auxiliary is downstairs, with more opinions than baked goods, and that's saying something."

They went downstairs to see the committee at the foot.

Diminutive Mrs. Erickson, who was in her eighties, had been the third-grade teacher in town for forty-seven years. She'd been his third-grade teacher and she never forgot an embarrassing moment of any student. She might set off a fire-alarm baking cookies because she forgot they were in there, but her teaching career was still very clear.

Next was Ruth Tisdale, the biggest gossip in town, she always gave her opinion on his sermons, she was in her late seventies, tall and slender with dark black hair, most of the time, but occasionally her snow-white roots showed. Since Maureen had warned Nicole about the woman, he figured she'd be on guard.

Carol Anderson who was the former mayor and now ran a B&B was also a member, Scott thought she was on the Auxiliary simply to keep the others in line. Sylvia Smith, who Nicole had talked to was also present. Several ladies were missing, and he wondered what had kept them away.

Sylvia answered the question he didn't ask. "The rest of the women are home watching their stories, apparently there is something juicy happening today. Of course, the TV people will string it out for a week or more, but the ladies couldn't bring themselves to miss this episode."

Ruth nodded. "I made the sacrifice. I can always watch it later now that my grandson has it programmed to record. He's a good boy."

Scott wanted to laugh, the boy was older than he was by six or eight years. They probably thought of him as a boy, too. He made the introductions and then came up with an excuse to escape. Not that he was afraid of the women.

Who was he kidding, he sure *was* afraid of them, especially when they were all together in a gaggle.

CHAPTER 9

Nicole hadn't seen Scott move that fast since she'd arrived in his church. She couldn't figure out what the hurry was.

Mabel Erickson spoke up, "Don't worry about him, we deliberately start talking about elderly women's ailments when he stays around. We figure it's good to humble the boy."

Ruth Tisdale cackled. "He sure does turn a little green when we talk about boils and bunions."

Carol Anderson shook her head. "You shouldn't pick on him so much. He's a good man."

Mabel nodded her head. "Yes, of course he is, but it's still good for him to realize he's human like the rest of us."

Sylvia finally took control of the group. "Come on ladies, let's find a nice place to chat. Let's use the dining hall, we can sample all the baked goods. That way Nicole can get a taste of all your goodies and save the rest for later."

Nicole was shocked when each of the women took hold of rolling carts and bags of food. There was enough for a small army. They went into the kitchen which still had warm coffee from the earlier meeting and those women put out a spread that Nicole was certain could feed the whole town. Scott hadn't been joking about the baked goods, which made her kind of afraid to hear the opinions.

Sylvia brought out plates and forks and napkins and butter from the kitchen to add to the feast. Once all of them had coffee, or tea as Mabel Erickson preferred, and a plate of snacks, they sat down to talk.

Nicole took a taste of a blueberry crumble that was to die for, it had come in a nine by thirteen cake pan so she would be able to have more. Whether she could finish it was doubtful, but she could share with Scott and any other people who came by during the week. Some of the items looked like they could be frozen and saved for later.

When everyone had eaten a few bites, Carol said, "So start by telling us about yourself, dear."

"All right. Well, Scott told you my name is Nicole Roman. I'm from Denver, Colorado and I just got here three days ago. I'm trying to find my brother. Our parents died about nine months ago and he's struggling with that." She didn't want to mention the pyromania yet, they would all know soon enough, but it wasn't something she wanted to talk about.

Mabel said, "Oh, you poor dear. It's very hard to lose parents but your brother having trouble isn't helping with that. So, is he here in town also?"

Nicole nodded, her throat was a little tight from the compassion she saw on the women's faces. She cleared her throat and said, "Yes, he's working at the amusement park. I haven't seen him yet, since today is his day off, but I will tomorrow."

Sylvia asked, "How did your parents die? Was it sudden?"

Nicole tried not to think about the night that her parents hadn't made it home and police officers had arrived at her apartment. "Yes, it was sudden. They were in a head-on car collision. We were told they died instantly when a truck swerved into their lane."

Ruth shook her head. "Oh my, you hear about things like that but never think it will happen to you."

"Yes, they had gone out on a date night and were headed home after seeing a movie, when it happened. I was instantly terrified when two police officers knocked on my door."

Carol said, "Well their last memories were good ones and they didn't suffer, so there is that to be thankful for."

Nicole knew she was trying to be nice and she appreciated it, but the horror of the news and the subsequent troubles were so strong that she hated that night and wished her parents had stayed home. She mumbled, "Thanks."

Sylvia cleared her throat, "Let's talk about something else, shall we? How did you meet Scott and take the job as his admin?"

Nicole didn't know exactly what to say. She wanted to stick close to the truth but still didn't want to talk about her brother. "I came to the church to ask some questions. When I mentioned I was going to need a job, Scott hired me on the spot."

Sylvia nodded. "He isn't much inclined to having to fend for himself. Since Maureen had been gone a few days he was probably desperate." She stopped and looked horrified at her words. "Not that you won't do a fine job and he's lucky to have you. It's just he's..."

Carol patted Sylvia's hand. "It's okay just let it drop. Nicole doesn't seem to be offended."

Nicole smiled. "No in fact I'm glad he was desperate, it saved me a good amount of job hunting. And apartment hunting also, since I'm staying in the rectory. His desperation was a godsend, which is quite appropriate for a church."

All the women chuckled at that.

Sylvia nodded her head. "God does work in mysterious ways."

Nicole had to wonder about that. It did seem like she had landed in a nice place even though the reason for being here wasn't pleasant.

Carol said, "So what can we tell you about our town?"

Nicole would be happy to let the focus change from her to something else, so she said, "Oh, tell me everything. Maybe start with the amusement park. This town seems very remote to have such a large park."

Carol laughed. "It's my favorite story. Six years ago, people were leaving our lovely little town for greener pastures. The economic downturn had hurt us severely, so I held a town meeting. I was mayor at the time and desperate to save the town. You see someone in my husband's family has been the mayor of Chedwick for generations and I was not about to let it die on my watch."

As Mayor Carol told the story of how the *Adventures with Tsilly* game had been born in the town with her daughter Sandy. And then Chris Clarkson, whom she'd met, had come up with the idea of the park, Nicole was enthralled.

It was a fascinating story, the other ladies would interject occasionally, but a lot of it had hinged on Carol leading the charge and an old newspaper man named Gus Ferguson. They'd started with the park and the town using *Adventures with Tsilly* as a draw for the millions of people who loved the game and books. But the town had evolved to also be a wedding destination and they had an art gallery that had glass art by the world-famous Lucille Thompson. It also had quilts and homemade soap and wood carvings, so it wasn't strictly an art gallery.

Nicole's hands shook when she realized that Nolan Thompson, the cop, was Lucille Thompson's son. He'd been the one to suggest a way for her brother to focus his obsession with fire to something constructive. She'd been thinking little glass blown knick knacks and he'd been talking about world class art. Her heart was pounding at the thought. It would be a miracle and nothing less, if it actually happened. Now that would be God working in mysterious ways for sure.

Nicole didn't hear much more of what the women said as she was totally focused on her brother studying under someone like Lucille Thomson or at least her son. They said something about a web developer that moved to their town after some forest fires had brought him in as a hot shot firefighter. And they also talked about a huge fundraiser Greg Jones had just put on. He was the assistant fire chief and she'd met him several times. She did notice through her fog of thought that he was dating or engaged or something to Carol's daughter who had invented the video game.

The women stayed a while longer, talking about the town and the best places to eat, and how to get things shipped into town if they didn't have them, and then devolved into gossip. But Nicole just let their words run over the top of her. She knew Scott would help her with anything she wanted to know.

When the ladies finally stood and started wrapping up the baked goods, she noticed they seemed to be making a plate of some of the items. The rest they sealed up tight, putting some in the refrigerators and some on the counters in the industrial kitchen.

Sylvia pointed to the plate they made. "It's for Scott, he'll be starving by now and salivating for all his favorites."

Nicole laughed, and the ladies took their leave. Before she could walk back to the kitchen, she saw Scott was there with the plate and a fork in his hand devouring the food they'd left for him. She shook her head and went over to him. "Shame on you for not telling me that Nolan is Lucille Thompson's son. He's not offering to show my brother how to make little cutesy crap, but to create amazing art."

Scott swallowed and grinned. "I wish I could have seen your face when that little tidbit came out."

"I wondered when you all laughed about my glass blowing comment, and you promised to tell me."

He nodded. "I did, but then we've been kind of busy actually finding your brother, so it slipped my mind. Sorry."

"But Lucille Thompson, do you know how famous she is? Is her son as good as she is?"

"Yes. In fact, Lucille says if her son hadn't stopped working in glass for over fifteen years, he would have far surpassed her by now."

"Why did he stop."

"It's a long sad story and not really mine to tell. But suffice it to say he stopped to become a cop, because his sister was murdered. The only thing that drew him back to the art was falling in love with our resident jewelry designer and being forced to help her with the art gallery."

"Oh, his sister was murdered, that's awful. No wonder he wanted to be a cop to stop people from killing others."

He nodded. "Yeah. I think I'm brave running into a burning building. But running into a gunfight, so not me."

"I couldn't agree more, in fact the burning building sounds scary to me."

"Well, we're not going into it without a lot of training and the proper gear, so that does help."

Nicole nodded, she supposed that would make some difference, but she wasn't sure it would be enough. "I just hope this idea of Nolan's works out for Kent, that would truly be a miracle."

"God's still in that business, so it would be a good thing to pray for."

"I will. I'm so glad I came here. This all seems like a bit of a miracle to me. Sylvia said something that's been floating around in my head. She said God works in mysterious ways. I think she's right about that. Now I'm going to get to work. I haven't done anything today but eat and listen to people."

SCOTT WATCHED the pretty young woman walk away from him as her statement pounded in his heart and brain. God did work in mysterious ways and he wanted to ask God just exactly what he had planned. But he knew that sometimes God didn't answer questions like that. In fact, most of the time it seemed like he bumbled around in the dark and nearly by accident bumped into God's plan for him.

He supposed God called that free will. He shook his head as he finished the food on his plate, sometimes free will made things a lot harder.

He thought about free will and the mysterious ways of God. He was just glad he didn't have to figure it all out. He could barely handle his own life and thoughts and feelings, let alone trying to orchestrate everyone in the world.

That's part of the reason he preached on God's love for people and not on hellfire as Old Man Peterson would prefer. Because Scott had no clue how God was working in another person's life or where they were along the path of faith.

He barely knew where he was at, let alone the people who sat in his church on any given Sunday.

Scott supposed he should get back to working on his sermon for this Sunday, he'd been very preoccupied with the other events going on and hadn't given it a lot of thought over the last few days.

He was happy that Nicole seemed excited about her brother working with Nolan. Now all they had to do was capture her brother and convince him and all the authorities it was a good idea. Easy peasy, right? He sure hoped so.

CHAPTER 10

The next morning Scott picked up Nicole early in the morning, so they could be in place, well before Kent would be arriving for work. She'd clearly just showered because her hair was damp, and she smelled delicious. He tried to keep his body from reacting to her scent or her beauty as she slid into his car.

Nicole had brought him out a plate with some of the food the ladies had dropped off yesterday. They'd brought plenty and he was happy to share the task of eating it with her. Sandy had made an amazing coffee ring. Carol had said she'd made an extra one for the church since she was still helping out baking for the B&B in the mornings. Sandy had come from Seattle the first part of the summer to help Carol when she'd had to have surgery. Since Sandy loved baking, she'd kept on doing that even when her mom was back running the B&B. Scott wasn't about to turn down the blackberry and raspberry coffee ring Sandy had made, and then there were also some scones, and a banana walnut muffin.

"I'm not sure I can eat all that."

"Try. Those women brought enough food for an army. It's

delicious but if I ate all of it, I wouldn't be able to get through the door."

Scott slid a look at the sexy woman sitting next to him and didn't think she had anything to worry about anytime soon. "Did you freeze some of it?"

"Yes, most of the muffins and scones. Half the cookies and the breads. I think there is banana, pumpkin, and zucchini breads. I don't think the blueberry crumble, or this berry coffee cake would freeze well. And then there's that dessert thing with cream cheese, chocolate and whipped cream on top, that wouldn't at all. Or the banana cream pie."

"I hope you plan to stay long enough to eat all those goodies."

"I've been thinking about that. If Kent ends up getting to work with Nolan on some kind of reduced sentence, then I would like to stay close. If he gets shipped somewhere to a penitentiary, then I'll need to go with him. I doubt it will be a super long sentence since he did manage not to hurt anyone. Still I wouldn't want him to be alone with no visitors."

Scott felt a great disappointment at the idea of her leaving, and he hoped her brother would get a deferred sentence with a work release. Then both of them would stay. He wanted to believe it was all about what was best for Kent and that Nicole would continue to be his admin. But that wasn't the only reason he wanted her to stay. He really liked her, and he wanted to get to know her better.

He'd even wondered about the strong attraction he felt for her. Was this the kind of attraction that led to marriage and a life mate or was it just some kind of powerful lust? He really didn't know for sure, but he'd decided that he wanted to find out.

That idea kind of surprised him, he'd not really thought about a wife, but the image was surprisingly pleasant when he pictured Nicole in the role. He'd never dated anyone else that fit there. A woman in college he'd dated had tried to convince him she was the one, he'd tried to make it work in his heart, but it simply wouldn't, so he'd eventually broken up with her. She'd found another pastor in training and they'd been engaged in a few months. So apparently it had been the job that attracted her, and not the man. She'd clearly wanted a starring role as a pastor's wife.

He thought the couple were still married and they were running a church in San Francisco, so he was happy for them and glad he'd dodged the marriage bullet. But now it didn't seem like such a bad idea. He knew he was getting way ahead of himself, since he'd only known Nicole a few days, but he could see that stretching out. Providing she got to stay.

But first they had to catch her brother. That was the first step, then there was a lot of steps after that, before he would even know if the woman was staying in town.

He realized he'd been thinking too long and hadn't replied. "I would be more than happy to have you stay on, but if you have to leave, I understand. Family comes first."

She relaxed. "Thanks. I'm so worried about all of this."

"I know, do you want to pray about it?"

"I would be more than happy if you would pray for it."

Scott chuckled. "Oh, don't you worry about that. I have been and will continue to."

Scott put the rest of his snacks on the console and started driving toward the amusement park. He noticed Nicole broke off tiny bits of the scone as he drove. She probably didn't even know she was doing it. He guessed it was nervous eating. He thought it was a cute habit. *What a sap.*

NICOLE RODE ALONG IN SILENCE, the only thing she could think was, please, please, please. She supposed it was some kind of prayer. Please let them catch him. Please let him be caught peacefully. Please let him not be mad. Please let him get a deferred sentence. Please let this all work out. Please let them stay in this little town that was so loving and kind to her. Please let her keep working for the hunky pastor. Just please, please, please.

They turned into the amusement park's lot and her hands got cold. She was so damn worried everything would go wrong. What if her brother had left town and she'd missed him? What if he resisted arrest? What if? No, she couldn't go down that path, she was better off with the please, please, please.

Scott put the car in park, turned toward her and took her cold hands into his warm ones. "It's going to be all right, don't let your imagination run wild with all the bad things that could happen. Focus on all the good things that might transpire."

How did he know exactly what she was thinking? She'd never felt so in tune with another person, even her parents or best friends. She felt her throat close but managed to say, "But I don't want to get my hopes up."

He squeezed her hands. "Getting your hopes up is way better than letting doom and gloom fill your thoughts."

"I think you're right about that, at least it doesn't scare the crap out of me by thinking about everything that could go wrong."

"Good. Now let's go in and get settled so we can get your brother the help he needs. Okay?"

Nicole nodded. "I'm ready."

"I'll be right there with you the whole time."

She felt such profound gratitude for him planning to stay by her side she could hardly speak. She finally whispered. "I appreciate that more than you know."

"You'll be fine. Your brother will be fine. It will all be fine."

"I sincerely hope you're right."

"Of course, I am. Well, at least I sincerely hope I am." He sighed and shrugged his shoulders, like he didn't really know how it would go. But she held on to his assurance like a lifeline.

He drawled out, "Let's get 'er done little lady."

Nicole laughed at his really bad John Wayne accent, but it did relieve some of the tension and for that she was grateful.

They were all situated by eight-thirty, Kent was due in at nine, but was often early by ten to fifteen minutes.

Nicole's eyes were glued to the parking lot entrance's camera. Occasionally she would glance at the others just to make sure he hadn't found another way into the building. There was one screen that showed the employee parking lot and she did scan that every few minutes, but she didn't see his car, so she turned back to the entrance camera.

She felt Scott tense and glanced up to see where he was looking and sure enough a car just like her brother's was parking. She watched as the man stepped out of the car, it was Kent. She murmured, "That's him."

Scott relayed the information that he would be walking in the door in the next few seconds.

Nicole's heart pounded, her brother looked broken, his shoulders were slumped, and he was walking like an old man. She stood and started walking toward the door, she had to get to him, he needed her, he needed a hug and her love. He wasn't dangerous to anyone, but himself, maybe.

Scott said, "You agreed to wait in here."

Nicole turned on Scott. "That's before I saw him. He needs me."

"I get that but..." He glanced at the monitor and saw that the men had Kent surrounded.

Nicole saw it too. "You delayed me just long enough." She turned from Scott and hurried to her brother.

She heard Nolan say, "We'd like you to come down to the station, so we can ask you a few questions."

Kent said in a weary voice, "I've got a job..."

A woman she'd never seen before said, "You go on in with the officers, Allen. We can manage without you for a bit."

Kent nodded. "Thanks. I'll be back as soon as I can." Then he looked up and saw Nicole, first affection flared for just a moment and then his eyes narrowed. "What are you doing here, Nicole?"

He looked back at the men that had him surrounded. "This is more than a few questions, isn't it?"

Nolan said, "That all depends on your answers. Now do you want to do this here in the hall where your friends and co-workers are coming in, or at the department?"

Kent shrugged but turned toward the door. "We can go."

Nicole was shocked at the anger she'd seen on her brother's face. She followed the men out the door, wanting to say something but not knowing what. Scott came up and took her hand, she welcomed the contact, but felt like a fool. She'd been so glad to see him and had felt sorry for him. But Kent's reaction was not of a similar vein, for a second yes, but overall no.

She sighed as she got into Scott's SUV.

He turned the key, so he could follow the patrol cars. "It will be all right, he needs some time is all."

She couldn't say anything, of all the things she'd imagined, this anger towards her had never entered her mind.

CHAPTER 11

Scott was worried about Nicole, she clearly had not been expecting her brother to be angry with her. She was working with law enforcement to get Kent stopped, which might mean jail time, so Scott wasn't too surprised at the guy's reaction. A case could be made that her brother would see her as turning him in. Everyone knew it was all with good intentions, but Kent wouldn't know that.

He decided he would wait and see how things unfolded, but he wouldn't be a bit opposed to clueing Kent in if needed.

When they got to the police department, Nolan already had Kent in an interrogation room, so he and Nicole waited.

She wrung her hands together, whether it was from nervousness or cold he couldn't tell. "Will they let me talk to him?"

"I don't know why not."

She said in a small voice. "He was so angry looking."

"Yeah." Scott felt like shit, he's the one that had pushed her to do this. It had been necessary, but he didn't like the hurt feelings she was having.

"I didn't expect that. I've missed him so much."

He took her hands, they were ice cold and shaking. "I know you have."

"He thinks I turned him in, doesn't he?"

What was he supposed to say to that? He couldn't lie to make her feel better. "That would be my guess."

Nicole whispered, "But I had to."

"I know, and eventually he'll realize that as well. But maybe not right now. He needs some help before he'll be able to think clearly."

She sighed. "Yeah, that's probably true."

Scott had to give her something to hope for. "It will be good in the long run. He's not done anything too horrific that will keep him in jail a long time. At least that we know of."

"And maybe he'll be able to work with Nolan."

He squeezed her hands. "That would be superior. He'll need to want to do that and agree to the terms."

"I don't think he's stupid enough not to want to. It would be a great opportunity."

"I agree, but I don't know his state of mind either. I don't think Nolan will push for it if Kent has a bad attitude."

Nicole frowned. "He's never been a cranky person. But I don't know how much he's changed. I hope not too much."

Nicole had shrunken into herself and looked dejected. He wanted to help but didn't really know how. He'd always felt like he knew what to do in nearly every situation, but he was at a loss this time and he didn't like the feeling. Had he been a cocky know-it-all before, always stepping in with just the right thing to say?

It was entirely possible. He wondered if maybe that was why his congregation had gone around him, to ask the board group to get them the bulletin board. Maybe he hadn't listened to why they wanted it and had shot it down too quickly. Scott didn't remember doing that, but that didn't mean he hadn't. Nicole and her troubles were shining light into his life that displayed areas he didn't like too much. Guess it was time for some rough edges to be sanded off in his own heart. Not pleasant, but probably good for him.

He thought back to what Nicole had just said. "Let's hope any changes are for the better. Sometimes tragedy helps us to reevaluate our lives." Or even a pretty woman who needed help and not pat answers.

She sat up a little straighter. "Yeah, I'm going to hope that's the case."

He wanted to get her thinking about something else while they waited so the stress didn't weigh her down. "So, tell me about Colorado. I've never been there. Are the mountains like ours here?"

"No, not really. Well some of them are, I suppose. But the altitude makes them a lot different. Here you're starting near sea level and going up from there. In Colorado, the mountains start at a mile high. So, the altitude is a killer. Sometimes literally."

As she talked on about her home state, he noticed some of the sparkle she normally had, come back into her. She had funny stories to tell about living in Colorado and also going on vacations to see family on the west coast, where she had learned to deep sea fish. She'd done a lot of lake and stream fishing growing up near the Rockies but had really been excited the first time she went out on a boat to deep sea fish.

"The rod and reel are massive and have to be mounted to the boat and the fish are enormous. I caught one and I was hooked. It splashed me, and I got covered in ocean water, so I was glad it was a hot summer day. The rest of the family enjoyed it, but I fell in love with the thrill of bringing in those monster fish. My uncles entered me into competitions whenever I could get away from school or work. I won several of them, too."

Scott could feel her excitement. He'd seen some pictures of her winning contests, but didn't know if he should admit to googling her. "We should definitely go out on a boat here on the lake and see how you like fishing on it. It's not the same as the ocean, but it's a big darn lake so it's probably a lot different from your Colorado lakes."

"Oh, that would be so fun! I would love it. Our lakes are not nearly the size of this one. Width wise maybe, but length wise, no way. Let's do it soon."

She smiled at him and he literally saw the moment she remembered why she was here. The smile faded, and the sparkle drained away. She said in a small voice. "If I'm still here that is."

He squeezed the hand he still held. "If you move away for a while you can always come back for a vacation and I'll take you. Even if we're both old and gray."

Nicole looked him in the eye. "I'm going to hold you to that."

"Good. I'm going to hold you to coming back. If you leave that is. Deal?"

"Deal."

THE DOOR OPENED to the interrogation room and she froze, her breath caught as she waited to see what would happen. She saw them lead Kent out of the room and toward the back. He didn't even turn her direction and her heart cracked right in half. What had happened to her sweet brother?

A few minutes later Nolan came out from the back and brought them into his office. "Nicole, your brother confessed to starting the fires. He acted like he didn't want to, but we didn't really ask many questions before he told us it all. It was almost like he wanted to get caught."

"Can I see him?"

"In a few minutes, yes. We didn't discuss the idea of a work-release program. We need to see what the other states are willing to do before we go down that road. If they want to extradite him to face charges in their jurisdiction, it could circumvent the idea."

"So, I shouldn't mention it?"

Nolan shook his head. "Not yet, no. We don't want to give him a false hope until we've gotten some idea of what might happen. But he was very cooperative and that will go in his favor. Greg is going to talk to some lawyers he knows. Kent indicated that he didn't have any assets and I've gathered the same from you."

"No, at least I don't know of any. I should probably call my parents' lawyer and see if the house has sold. That might give us some, I don't know how much equity they had. It wasn't paid off, so there might not be any at all. I can let you know what they say."

One of the other officers knocked on the glass to Nolan's office and gave him a thumbs-up sign, as he continued walking toward the door.

Nolan said, "Your brother has been processed and you can go see him now."

She cleared her throat and still her voice came out small. "In jail?"

"In a holding cell, yes." Nolan stood. "Come with me, it's not that bad. Scott, you can come too if you want."

They all walked down the hall to the holding cells. Kent was laying on his bunk with his back to the door.

Nolan said, "Kent, your sister would like to speak with you."

"I've got nothing to say to her."

Her breath caught in a gasp.

"No, wait, I do." He turned and stood. He pointed at her

as he stalked over to where she was standing. "You ratted me out."

"No. You needed help."

He gave a mirthless chuckle. "A jail cell is helping me?"

Her heart was breaking, but she wasn't going to back down. "You can't hurt anyone in here."

"I didn't hurt anyone."

"You almost did with the Howe's."

Kent shook his head. "That was an accident. I didn't know anyone was in there. That place had been abandoned when I'd seen it earlier."

"But it was a home for sale, and you burned it."

"So, you turned me in?"

His anger radiated off of him, but she knew she'd done the right thing. "I had to, you could have hurt those people or killed them. Then you would go to jail for murder."

He scoffed. "So melodramatic. Well you've done your duty to society Nicole, so just go on and leave me to rot in jail."

"But I want to help."

"You've helped enough. I don't need your kind of help."

Kent marched back and laid back down on his bunk with his back to her again. She was torn between sorrow and anger. She had not been the one to set fires, to break laws. But he was her brother and she loved him. He hated her. She had no family left.

CHAPTER 12

Scott was pissed at Kent's attitude toward Nicole and he might just come back to have a chat with him. But not today. Nicole needed him. He followed her down the hall and out the door.

"He's angry now, but he'll get over it. You still need to see about the house being sold. He'll still need a lawyer. Maybe after he has some time to think he'll see the truth. Or if he can work with Nolan..."

Nicole didn't answer him she just walked over and got into his car. When they got to the church, she turned to him. "Will you be all right if I take the rest of today off? So, I can make phone calls? I know tomorrow is busy with people coming and going. Saturday wouldn't be good for calling anyway."

Scott didn't want her to wallow, but he supposed she needed time to think. "That would be fine. But if you need someone to talk to, I'm all on your side." Of course, he's also the one who'd set the whole thing in motion, so she might be angry with him.

She gave him a tiny smile. "I'll keep that in mind. See you tomorrow."

As she walked away Scott prayed that was true and he hoped the tiny smile meant she wasn't mad at him.

It might be a good idea for her to spend some time alone, he had some ideas of his own to investigate. If the Roman's didn't have any assets they could draw from, he wanted to see what other options were available. Maybe a church fund of some sort was out there for this type of special need. A fundraiser could be started, but they'd just had that huge one here in town, for the helicopter flights to Chelan when people needed medical attention beyond the clinic's scope. It had been very successful but a second one on the tail of it probably wouldn't do well. Maybe a Go Fund me thing on the internet would work.

He decided to start making some phone calls to see what was available. His first call would be to his father.

His dad picked up on the first ring. "So, how did it go this morning?"

Scott realized he should have called his dad hours ago. "It went well, actually. Kent didn't fight and confessed to all of it. In fact, Nolan thought he was somewhat relieved to be caught."

"Good. I'm glad to hear it."

"He's not happy that his sister was involved."

His dad made the humming sound he did when he was thinking. "He probably sees it as betrayal."

"No doubt, but Nicole was crushed by his attitude."

"I don't see her as staying crushed for long. I think she'll bounce back pretty quick, don't you?"

Scott had to admit his dad had a good point. "Yeah, I do too. She's not too much of a fragile flower."

"No, she's not. I'm glad you called to let me know."

"Dad, I also wanted to ask you about ways to maybe help

with the lawyer costs. You know Nolan was thinking to maybe mentor him on glass art, to teach him to use fire in a constructive way rather than destructive. But a good lawyer to present that idea is going to cost. Especially if they need to convince the other states not to extradite."

"True. Does Nicole or her brother have any assets?"

"Nicole is calling the lawyers of her parents to find out. They did have a house that they put on the market, but she doesn't know what that would bring in, if it sold, or what they still owed on it."

"I see. Well let me think of what might be available. I'll call you back if I think of anything. It might be worth trying to contact Maureen, she would know. I don't know where on their world tour she is, so email would probably be the most efficient."

"Thanks, Dad. I'll do that. Let me know if you think of anything."

"Will do."

Scott immediately drafted an email to Maureen. She would be a great source, the only trouble being, the clock was ticking, and no one knew for sure where she was in the world or more importantly what time zone, she was in.

Scott continued to make a list of his own ideas and how to go about investigating those. He would talk to Nicole about his thoughts tomorrow.

NICOLE NEEDED SOME ALONE TIME, she walked into the rectory. It was so cozy, but not what she needed. She wanted some open space, it was easier to think things through when surrounded by nature, so she got out the maps she'd accumulated. There was a road that went up the mountain, but it was marked as a dirt road and she wasn't sure her car would be the best for that. She wondered if that was why it seemed like most people drove trucks or SUVs. She hadn't seen many regular cars especially hybrids, which seemed unusual these days.

There was also a road along the lake that ended at a park, that looked like the better plan. She got a bottle of water, a sandwich, her journal, her sketchpad, and a sweater. Those should keep her for a while, if she found a good place to sit and think. If she didn't, she could always come back. She did need to make phone calls, so she would have to stay in cell range.

She followed the map although it wasn't exactly a difficult route, basically head south-east and keep the lake on the left. The streets all converged where the mountains rose up and there was only one road left that led out of the town, even that, was only a mile or so long. When she got to the park, she could see why the road ended. There was a large stream, possibly a river and then on the other side of that the mountains rose high and rocky. There was nowhere else for a road to go unless someone blasted the mountain and built one deliberately.

It wasn't really much of a park even, just some grass, two picnic tables, and what looked like primitive bathrooms. The parking lot would hold maybe a dozen cars, but it was empty now so there was no competition for a good spot. Nicole pulled into one of the spaces that faced the lake, and simply sat in the car for long minutes, watching the clouds reflecting on the lake's surface.

She gathered her things and stepped out of the car, there was a slight breeze, so she was glad she'd brought her sweater. Setting all her thinking paraphernalia on the table Nicole pulled on her sweater and sat on the bench. It was clean enough with only a few carvings in the table top, fairly typical for mountain tables. She traced her finger over some of the carvings and wondered if she'd met any of the people who had declared their love in these table carvings.

Deciding to make the phone calls first she scrolled through the numbers on her phone to find her parents' lawyers. She was disappointed when all she got was an answering service saying the office staff was not in today, but that she could leave her name and number and a brief message. If it was not urgent, they would call her back on Monday. Urgent calls would be returned over the weekend at double the normal rate.

Nicole shook her head at the policy and left her non-urgent message. She pulled out her sketch pad and colored pencils and drew a picture of the lake, she couldn't get it to look quite as serene as it did in person, but it was close enough. A grey squirrel was sitting on a rock close by probably hoping for a snack. Nicole drew him too and then decided he'd been so patient she would toss him a crust from her sandwich.

He jumped off the rock to where the bread had landed and then went back up on the rock to eat it. She wondered how often he received a snack from posing on the rock for tourists to snap pictures of, she decided she might as well take one of him eating her bread crust.

When he'd finished it and didn't get any more tossed his way he scampered away. Nicole was charmed by the little guy. She wrote about him in her journal and how he'd brightened her mood after a challenging day. Then she wrote out her feelings about capturing her brother and his attitude.

As she wrote she began to see things from Kent's point of view and realized he'd felt betrayed, when that wasn't at all what she was doing. He wouldn't be able to see it from her point of view, at least not yet, because he was still caught in the pyromania cycle. Which meant he didn't see the fires as destructive but as a harmless action that helped him cope with stress.

Kent would never mean his actions as malicious or to hurt anyone, but fire was unpredictable, and no one could completely control it. Just look at all the wildfires they'd had the last few years. This town was completely surrounded by forests, if a fire got out of control it could be devastating.

No, she'd done the right thing, and if Kent couldn't understand that right now, maybe he would in the future.

Nicole was glad she'd brought her journal, so she could write out her thoughts and feelings. Having to actually write them down clarified them for her and she could look at them more objectively.

She realized she was hungry again and ate the rest of her sandwich, feeling more relaxed than she had in days. Her brother was now prevented from committing any more crimes and that had been pressing on her for months. The constant worry and fear was finally over. Not everything was worked out by any means, but her cross-country trek was finished.

She could very easily stay here in this town. There was nothing calling her back to Colorado, her job was mediocre, her childhood friends were either married with kids, gone, or leading a wilder life than she was interested in. She wasn't that fond of anyone she'd been dating. No, she really had no reason to return. The only reason she'd be willing to leave this town would be to go wherever her brother was taken.

She couldn't do anything more for Kent today. She'd left a message with the lawyers, Greg was looking into finding a good defense attorney. Nolan was contacting the other states where her brother had started fires. Kent was safely in jail.

Nicole didn't have anything else to do, she could read the novel on her phone, but the picnic table was not very comfortable for that kind of activity. Too bad she hadn't thought to bring a blanket. She'd seen what looked like a park blanket in the bottom of the linen closet on top of an old-fashioned picnic basket and mid-sized cooler. Maybe next time. She could go back to the cozy cottage and read in one of the over-stuffed chairs. It would certainly be a lot more comfortable than the wooden picnic table.

Then again maybe she should stop by some of the shops in town. She didn't really have any money to spend at the moment, but she could window shop and maybe meet some people that weren't either police officers or firefighters.

She pulled out the tourist map and looked at the selection. Maybe the art gallery. They probably had people who browsed.

The art gallery was not at all what she expected.

CHAPTER 13

Nicole hadn't gotten three steps inside the door of the old Victorian house, before a spunky young woman who was enormously pregnant greeted her.

"Hi, I'm Mary Ann, welcome."

"I'm Nicole. This isn't your typical art gallery is it?"

"No, it's not. But that just makes it better. We've got mostly local artisans in here and we carry whatever it is they make. The ones that aren't local have some kind of connection to Chedwick. Our landscape photographer, Rachel Reardon-Kipling was born and raised here, but then she went off to Colorado, fell in love and stayed. Lucille Thompson is in our gallery because her son lives here."

"I'd heard that Lucille's son lived here. Do you have any of his work?"

"We do. Not many people know he's producing yet. Did you meet him?"

"I did. I'm working at the church."

"Did you take Maureen's place?"

Nicole nodded, and Mary Ann kept right on talking.

"That's good, Scott's a great guy, but sometimes he needs a keeper."

Nicole personally believed that was not true, the man was extremely resourceful. Maybe he perpetuated that belief deliberately. She wasn't quite sure about that.

"Maureen left very detailed and helpful instructions, so it's been easy. But I just got here a few days ago."

"Well that was quick work on your part to land the job, or maybe I should say, on his part."

"A little of both actually. I needed a job and he needed a secretary. Although my first task was ordering pizza."

Mary Ann laughed out loud. The woman had a huge laugh and Nicole felt herself grinning along with her. Mary Ann had been walking while they talked, or maybe Nicole should say waddled. They'd ended up in front of some lovely glass sculptures, but Mary Ann was puffing a little and that took Nicole's concern from the glass to the woman.

"When is your baby due?"

"Yesterday, but she is not cooperating."

"Oh my, should you be working and on your feet? Yesterday? Really?"

Mary Ann laughed again but this time it was a bit breathless and Nicole put her hand in her pocket on her phone in case she needed to call nine-one-one.

"I'm fine, but I do get a little winded from time to time."

Nicole was completely freaked out now. "Maybe you should sit down. Put your feet up. Have a drink of water. Call the hospital."

Mary Ann shook her head. "I'm fine, really." She pointed to the glass sculptures in front of them. "One is Lucille's, one is Nolan's, can you guess which is which?"

Nicole forced her eyes away from the pregnant woman to where Mary Ann had pointed. There were two gorgeous sculptures in front of her. One was more fluid and felt feminine and the other had sharper angles and darker colors. She pointed to the more fluid one. "I think that one is Lucille's and the other is Nolan's"

Mary Ann clapped. "Good job, Nolan's work is a little fiercer than his mother's. Since he's a cop and seen some things, it's not a big surprise. However, I imagine Lucille could have some fierce in her if she wanted."

Nicole grinned. "Yeah, not all of us ladies are soft."

"Lucille's been here a lot in the six years Nolan's been on the department, she's an amazingly humble woman most of the time. I've seen her get her back up a time or two in mama bear fashion, mostly over her grandkids."

"Oh yeah, you don't want to mess with a woman's grand-kids. Not healthy."

Mary Ann laughed and then looked down. "Oh no. I guess you were right. I should have been sitting with my feet up."

Nicole looked down at the growing puddle around Mary Ann's feet and nearly had heart failure. She whipped out her phone so fast it was nearly a blur.

"No wait. You'll scare everyone to death if you call nine-one-one. They'll tone it out over the damn radio and every fricken firefighter in the town will be storming the place. Let me call my husband first, and if he can't get here, you can call them."

That idea scared the crap out of Nicole, but she guessed maybe it was a good idea. She wanted to call Scott though, he wasn't far and probably could at least help in some way. Mary Ann was listening to the phone ring and frowning, so Nicole called him.

"What's up, Nicole?"

"I'm at the art gallery and Mary Ann's water broke. She's trying to call her husband, but he hasn't answered yet. She doesn't want me to call nine-one-one. Something about the firefighters storming the building."

"I'll be right there. If you think you need to call it in, do it. You can't always listen to the victim."

Nicole looked at Mary Ann who had hung up the phone. "I didn't call emergency, but I did call Scott. The church isn't far from here."

Mary Ann nodded and then started breathing hard.

Nicole watched in horror. "I'm calling it in."

Mary Ann puffed out a huge breath and nodded. "Go ahead."

Nicole's hands were shaking as she dialed the emergency number.

"Please state your emergency," the voice said.

"I'm Nicole and I'm at the art gallery and Mary Ann's water broke and her husband didn't answer when she called. Can you get an ambulance or something? Scott Davidson is on his way."

"Yes, please tell me your full name."

"Nicole Roman. Do you need the address? Or Mary Ann's last name? I don't know either one of those, but I can ask when Mary Ann isn't breathing so hard."

"Mary Ann is breathing hard? How often?"

"Um, maybe every five to ten minutes?"

"I'll get help there right away. See if you can get her to sit down and elevate her feet. We need to slow this down a little."

Nicole shut her phone. She looked around the room for a chair. "The dispatcher said for you to sit down and elevate your feet. She wants to slow the labor down. I don't see a chair anywhere."

Mary Ann took her hand. "Help me sit on the floor. I can't walk to a chair. I think this baby is coming fast."

"No, it can't, we need to get a doctor."

"Nicole, please just help me sit. Get behind me and help me lower to the floor."

Nicole hurried around behind Mary Ann and helped her sit on the floor. And then assisted her to lay down all the way which effectively raised her feet.

Mary Ann let out a whoosh of relief. "Nicole, now help me get my pants off. When anyone ever fricken gets here, I want them to check on the baby."

Nicole helped Mary Ann get the pants off just as a tiny dark-haired woman came rushing in the back door. And Scott charged in the front.

The woman screeched, "Why didn't you call me?"

Mary Ann was panting again, so Nicole said, "She didn't have time. The water broke, and she started this breathing."

"Well, fuck." She looked at Scott. "Can you check to see what her cervix looks like?"

"I've never done it in real life before, but I have in training."

"You win then. I'll get towels."

Mary Ann had stopped panting. "Hurry Scott, I don't think she's going to be waiting long."

Scott pulled on some plastic gloves and knelt between her knees. He leaned down, so he could see. Mary Ann pushed her hips up off the floor to give him a better view. He said, "I need light."

Nicole turned on her phone's flashlight and tried to aim it in, so he could see. He helped aim it and then used his hands to open the passage enough to see inside. "Damn, Mary Ann. She's coming. I can see at least an inch of scalp."

The dark-haired woman rushed back just as he said that with towels, scissors, a big bowl, and a flashlight. "Well fuck, where in the hell is Trey? Or Nolan? Or the doctor? Or any damn body besides us? For fuck's sake, Trey came back from fire season early to be here for the baby's birth and now he's not even here!"

Mary Ann said firmly, "Calm down, Kristen. Hysterics isn't going to help us now."

Kristen looked like she wanted to kick something, but she took a deep breath and said calmly, "You're right Mary Ann, this is a natural process, and Scott has EMT training and I'll just bet a half-dozen firefighters will be storming in the door any second."

"No, Kristen! You go keep them all outside except for the essentials. We don't need all those dirty guys in here, not where I'm having my baby."

Kristen looked relieved that she was given another task and marched off to protect the cleanliness of the area.

Nicole could have kissed the man and woman who came in with a doctor's bag and a gurney.

Scott looked up and Nicole saw relief spread over his face. "The baby's coming, Doc. I saw her head, no time to get Mary Ann to the clinic."

"Ok let's get her on the gurney, so we can see better, and I'll take a look."

Nicole watched in awe as they lowered the gurney and quickly got Mary Ann onto it and raised up to a better height. Mary Ann moaned as another contraction started. The doctor quickly looked inside. "You're correct Scott, no time to get to the clinic. Can you get some water heating upstairs, so we'll have something sterile for the baby? We can use the towels Kristen brought down to clean up. Scott, see if you can find a clean baby blanket up there, not a fuzzy one, as least fuzzy as you can find. Kristen and Nolan's kids aren't that much older, there should be some around."

Another man rushed in the room just as Mary Ann's contraction ended. "Well it's about damn time you got here Trey, where the hell have you been?"

"I'm sorry, baby."

Mary Ann burst into tears. "I needed you and you didn't

answer. My water broke, and the contractions started, and Nicole helped me sit on the floor, and Scott had to look to see what was going on, and the baby, she's just not waiting to even get to the clinic. I was so scared."

"I know, sweetheart. But the doc is here and I'm here and that's all we need. So, don't be scared, let's have our impatient little girl." He kissed her forehead and Mary Ann relaxed instantly.

She smiled up at the man and it was a beautiful sight. "All right, I'm ready."

Nicole and Scott went upstairs to get some water heating. She'd always thought that heating water was something people were told to do when they wanted those people out of the way, but maybe there was a purpose to it.

Scott said, "I'll get the water going. You go see if you can find a baby blanket."

Nicole nodded and went down the hall to search. This place was very odd. The rooms were fully furnished, and she found a baby room. But it didn't look lived in. It was too neat and tidy, nothing was out of place and there weren't many things in the room. She looked through the baby dresser and there were only a few items in each drawer. She did find some baby blankets and took two with the least amount of fuzz, back to the kitchen. She glanced in the other bedroom, and it didn't look lived in either.

When she got back to Scott, she tried to act casual, but she was kind of freaked out by the house. Finally, she asked, "Is this Nolan's house? Is he married to Kristen? Do they live here?"

"Nolan is married to Kristen. But this is Kristen's work house. They don't live here. When she's working, they sometimes come and have a meal or give the kids a nap or whatever, but they have another house that they live in, that Nolan purchased when he moved here."

Nicole relaxed and decided she'd been silly to be freaked out. "Oh good, because this house has no real appearance of being lived in. It's too neat and there isn't much in the drawers."

Scott grinned. "Kind of spooky was it?"

"Yes. No. Yes, it was. But now it makes sense. What does Kristen do?"

"She makes jewelry."

"Oh, I saw some very unique jewelry down there before Mary Ann's baby became impatient."

"Yes, that was either hers or Mary Ann's. Kristen taught Mary Ann how to make jewelry too."

"I'll come back some day and look closer. Mary Ann was showing me Nolan's work."

"Let's get these supplies downstairs. I think that baby probably will have been born by now. She wasn't waiting."

When Nicole opened the door, so Scott could carry the water down, she heard a newborn's cry. Yep, the baby was born. She'd been in the building about an hour and look at all that had happened.

They took down the supplies and gave them to the nurse who put them to good use as the doctor delivered the placenta. Nicole was both fascinated and horrified at all the proceedings. She'd never seen anything like it.

Scott had amazed her, he'd not hesitated to come to help, then he'd calmly gone about doing something he said he'd never done. Only in training, which was a completely different ball park. He was such a nice man.

SCOTT WAS COMING down off the adrenaline rush. He'd been scared absolutely shitless when he'd walked in and seen Mary Ann on the floor panting. He'd thought on his quick drive over that he would get Mary Ann in his truck and on the way to the clinic, even if he needed to carry her. She was a tiny little thing so even with the baby weight he could carry her easily.

When he'd walked in the door and realized the labor was too far along to drive her to the hospital and Mary Ann and Kristen had insisted he look and see what was going on he'd been terrified. Training with a dummy was completely different than looking at a real live person, who you'd known all your life.

Adrenaline had shot through him and he'd wanted to run. But he'd sucked it up and been a man, so he didn't scare the hell out of the three women who were putting their faith in him. Then when he'd seen that scalp peeking through her cervix, he'd about had a heart attack, thinking he might actually have to deliver the little one. He'd been praying up a storm for God to get the doc, or anyone who knew more than he did, there.

Training was great, but having to use it, not so much. He'd been thrilled to death when Doc Sorenson and Wendy had come in the door with the equipment they would really need and a gurney to get Kristen off the floor. He'd been worried about her having the baby on the dirty floor. Not that it looked dirty other than where Kristen's wet pants were soaking up the amniotic fluid, but still.

Trey finally arriving had been the final link to set him free from any responsibility beyond finding a blanket and heating water. When he'd gotten the water on to boil, he'd put his elbows on the counter, hung his head into his hands, and thanked God for getting the others there in time.

Was this another place God had been showing him he'd been cocky? By thinking because he had training it would be easy. Maybe it was. He was sure learning a lot about himself this week. God clearly wasn't finished with him yet.

CHAPTER 14

Well, Nicole had certainly met some new people, several more firefighters since she found out Trey was a firefighter both for the town and on a team who went around to put out wild fires and forest fires. Then when they'd left a whole bunch of men were gathered in the yard, many of whom she recognized but several more that wanted to thank her for helping Mary Ann, Scott had introduced her to them all.

Kristen had about hugged the stuffing out of her for being with Mary Ann when it all started and then another woman that looked nearly identical had done the same. Nicole had learned the second woman was Barbara, Chris's wife and Kristen's sister. She owned the wedding and costume shop next door and had been the one to alert Kristen.

Nicole lost count of all the people she met as she went from group to group. But they all thanked her for helping Mary Ann. Nicole started to feel like a fraud, since she hadn't done much more than help the woman sit down and called the emergency number. It didn't seem like much in the grand scheme of things, but she supposed maybe just being there had been part of it. She could imagine how scary it might have been for Mary Ann to be all alone.

Oh, what a circus the street had become, clearly Mary Ann was a town favorite based on the multitude of people filling the yard and street. Cars were parked haphazardly, and people were standing everywhere. She was a little surprised by the number of bystanders since it was a Friday afternoon, didn't people have to work? Did the whole town close down when something like this happened? Had this kind of gathering taken place during the fires her brother had started?

When they got somewhere quiet, she would ask Scott. But she wasn't going anywhere soon since she'd only met about half the people, and Scott was directing her towards the other side of the yard.

She greeted Carol from the ladies' auxiliary and her daughter Sandy, who had made the delicious coffee cake. Sandy was newly engaged to Greg, the fire chief, it was interesting to see how the people were paired up and what their jobs and roles were in the town. Nicole decided she might want to draw it all out in her sketch pad or maybe put notes on the town map, so she could remember them all.

Her head was spinning a little from meeting so many, when a cheer rose up. The doctor was bringing Mary Ann out of the door on the gurney, Trey was walking beside her carrying the new baby.

The doctor hollered out, "Just taking Mary Ann in for some stitches and the baby to be weighed and officially checked out."

Trey looked right at Nicole and said, "Our little Nicole Scotti Peterson might need the jaundice lights."

Nicole gasped, they'd named the baby after her and Scott. Why would they do that, she'd done almost nothing.

Trey walked over to her and gave her a peek at the baby. "Thank you so much for being with my wife. You helped more than you could possibly imagine. Please come by for a visit, and so we can get to know you."

He looked at Scott, who nodded. "I'll bring her by your place in a few days."

Trey cleared his throat, "Thanks, man, for everything." Then he turned to climb into the back of the ambulance. Somehow miraculously the road cleared, and the ambulance drove slowly away.

Soon the people standing around started to dissipate until only a handful were left. Nolan and his wife Kristen, Barbara and her husband Chris, and Greg remained. Scott and Nicole joined the group remaining.

Nolan looked her way. "You know you're now a town hero. You helped one of our own and it won't matter when or how the news of your brother comes out. People won't give two hoots about that. You're one of us and will always have a soft place in our hearts."

Nicole was warmed by the words, but she still felt like a fraud. "But I didn't do anything. I helped her sit down and called the dispatcher."

Chris shook his head. "No, you paid attention and helped her get her pants off and knew how quickly the contractions were coming. Without those things the dispatcher would not have had all the information."

Kristen's voice was watery when she said, "Most of all you were there by her side lending her your strength. She just needed someone by her side until Trey and the doc got here. That was all you, Nicole."

Barbara nodded. "If she hadn't felt that way, she wouldn't have named the baby after you."

Greg nudged Scott. "Nicole Scotti Peterson. I guess she was grateful to you too, preacher-man."

Scott grinned. "Can't complain, although I thought I might pass out when she asked me to look to see how far along she was."

Chris laughed. "Hell, I've got three and still nearly pass out every time."

Nicole looked at Barbara who was slender and didn't look like she'd had three kids. "Three? Really? You look great Barbara, how old are they?"

Barbara preened for one second and then said, "Four, two and eleven weeks."

"Eleven weeks? You're joking."

"Not at all, want to come see the little monsters? We've got a daycare area set up on the third floor, so we can all keep an eye on them." Barbara looked down to her chest. "Um, maybe later would be better, the baby just woke up and is hungry." Then she turned and hurried back to the house.

Chris said, "If one is up, they all are. Guess I'll see if I can corral the older two to let the baby eat in peace." He caught up with his wife before she got to the door and slung his arm around her waist.

Kristen looked up at Nolan. "Are you off now?"

He nodded still looking toward where Barbara and Chris had disappeared.

"Good, you can come help me clean up the mess. They were looking at your art, when Mary Ann's water broke."

Nolan looked at Nicole, who nodded. "Damn. I should have said I was still on duty."

Kristen grabbed him by the arm. "Too late buster, come on."

Greg chuckled. "Have fun, guys. I gotta go open the bar. Scott, bring the lady in tonight. I'm sure the town will be celebrating the baby's birth, might as well have the hero and heroine of the hour join in the fun."

Nicole wasn't sure she wanted to be the center of the

celebration, but at the same time it might be fun to meet a few more people. "I'm not much of a drinker."

Greg said, "No worries. Scott doesn't drink very often either. I've got soda and sparkling water, all the usual things. And I make a mean Arnold Palmer."

Nicole laughed at that. "I do enjoy me a good Arnold Palmer."

"Excellent, the first one is on the house. You too, Scott."

Scott rolled his eyes. "We'll see."

~

SCOTT WOULD BE happy to escort Nicole to Greg's if she wanted to. She'd been looking a little overwhelmed with the crowd earlier and he didn't want to cram the town and their friendliness down her throat.

She'd been invited to see Chris's kids, the new baby, the bar, a book club, and a quilt sewing circle. She'd met half the town in a very short period of time and there would be even more at the bar tonight.

"Let's get back to the church before Kristen drags us in to help clean. I think we've done enough for today, don't you?"

"Yeah. I'm good on skipping out on the cleaning. In fact, I'm feeling a little tired, can I just ride with you and get my car later?

"Sure. The adrenalin rush is wearing off, you could probably use a soda or a snack. Did you eat lunch?"

"I had a sandwich. Let's go to the rectory, there are a ton of snacks there."

He laughed. "That's for certain."

Scott noticed she looked tired and she leaned her head back and shut her eyes on the short drive to the church. When they arrived, she just sat there like it was going to be too much trouble to walk the twenty steps from his car to the rectory.

He got out and went around to her door and opened it. "Want me to carry you?"

"No, don't be silly. I'm just trying to summon enough energy."

Scott took her hand and it was ice cold, was she in shock? Or just drained. He leaned in and lifted her easily in his arms. "I think your blood sugar has bottomed out or you might be in shock, let's get you inside."

She tried to complain but he simply started walking, kicking the car door shut behind him. She pulled her keys out of her purse, but her hands were shaking. This was beginning to worry him, so he moved quicker. Scott put her on the couch and covered her with a blanket that hung over the back of the couch. He elevated her feet and then hustled into the kitchen to see what instant sugar she might have.

He found lemonade in the fridge and was relieved. It seemed she really did like Arnold Palmers because she also had a container of iced tea. Well she was getting the lemonade straight this time, so it could get her sugar up. He poured a glass and took it into the living room where she hadn't moved.

Scott knelt by the couch. "Nicole, drink this."

Her eyes fluttered open and he propped her up. He held the glass to her lips, and she drank deep. He waited another few seconds and had her drink again. When over half the glass was empty, he helped her sit up and handed her the glass. "Keep sipping while I get some food."

She didn't complain, just nodded.

He went back to the kitchen and loaded some of the sweets on a plate, but then decided she should have some protein to counteract the sugar, he rifled through her refrigerator to find some cheese and lunch meat. He found crackers in a cupboard and a can of mixed nuts.

Taking the feast out into the front room he noticed her color was better and the glass was nearly empty. He set the food down and they both started munching, because he noticed he was feeling a little shaky, too. He'd brought the lemonade with him, so he refilled her glass and poured one for himself.

"You might need to get more lemonade to go with your tea, since we're drinking most of this one."

She nodded. "That's fine, it helped a lot. I was feeling very odd."

"Yeah not a surprise, in fact it's quite common. I should have thought about it and gotten something in both of us before we stood around in the yard meeting half the town."

"I was wondering about that, does everyone stop whatever their doing to turn out at something like that?"

"Not everything that goes out over the radio, but anything important. We're a close-knit community. I'm sure you noticed in just the few minutes you were with her, what a nice person Mary Ann is. Everyone loves her.

"She volunteers at the school, helping teach practical use of mathematics. Plus, Trey has worked with everyone on their web pages and was on the crew that helped save the town from a forest fire a few years ago. So, their baby coming at the art gallery instead of the clinic drew everyone that could get away."

"Which is why Mary Ann first told me not to call it in and I called you instead. She didn't want everyone showing up."

"I can understand that, not exactly the kind of an event you want to have a crowd for."

"So, the fires? Did they draw that kind of crowd?"

"Yeah. The one at the Howe's house was pretty much the entire town. Of course, a lot of those were support. They brought food and drinks to keep the firefighters going during the long night of putting out the fire."

Nicole just looked at him. He had to assume she knew nothing about the work involved in her brother's stunts. "The abandoned building didn't draw quite as much attention and it was put out quicker since only the structure burned, not rooms full of furnishings. Plus, there was no worry about any people involved or their pets. The Howe's are elderly, and they have three dogs and some cats."

Nicole gasped. "Oh my God, he could have killed them or their pets. How did they get out?"

He didn't want to freak her out, but she probably needed to know. "She climbed out the bedroom window, and he went into the other bedroom to let the animals out through that window, and then followed them. Fortunately, both of them are active and could manage the climb and they had old-fashioned large windows, so they could raise them and get out without having to break the glass."

"The doors..."

"They were completely blocked by the fire."

Fury covered her face and she said harshly, "My brother needs to be slapped. He could have killed them. Does he even realize that?"

"You heard what he said. He didn't know, which I took to mean, that since he didn't know it wasn't his fault."

She folded her arms, her knuckles turned white where she was clutching her arms. "If he ends up going to jail, he will definitely deserve it, and if he gets to work with Nolan, I'm going to remind him of just how lucky he is to get a second chance. Not only that, but I am going to watch him like a hawk. He starts acting out and he's going to jail. I will turn him in myself."

She was fierce. Her eyes were flashing, and her skin was flushed. It was beautiful to see, and his body agreed as lust shot through him. He forced himself to look away at the plate of food and take a bite of something he wasn't sure he could force down his throat.

Before he ate it, he said, "We'll all be keeping an eye on him if he's released to work with Nolan." He motioned toward the plate. "Keep eating, you need to get your blood sugar stable."

She unfolded her arms and reached for some cheese. "Thanks. I'm feeling a lot better, even if I *am* horrified by my brother's actions. Thanks for taking care of me."

He looked up and into her chocolate-colored eyes. "Any-time, Nicole. I mean that."

She blushed and this time it wasn't in fury.

CHAPTER 15

Scott and Nicole did end up going out. After they'd eaten, he'd gone home to clean up, and she'd said she was going to rest for a while and would call him to let him know if she wanted to go out.

He'd showered and changed his clothes that he hadn't even realized had amniotic fluid on them. Then he'd looked over his sermon and made a few changes based on some of the things that had happened this week. It had been a busy few days.

He'd started wondering about what to have for dinner when Nicole called and said that she did feel like going to the bar.

"Great, do you want to get some dinner first? Greg has anything in the world that can be cooked in a deep fryer. Or the café has good food, we went to the casual side that has the salad bar, for lunch the other day. But in the evening, they open the other side that has white tablecloths, candles, and fancier food. So, you can take your pick of casual or fine dining. Plus, there are a couple of smaller places in town."

"Let's eat at the café, a salad bar sounds terrific."

Of course it did, he'd decided the woman was part rabbit. "Perfect, and we can grab your car on the way back from the bar. What time shall I pick you up?"

"I'm ready now. I didn't call until after I'd showered to see how I felt, but my nap restored me, and I decided it would be fun to hang out with some people."

"Excellent, I'll be right there."

He jogged out to his SUV and slid in, he knew this wasn't really a date, but it still felt like one and he was excited to be going out with her in a non-official capacity. He'd put on a nice shirt and his good jeans earlier when he'd showered, and he realized it was in hopes she would want to go out.

When he knocked on the door, he almost swallowed his tongue when she opened it. She was gorgeous. She had on a brick-red dress with long sleeves and a scoop neck. It was short, and clung to her curves in a way that made his mouth water. She'd done something to make her eyes look mysterious and smoky. And her lips matched the dress. Her black hair hung down her back, he'd only seen it in a pony tail so far, it was gorgeous, he wanted to sink his fingers into it. He couldn't move, he just stood there staring at the vision in front of him.

She fidgeted with her neckline which broke him out of the trance. "You look amazing."

She gave him a slow smile that made his blood heat, and he knew if he didn't get them on the road, and into a public setting he would be putting his convictions about sex before marriage to the ultimate test. He wanted to take her right there in the doorway, and he didn't care that it was only a dozen yards from the church.

He shook his head and cleared his throat and it still came out tight, "So, are you ready?"

She patted him on the chest. "I know how you feel. You look mighty hot yourself."

That got his attention. "Really?"

"Really. Now let's get going, before something we're not ready for happens in the front door a dozen yards from the church."

He huffed out a laugh. Had he said that out loud, or was she thinking the same thing? He was afraid to ask. So, he took her hand and they walked to his truck. When she slid in, his mouth went dry, as the hem of her dress hiked up a couple inches, revealing more of her smooth bare legs. He wanted to lick them from the toes of her peekaboo sandals upward.

He carefully closed the door and walked around the back of the truck ordering his body and mind to calm down. Maybe he should start quoting scripture to himself, specifically the ones about lust, but right at the moment he couldn't think of one single verse on the subject. So instead, he gave himself a stern talking to, finishing with, *you are such a dumbass Davidson, get it together now.*

Not that the stern talk helped, because it didn't. When he got in the driver's seat, he could smell her, and she smelled as good as she looked, and he couldn't for the life of him say what the scent even was, because in his brain it was simply the smell of her, and maybe lust.

Restaurant, he had to get to the restaurant. Where there would be people and light and the smell of food, and they wouldn't be enclosed in his car. Now if he could just remember how to turn the darn thing on and drive.

NICOLE COULDN'T FIGURE out what was wrong with Scott. She'd seen his reaction at how she looked and had felt pride in her appearance. It wasn't anything truly special, but she'd pulled on a pretty dress, left her hair down, and fussed with her makeup a little. She supposed he'd not seen her at her best so far, but she didn't think it was that spectacular.

Scott was looking pretty sharp in her opinion, too. He had on a medium blue button shirt that made his eyes pop. He'd had a shower and trimmed his beard and he smelled clean and sexy.

She'd wanted to drag him inside and do wicked things to him. But he'd clearly been fighting that idea, and when she'd smarted off about having sex in the doorway, he'd looked like she'd read his mind. Now he was sitting in his truck not moving and she wasn't sure what she should say or do.

"Scott?"

He looked like he'd just come out of a trance as he reached to start the SUV and get it moving.

"What's wrong?"

He huffed out a breath. "I was just berating myself for being a know-it-all with the men that have come to me with lust problems. I probably shouldn't even be saying this, but until I met you, I never once felt lust like this."

Her breath caught but he continued on. "I mean I've been attracted to women in the past. In high school and college, I had sex with a couple of long-term girlfriends. When I became a pastor, I decided I would remain abstinent until marriage. Thinking it was no big deal. So, when other guys came and told me about the lust they were feeling I would give them pat answers and a few tools to help them."

He shook his head. "I didn't know squat. Since the first moment I met you I've barely been able to think straight. You draw me like no other woman I've ever met, and I can't figure out what to do about it."

Nicole didn't know what to say other than a tiny "Oh," that escaped.

"So that guy, with the pat answers, was a total fraud and I want to go back and slap him upside the head."

A nervous giggle escaped at that.

He huffed out a breath as he pulled into the parking lot at Amber's café. "So just punch me if I get out of control. Or dump cold water in my lap. Or something."

She didn't really *want* to dump cold water in his lap and she'd gladly take him to her bed, but she didn't want to go against his convictions. She wasn't a virgin, but she'd only been with one other guy, so she knew a little about where he was coming from.

She cleared her throat. "Well now that that's cleared up, maybe we should go into the restaurant where there are other people, so I don't try to convince you to go against your principles."

"Do you want to convince me?"

"Oh, yeah. You do something to me, I've never felt before either, but I don't want to be your downfall."

He shook his head. "It's not that I feel like it's a terrible sin. It's more like I want to be a good role model for others. It's kind of the pastor's job to do that kind of thing."

He was so earnest trying to do what was right she had to try to help him. "I'll wear baggy ugly clothes from now on and not shower so I stink, how about that?"

He laughed and the tension in his expression and body eased. "It wouldn't help at all. I think you could be caked in mud and I'd still find you attractive."

"You're silly. Let's go eat."

"Yes, ma'am."

Nicole was a little shocked at all Scott had said, she'd never had a man straight out tell her he was lusting after her. Maybe the fact that he wasn't planning to act on that lust had something to do with it.

She had to admit she was a little disappointed that he

wasn't going to act on it. He was a sexy man and the attraction she had for him was off the charts. But at the same time, she knew she might be leaving at any moment so maybe not starting a relationship was a good idea.

Not totally convinced of that she wondered what he'd be like in bed, not that she had a lot to compare it to, unless a person was counting reading. She'd read a lot of romance novels since her first sexual encounter and realized she'd missed out on some things she'd like to try. She'd gone with the guy for six months after their relationship became sexual.

It hadn't been a hardship when they had parted ways. He'd been going off to college in another state and she'd planned to attend an in-state school. Colorado had some good colleges and she hadn't felt any need to go elsewhere. She'd worked and attended classes, going out with friends to parties and spending holidays at home. Nicole hadn't had any relationships that she'd been committed to enough to lead to sex.

Casual sex didn't interest her, so she'd not dated like most of her friends had. A lot of them were married now with kids and she'd wondered if she'd find someone, that she wanted to spend her life with. So, this thinking about sex with Scott was a very different occurrence for her.

She certainly didn't know him well enough to want to spend the rest of her life with him, so why was she suddenly interested in having sex with the man?

This wasn't the time or place to be pondering that however, so she put it aside to think about later and followed him into the restaurant. She was only a little surprised when he greeted everyone by name, from the hostess to the busboy and many of the diners. He introduced her as his new admin to many of them and practically every one of them thanked her for helping Mary Ann out earlier in the day.

An old guy in the back waved them over to his table. The

hostess who might have also been the owner whispered, "No good deed goes unpunished."

Nicole had no idea what she meant, but Scott clearly did, because he shrugged and changed direction toward the man. Leaving the hostess to return to the front.

The old guy waved them to a seat and said, "Scott and Nicole, isn't it, please join me. I'm almost finished and then you can keep the table."

Scott said, "Thanks, Gus. This is Nicole Roman, my new admin and current town heroine. Nicole, this is Gus Ferguson the town newspaper mogul."

Gus laughed at the description and Nicole had to wonder about it. The town wasn't big enough to have a newspaper mogul. She'd even seen the local paper, which was a couple dozen pages or less, including all the sports statistics.

Gus pulled a small notebook and pencil from somewhere and started jotting down notes. He asked a few questions about how she'd come to be in the art gallery. Where she was from originally. How had she felt during the incident and a few other questions. Then he turned his attention to Scott and asked him some similar things.

When he was finished, he thanked them, put the leftover jelly and sugar packets in his pocket, stood and walked out, leaving the bill on the table.

Nicole watched him leave and then turned to Scott. "Did he just steal sugar and jelly, and leave you the bill?"

Scott nodded. "That's exactly what he did."

"But..."

Scott shrugged. "It's just his way. He does it to everyone, hence Amber's comment."

"But why does everyone allow it?"

"First, because he's rich as Midas and has helped nearly everyone in town out, from time to time, and second because he's been doing it for so long, even before he was rich, no one has the guts to question him on it."

Nicole decided this town was like Oz or maybe Alice's Wonderland, nothing worked quite the way she expected it to.

CHAPTER 16

Greg's bar was no exception.

After a very tasty dinner including a to-die-for piece of Chocolate French Silk pie that Scott had shared with her, they had walked to the bar. It wasn't far, and it was a nice night, and they'd used the idea of walking to justify the pie.

Nicole had enjoyed the evening as they talked about everything. Their likes and dislikes. About growing up in such completely different homes. When they got to their talents, Scott had been thrilled to find out she'd come from a family of musicians and could play the drums.

She'd been in an all-girl punk band in high school.

Scott's eyes glowed with enthusiasm. "You really play the drums? How would you feel about using that skill on Sunday morning? My mom plays the piano and I play guitar, but we really could use drums or a bass guitar to make it more of a complete sound."

She hedged at the idea, not sure she was quite ready to be on a worship team, she wasn't the most spiritual person and it seemed weird. "Kent plays the bass guitar."

"Oh, even better, if he gets to stay here maybe I can get Nolan to make it part of his rehabilitation to play bass on Sunday's."

"That's kind of manipulative."

Scott shrugged. "Not really, he'd probably be going to some kind of church if he was in prison, just to relieve the boredom, if nothing else. You can think about it. We do have a quick run through practice on Saturday, so you can come in and watch tomorrow, and see if you want to join us."

"I can do that. Speaking of Saturday do we need to be there to let all those different people in?"

Scott opened the door to the bar as he said, "Not really, I am usually there, and so was Maureen, but most of them have keys so they can come and go when it fits their schedule."

"I was mostly wondering about the bakery delivery. It seems like weekends would be busy, do they deliver early, before the rush or in the afternoon after it?"

Scott looked over her head at the other couple coming in behind them and grinned. "Samantha, would you like to answer Nicole's very insightful question?"

Nicole turned and saw a pretty woman and handsome man behind them, she thought she'd seen them at the art gallery, but she wasn't sure.

"Nicole this is Samantha and Kyle. Samantha owns and runs the bakery, and Kyle is our resident real estate agent. Samantha, Kyle this is Nicole my new admin."

Samantha shook her finger at Scott. "She's more than that Scott Davison, she's our newest heroine, she helped Mary Ann this afternoon, when Trey was out doing God knows what, instead of being with his wife when she went into labor."

Kyle rolled his eyes. "Dramatic much, the man has a job.

Nice to meet you Nicole, thanks for lending a hand." He looked at Scott. "You too bud, better you than me."

Samantha sniffed. "I suppose thanks are in order to you too, Scott." She looked back at Nicole. "We didn't get to meet you this afternoon because Trey and Mary Ann came out and interrupted the introductions." Samantha's eyes filled, and she grabbed Nicole in a bear hug. "Thank you so much for helping Mary Ann. She's one of my best friends."

Nicole could barely breathe. The woman was strong for her size. Nicole wondered if it was all that bread kneading.

Kyle said, "Let the woman breathe, Samantha, her eyes are bugging out from lack of oxygen."

It wasn't quite true, yet, but she was relieved when Samantha let her go.

"Sorry. I sometimes forget my strength. I've been working in the bakery for years and went from a skinny lightweight to being kind of strong."

"Freakishly strong, Samantha." Kyle said with a grin, "The woman can squash me like a bug if we arm wrestle."

Scott gave the couple a sly look. "Is that what you kids are calling it these days?"

Kyle laughed, and Samantha turned beet red.

Samantha waved her finger at Scott again. "You are not a nice man."

Scott grinned. "Sure, I am."

Samantha turned and dragged Kyle with her.

Nicole said, "You embarrassed her, and she never answered my question."

"She'll be back to answer it later, when she gets over being embarrassed. Besides she's fine, the two of us have known each other since we were babies. She was my first kiss and I was hers. I think we were twelve."

Nicole looked at Scott and back toward Samantha. First

kiss, huh? Kind of a powerful moment in life. She wondered what he'd kissed like then and how much he'd improved.

As if he'd read her mind he said, "It was awkward. We eventually got better at it and then she moved on to someone else, a guy in the grade ahead of us who had a big brother with a car. That family moved away when the town had the economic issues. I don't think she was sad about that."

Nicole thought about her first kiss. It had been awkward, too. Maybe all first kisses were required to be awkward. They moved further into the bar and nearly everyone thanked her for helping Mary Ann. She met new people and was reintroduced to others she'd met earlier. She probably wouldn't remember half of them.

Greg brought her an Arnold Palmer and Scott a coke, before they even asked or found a table. Nicole was a little surprised by the bar, half of it was a completely typical bar, but the other half was a game room and the game room had windows with twinkle lights in them. The pool tables were near the windows and there was a dart board on a wall toward the back.

Scott was heading toward the dart board like a homing beacon. Clearly that was his favorite part of the bar. There were a group of people playing darts and they asked him if he wanted to join on the next round. One of the guys, she thought his name might be Matt, gestured toward Nicole. "We're playing couples, so your lady can join in."

Scott turned toward her. "Are you interested?"

Nicole thought it might be fun, but she hadn't played darts since she was in grade school. She said, "I could, but I will be really awful. I haven't played in maybe fifteen years."

Scott grinned. "That's fine, it's all just for fun."

Matt's eyebrows shot up and a woman Nicole assumed was his wife laughed out loud. "That will be the day, Scott

Davidson, when I know hell has frozen over, when you don't take darts seriously."

"Lori, shh, we don't want to scare her off," Scott said in a stage whisper loud enough for everyone to hear.

Lori laughed again. "Come join the fun, Nicole. If he gets out of hand, we'll sit on him. Or better yet, we'll tell Sylvia on him. She'll straighten him out right quick."

Scott shuddered dramatically. "That's just mean, Lori."

"Someone's got to keep you under control, pastor."

~

SCOTT WAS HAVING A GREAT TIME. Nicole seemed to be game for anything. Her first few throws nearly missed the dart board, but she got the hang of it pretty quickly and the two of them gave the other couples a run for their money.

After they had played a couple of games, he noticed she was rubbing her arm, and decided she'd had enough, so he asked her if she wanted to dance or just chat.

When she nodded and thanked everyone for putting up with her, several of the other women dragged their men to the other half of the bar, too. It seemed like the couples' dart night was over. Scott didn't mind in the least, he would be happy just talking or dancing with Nicole.

He saw several tables with friends and was trying to decide if they should join one of them. She'd met some of the different groups, but he didn't know if she had any favorites yet.

Scott decided to ask her if she had a preference. "Do you see anyone you would like to sit with?"

She looked around the room and eventually nodded. "Yeah, let's see if Samantha and Kyle would mind if we join them. I liked her, and I still need an answer to my question."

"Great, but fair warning, they dance more than they sit and chat."

Nicole smiled. "I like to dance, if you do."

"Dancing with you would be my pleasure. Let's go before they leave their table."

He put his hand on the small of her back and they weaved through the tables and people. He liked the feel of her under his hand and hoped she didn't mind.

Scott just smiled when she got to his friends' table. She was already asking if they could join them. Samantha smiled in welcome.

Kyle nodded and stood. "Let me get another chair. Why does it always seem like there is only three chairs?"

Scott looked around the room for a spare chair. "Maybe because they're small tables."

"Still, nearly everyone pairs up, don't they?"

Scott grinned at his friend, knowing he'd stepped into it. "Well, unless you're into ménage."

Kyle's head snapped back to Scott. "You shouldn't even know about things like that, let alone talk about them."

Scott laughed at the shock on Kyle's face. "I don't live under a rock, Kyle."

"I don't care, that's not something I want to hear coming out of my pastor's mouth."

Scott frowned. "Since when do you come to my church?"

His friend shrugged. "Well I don't, but I still consider you my pastor."

Kyle had stepped into his trap again. "Well then you need to start tithing, to keep the doors open for when you do decide to grace us with your presence."

Kyle punched his arm as he pointed to a lone chair at a table where a couple should have gotten a room by now. Scott walked over and took the chair and the couple never even noticed.

Kyle huffed out a breath. "You didn't even ask."

"Nope, they will never remember it was even there."

Scott noticed Samantha and Nicole were deep in conversation, their heads together so they could be heard over the music. Samantha glanced at him as he and Kyle sat back down. She whispered something to Nicole who looked up at him with something like a smirk and went back to talking with Nicole.

Kyle leaned over. "I don't trust them. Are they talking about you?"

"Probably, do you think I should be scared?"

Kyle nodded sagely. "Very, very scared."

"Maybe we should distract them on the dance floor."

Kyle looked that direction and then back at Scott. "Not a bad plan. If we can get their attention that is."

The waitress came up to see if they wanted to order something. Scott said, "Sure I'll take another coke, Nicole would you like another AP?"

She didn't stop whispering to Samantha, but she did nod and shoot him a thumbs-up. So, he ordered, and Kyle did the same. He and Samantha had switched from beers to water and sodas a little while ago. Samantha still had to go into work at four in the morning to get the donuts and morning baking done.

Scott asked the waitress to bring them the appetizer sampler which had fried cheese, onion rings, fried mushrooms, and deep-fried pickles.

While the girls were slightly interrupted by the waitress, Kyle pounced. "You girls want to dance?"

Nicole said, "Yes, but I need to use the ladies, first."

Samantha nodded. "I'll come with you."

Kyle raised his hands in supplication. "I tried."

"You did. You're a good friend."

Kyle said, "They might not be back for a while."

Scott wondered what the in-depth conversation was all about. Then he questioned if he really wanted to hear. Maybe he didn't. "I know."

Kyle shook his head. "Maybe I should have ordered a beer."

Scott agreed with the sentiment. "Maybe *I* should have."

Kyle looked at him with pity. "Yeah, you probably should have."

Scott huffed out a laugh. "It can't be that bad. Can it?"

"Hard to say with Samantha bro, hard to say."

It didn't take the women as long as Scott had thought it would, and they didn't even stop they just walked by the table, grabbed the men's hands and pulled them onto the dance floor. The first two songs were fast and wild. When those finished their appetizers and drinks had arrived, so they sat the next few out, talking and eating.

When they had polished off the platter of deep-fried goodness, they decided they better get back out on the dance floor and burn off some of the calories. So that's exactly what they did. Everything was fine and dandy until a slow song came on.

Scott didn't hesitate to pull Nicole close. He loved having her in his arms. But he realized his mistake quickly as his body reacted to that nearness. He could smell her, and it was delicious. Nicole felt like heaven in his arms and he wanted to pull her even closer and kiss her long and slow.

She looked up at him and he could see the same desire in her eyes. He didn't know whether to run or to lean in and take that kiss. It was like there was only the two of them in a place of desire and passion. The rest of the room faded away and he drew her in closer. Her breath caught. He saw her pulse beating madly in her throat. She wouldn't push him away, that was clear.

Someone laughed, and it reminded him of where they

were. He pulled back and looked around. She did the same and probably appeared as dazed as he felt.

She smiled up at him and he very nearly pulled her right back in.

She pushed back a little. "Maybe we should stop and have something to drink. Something very, very, cold."

He smiled softly at her and ran one thumb over the knuckles of the hand he held. "I don't think a measly drink is going to help. But it's a place to start."

She turned and led him off the dance floor. Nicole could have led him anywhere. He would have gone quite willingly anywhere, anywhere at all. But she took him back to their table.

She picked up her glass and drank deeply and he was mesmerized. He supposed she could do just about anything, and he would be enchanted by her. He really needed to get a grip.

CHAPTER 17

Nicole rushed through her morning, she'd slept later than normal, after her evening out with Scott. She'd had a lot of fun and they had managed to keep their hands and lips off of each other. Which was in itself something of a miracle, to her mind.

He'd wanted to kiss her right out on the dance floor in front of God and everybody. And she would have let him too. She'd been glad when that guy had laughed and broken the spell. After that they'd, by some unspoken agreement, only danced during the fast songs and sat out the slow ones.

As the night wound down to more and more slow ballads, they'd decided to call it a night. Kyle and Samantha had left at the same time, so it wasn't awkward. Of course, Samantha had to get up really early to go to work, but it was still a good time to leave, even if Nicole didn't have to get up early.

When Scott had driven into the parking lot, she'd jumped out of his SUV before he could turn it off and told him not to get out, saying she'd see him in the morning. She'd known without a shadow of a doubt that if he'd gotten out of the truck and walked her to the door, there would have been kissing, and who knew what else?

She'd decided on the way home, that it probably wasn't the best idea to get involved right now, when she and her brother's lives were in upheaval. So, it was best to circumvent anything getting started by keeping Scott at arm's length. How long she would be able to avoid it she didn't know, but one day at a time was a good place to start. Maybe it was really one hour at a time.

Nicole had not gotten to sleep for a long while, as she'd thought over her evening, and all the things that had happened since she'd gotten off that ferry, not even a week ago. The feelings of belonging here, just didn't make sense. How on earth could she possibly feel at home in a town half way across the country in a place she'd been for a few days. It should be impossible, but it was exactly the way she felt.

Even her talk with Samantha had seemed like they'd known each other all their lives. They'd not been talking about anything terribly significant, although they'd plotted to make Scott think they were talking about him. Samantha thought it would serve him right from embarrassing her earlier. Nicole had been happy to play along.

Everyone in the bar had treated her like their best friend. She knew a lot of that had to do with helping Mary Ann, but she wasn't convinced it was all that. This was simply the friendliest town she'd ever been in. She wondered if she'd stumbled into a movie set rather than a real town.

Nicole sighed as she thought about her brother, she didn't have any good news for him yet, but she knew she should go visit him. Even if he ignored her. She'd do that after working at the church. Maybe she could take him some of the treats still filling her refrigerator and freezer.

Someone had brought a pan of fudge and she knew that was a favorite of his. She liked it, but she was more of a baked goods fan than candy, so she would take him some as a peace offering. It might work, and if it didn't, well he would eventually get over blaming her.

She pulled her hair up into her characteristic pony tail and slid on her shoes. She still wasn't sure if she was supposed to be around for all the cleaning and deliveries today, so she wanted to get there before it all started, just in case.

She had asked Samantha about when she brought in the morning pastries for the congregation and she said not to worry she had a key because she brought them in very early Sunday before she opened her shop. Nicole had marveled at how early the woman started her day.

Nicole had also made a platter of goodies to have in the kitchen today, so that people could help her eat some of them. When she opened the door to the rectory, she saw Scott's SUV was already parked in the lot. Well, so much for needing to be there early.

The back door was unlocked, and she could hear a vacuum running. The cleaning people didn't mess around in the morning. She took the snacks into the kitchen, which was already spotless, the floors nearly dry with only a few damp places left. *Good grief, what time did they start?*

She set down the tray and then wondered if she should make some coffee to go with it. But there was already a full container of it made. She went to Scott's office and found him reading over his sermon and making notes. He certainly took his preaching job seriously.

She didn't want to disturb him, but he seemed to sense her presence and looked up. "Good morning, Nicole."

"Sorry to interrupt. I brought some of the goodies with me this morning. I'm hoping some of the people that are in and out all day today will help me eat them. And you, too."

He stood and walked toward her. "Excellent. I was just

thinking about food, and that maybe I should have stopped at Samantha's this morning, but I knew the cleaning crew would have coffee on for me."

"What time do they get here?"

"I have no idea, I've never beaten them in yet. It doesn't matter what time I come in on Saturday they are always here with coffee on."

"So, I shouldn't even try to get here before them."

"No. In fact, I think they would prefer if we weren't here at all, so they can clean without being disturbed by us mucking up the place."

Nicole laughed. "Good to know. I won't hurry then. Should I tell them I brought snacks?"

Scott shook his head. "Nope, they probably already know and have sampled them. Did I tell you they are kind of scary in what they know and do?"

She decided he was teasing her, so she didn't answer him.

"You don't believe me. Come with me and I'll prove it."

She rolled her eyes but followed the silly man back to the kitchen.

He pointed to her platter with a flourish. "See. I told you. Scary."

Nicole was surprised to see that there were indeed several of the offerings she'd brought missing. She'd only been away from the kitchen five minutes, and they'd come in, eaten, and hadn't left even a crumb to indicate they'd been there. She had to admit, even if it was only to herself, the cleaning crew was a bit spooky.

"All right, you win. They are a bit like wraiths."

A laugh burst forth. "Wraith cleaners. I love it."

A diminutive woman peeked around the corner. "We are not wraiths, Scott Davidson. We are merely very intelligent and observant women. Now, don't make a mess in here. Or anywhere else for that matter. Nice to meet you Nicole, welcome to our town."

And with that the woman was gone, before Nicole could actually meet her.

Scott just laughed and said, "That's probably the closest you'll get to any of them."

"How many are there?"

"I have no idea. We pay them a flat fee. There might be one, there might be fifteen."

Nicole thought that was the oddest way to do business. "But..."

"My grandfather set up the arrangement. My father continued it. Who am I to argue?"

"Well, alrighty then." She certainly had nothing to say about it. But she did think she might try to meet them.

Scott grinned at the determined look she could feel on her face. "You can try. But I doubt you will succeed. I've been trying my whole life; those women are sneaky."

Nicole thought she heard a small huff far away and wondered if the women had listening devices. That was silly, so she decided it was her imagination.

Scott had filled a plate and asked her, "Would you be able to print up and fold the bulletins for me? I have it all ready. Well, mostly."

Nicole had seen instructions and even some bulletin blanks to print on, so she was certain she was able to do that. "Sure. That should be easy." She paused as she thought about it. "Unless it's in your chicken scratch."

Scott rubbed the back of his neck. "Well yes, it is hand written. But it's very similar to last week. Just a different scripture, sermon title and song list. Okay not real similar. But if you can't figure it out, I can help you."

She patted his arm. "Maybe we should teach you to type

up what you want. Word is easy to use. Or you could even put it in email."

He shrugged. "We can try… again."

She laughed and shook her head. "Never mind, I'll figure it out."

~

SCOTT TOOK his plate back to his office, careful not to leave any crumbs that the cleaning crew might find. He'd had fun teasing Nicole about the cleaning crew, he knew who they were, and for the most part when they came in. But they did like to be mysterious, so he played along.

As he ate the goodies he thought about last night. He'd enjoyed it far more than he had anticipated. Nicole fit in with his friends and seemed game for about anything. He'd been half relieved and half disappointed when she'd jumped out of his car last night when he'd brought her home.

He would have kissed her, if she'd let him walk her to the door, and while he did want to do that, badly, a part of him wondered if it would be better to wait and see what happened with her brother. That was the logical part of his brain that only engaged when he was away from her presence. When he was with her, that logic seemed to vanish into the ether, and he couldn't remember why kissing her was a bad idea.

It was a little easier when they were here in the church at work. Not completely easy, but better. Probably because they had other things to think about, like their jobs. Nicole came in and handed him the paper he'd written up for the bulletin.

Pointing at it she asked., "What is this?"

"A three."

"It looks like a one which is why I couldn't find it in the song book."

"Sorry sometimes the curves get lost, from the rush."

She shook her head at him. "That sounds almost naughty. But I'll keep it in mind when I'm trying to decipher your handwriting. Rushed means less curves."

She turned and walked out of the door, as he sat there thinking about curves and rushing and naughty. That woman was tying him in knots. He. Loved. Every. Minute. Right up until his phone rang with his mother's ringtone, and then he felt guilty, or maybe embarrassed.

"Hey, mom."

"Hi, Scotty. Would you mind if we pushed rehearsal back an hour? Your father and I started a project that's going to take a little longer than we anticipated."

"Sure, no problem. My new admin, Nicole, is going to join us at rehearsal to see if she wants to play with us on Sunday. She plays the drums."

"Oh, that would be nice, we could use someone on drums. Besides, I would love to meet her. Maybe afterwards we can all go out for dinner."

Scott wasn't sure that was a great idea. "I'll ask Nicole."

"All right. I'll see you later, your father is calling for me to come help."

"What are you doing? I can come help if you need it."

"No, you're busy on Saturdays. Got to go. Love you. Bye."

She'd hung up before he could answer. He wondered what his mom had dragged his dad into doing. She spent way too much time on Pinterest.

He went out to warn Nicole about dinner in case she wanted to come up with an excuse for not going. His mom and dad together could be intimidating. Nicole wasn't at her desk, he stood there stupidly wondering if he should go track her down or go back to his office.

It wasn't like this was something urgent he needed to talk to her about. But he didn't want to wait he wanted to see her now. Which is what made him decide not to seek her out, he forced himself back in his office, this obsession could not be good.

CHAPTER 18

Nicole made up the bulletin, printed it on some stock she found that had a pretty, late summer look to it and folded them. She didn't know what she was supposed to do with them, so she took the stack into Scott's office.

"What do you want me to do with these now?"

Scott looked up and a grin covered his face. "I guess I should have been more specific about how many to print."

"I just used all of one pattern I found in a box."

"Yeah, those patterns come in lots of two hundred, we'll have more than three quarters of them left over. Maybe we can send the extras to junior church and they can make paper airplanes out of them."

"Oh. Oops sorry. I just assumed the lots came in the number you needed."

"No worries. It's my fault I should have told you how many to print. You can put them on the table outside the doors."

"So, only half of them?"

"Sure, let's give everyone something to think about and

strive toward. The town only has about a thousand residents, including the kids. But we could try for a few more people and who knows, everyone might decide to show up tomorrow just to get a look at our new hero."

"Me?"

"Yes, you."

"You helped, too."

"Yeah, but everyone already knows me. So, my mom called to push worship practice back an hour, she's got dad working on a project and it's taking longer than it should. I'm sure dad is thinking about blowing up her computer and phone about now, to keep her off Pinterest."

Nicole let out a silvery laugh that shimmered through him igniting nerve endings. He shivered and continued, "Anyway since it's going to be later, mom also wondered if you and I would like to join them for dinner. You can decide after you meet them, but I wanted to give you a chance to think up an excuse, just in case."

Nicole frowned. "That's kind of mean. I'm sure your mom is lovely."

"Oh, don't get me wrong I love her, and she is wonderful, but you might get the third degree."

Nicole looked taken aback, and Scott realized she was thinking about her brother.

That's not what he meant. He hurried to add, "Not that dad would have said anything, getting any news or gossip out of him is never going to happen. He probably hadn't even told mom you were working here, let alone anything about your brother."

"Oh good. I suppose it will all come out soon enough, but I wouldn't mind it being later."

"I was more referring to mom wanting to know about you. Where you're from, what you like, where you went to school. Stuff like that."

Nicole smiled. "I can handle that."

"If you want to fine. If not just let me know and I'll figure out a way out of the invite."

"All right, but it sounds like fun. However, I was going to go see my brother after I sat in on your practice."

"You can go now if you want. I'll be here if anyone needs anything."

Nicole beamed at him. "That would be great. I probably won't be long. Especially if he's still mad at me."

"If he is, don't take it personally. He might need to pout for a few days. Plus, he doesn't know about any of our plans to try to keep him out of jail, so he's probably worried, too."

"Well, he should be worried. I've been worried for nine months. It's his turn."

"Yes, but he still might take it out on you."

She tossed her head in bravado, because it would hurt if he kept rejecting her. "It will be his loss then. I'll put these out and then go. Do you want me to bring lunch back?"

"That would be awesome."

"What do you want?"

"Surprise me."

Nicole wondered why people said things like that. What if she picked out something he didn't like? It gave her the freedom to decide though, so she let it go and if he complained about her choice, she would dump it in his lap.

SCOTT WATCHED NICOLE LEAVE. He'd been fascinated watching the thoughts flit across her face. She had an expressive face and she'd obviously never learned to school it. So, she was easy to read. He couldn't wait to see what she brought back for lunch. It had irritated her at first when he'd not picked something specific, but then she'd looked mischievous.

He was a little worried about her brother's reaction today. Kent seemed self-absorbed and not at all concerned about Nicole or anyone else he might have hurt with his actions. No one had been injured, but the Howe's had been questioned and lost equity in their house because of Kent's actions.

Maybe the insurance had helped, but they either needed to rebuild it, so they could sell it at the higher price or they would have to sell it as a fixer upper at a low price. Plus, all their keepsakes had gone up in flames. And that was only here in their town, Scott had no idea what he might have done before he'd gotten to the Chelan area.

Someone needed to lay it out for Kent, so he realized what he'd done. Scott wondered if Nolan had heard back from any of the other states. He would ask on Monday if he didn't hear before that.

He chuckled as he thought about all the bulletins Nicole had printed. He didn't think two hundred people had ever shown up at church. She was used to a big city where churches had huge attendance and even multiple services, although she'd never said if she was a church goer to begin with.

A lot of people their age did not attend regularly or at all. He supposed in some ways the church had failed this generation. It was hard to keep the different generations engaged. Even something as simple as the songs. The older folks liked the hymns from the song book, whereas the younger people liked the modern music they could hear on the radio. Scott always did one hymn from the book and a couple modern tunes. But that wasn't the only difference in the ages. Scott shook his head. He did his best and left the rest up to God.

It was about time for the flower delivery, so he went down to help tote and carry.

When Nicole came back, he could tell she was trying to be happy. "I went to the Korean barbeque place and got a variety. I decided we could share."

Scott let her bustle around and then took her hand. "Kent?"

"He's still angry. I took him fudge and everything, and he still wouldn't talk to me. Just called me Benedict Nicole."

Yeah, Kent needed a good talking to, that was for sure. Scott just might take it upon himself to set the jerk straight, he needed to treat his sister with the respect she deserved. But he didn't want Nicole to worry so he kept his anger buried. "Just give him time and maybe let him sit alone for a couple of days. It might do him good."

"Maybe. I just don't want him to feel the world has abandoned him or that he's completely alone."

"He knows you're there for him, if and when he gets over himself. Give him a couple of days, maybe we'll know more by Tuesday or Wednesday. Nolan should start hearing back from the other states after the weekend, about whether they want to extradite him or let him stand trial here. If they let him stand trial here, we've got a better chance to get him rehab, rather than jail time."

Nicole rubbed her forehead then nodded. "You might be right. If we have some good news for him maybe he'll stop being angry."

Scott kind of doubted that, but he didn't argue. "Let's eat before your yummy food gets cold."

She was still clearly thinking about her brother, but she started to put the food out and he got some plates and plasticware from the kitchen. He chuckled when he saw what she'd bought. "Well this is going to be quite the feast."

"Yeah, I probably bought too much, but I didn't know

what you liked, so I bought a little of many things, not quite everything on the menu but close to it."

"I like almost everything they have. All the people in town know me, so you can always just ask them."

"Well they did suggest egg rolls which I probably wouldn't have gotten otherwise."

Scott couldn't stop the grin from forming. "They're my favorite."

"I see, so I should just go into the restaurant and say, 'I'm feeding Scott' and they'll load me up with your favorites?"

He shrugged. "Pretty much. It's a small town and I've eaten at all the restaurants in town for my whole life, so yeah you could totally do that. Plus, I'm not fussy about what I eat so even if I get something different, I'll still eat it."

"Good to know. So, there isn't anything you don't like?"

"I'm not a huge fan of liver and onions, or tofu, but that's about it." She grinned at him, which made him happy that he'd managed to help her smile again after seeing her brother

. "Well, that's easy enough, no liver, no tofu surprise. Got it."

He chuckled as he finished filling his plate. "Yeah, I'm easy."

After he said that he realized that it could be taken a different way, but he decided to let it ride. A bit of pink had entered her cheeks, so he knew she'd thought about it, too. But addressing it might be more fraught with pitfalls than just ignoring it, so he did, and shoveled in a big bite of food.

Nicole watched as he chewed, and he wondered why she was looking at him with a sly smile. As he swallowed, he realized that he'd just eaten tofu. It was hidden in sauce and surrounded by vegetables, so he hadn't noticed, but her expectant look had clued him in.

"That was tofu."

She nodded happily, her eyes sparkling with mirth. "And you ate it."

"I did and if you hadn't been watching me, I probably wouldn't have noticed. The texture is what I don't like about it, but with it chopped up small, covered in sauce, and surrounded by vegetables it was hard to tell."

"So, tofu is okay if it is in small pieces and has crunchy stuff with it?"

"I suppose it is." He was enjoying her delight in tricking him. If it was going to make her that happy, he'd eat tofu every day. And maybe even liver and onions, once, but only once, he really didn't like it.

"But no trying to trick me with liver."

She scrunched up her face at that. "You won't have to worry about that one, it's disgusting. On that I am totally in agreement. And I hope you're not a cauliflower connoisseur, because that stuff is just nasty."

He laughed. "Good to know. I can take it or leave it. It's not my favorite by any means."

They continued to chat as they ate. He loved learning new things about her. He'd lived with all the same people for so long that there was hardly anything new to learn, so having Nicole around was a welcome change.

CHAPTER 19

Scott didn't have anything for Nicole to do in the afternoon, so she decided that it might be good to get warmed up on the drums. She'd been on the road for nine months and hadn't touched a drumstick. She also thought she might need to arrange the drums a bit to suit her size. She probably needed to pull everything in a little closer since she was only one inch over five feet. Depending on who used them last, there might be some changes needed. She might also need to tighten the drum heads, if they'd loosened them like they should have, when not being used regularly.

After she got everything arranged and ready, she sat down to warm up. She'd asked Scott for any music he had and when he said he didn't have any that he was aware of she took the list of songs and looked them up on the internet to print them out. She would practice with those and then decide if she wanted to use them when the others joined her. She didn't always follow the music exactly, sometimes she improvised and often it sounded better, to her ears at least.

She ran through her warm ups, then each of the songs a

couple of times. He needed better drumsticks and she wished she'd brought hers from home rather than putting them in storage with everything else. If she stayed here in town, she would order some and get them taped up like she liked them.

After she'd run through all the songs that would be played on Sunday, she let herself go and play whatever came to her. As the beat poured out of her, she closed her eyes and allowed her hands and feet to let the music and the tribal rhythm flow.

Nicole felt her burdens lift and fly away, to burn up in the sun. She wished she'd found a drum set weeks ago, to relieve the tension. The thunder of the drums started to fade, to settle, until the last of the sound, the last vibration ceased. Limp from the effort, she gloried in the feeling of lightness that washed over her, her fear and worries were gone, eradicated by the pounding rhythm.

She opened her eyes when she heard clapping. Scott and several other people were standing in the back of the room. Her raging sounds had drawn a crowd.

Scott walked forward from the others. "That was magnificent, Nicole. The sound and beat were pounding through me, to the point I couldn't breathe, from the magnificence."

Nicole ducked her head. She'd felt that way, but didn't realize anyone else would feel it. She said quietly, "Thanks. It felt good to let everything go into the rhythm. I feel lighter." She looked to the back of the room and whispered, "Who are all those people?"

He shrugged and said for her ears only, "Neighbors, my parents, people walking or driving by that heard or felt the vibrations. Some of which haven't been in the church in years. We might decide to have you do that more often."

He winked when he said the last, so she knew he was teasing, but there was a scheming look to his eyes. So, she wasn't quite sure what he was up to.

He turned back to the people gathered. "We're going to have worship practice now. Nicole might be joining us on Sundays, so if you want to hear more, feel free to come back tomorrow at ten thirty."

A couple of people looked around like they were surprised to find themselves in the church, others laughed and waved as they turned to leave the building. Scott's father and a woman she assumed was Scott's mother walked forward.

She stood to go greet the couple, and noticed her muscles felt a bit weak, but they held after she steadied herself.

Scott said, "Nicole this is my mom, Charlotte. You've already met dad. Mom this is Nicole my new admin."

Scott's mother was tall and thin with a short cap of curly brown hair that was graying gracefully. She wore a huge smile that reminded her of her son's smile.

"Call me Char. Nicole, that was amazing drum work. I do hope you'll join us, we've needed a drummer for years and you are far more talented than anyone we've ever had before."

Nicole didn't know what to say to that, so she just said, "It's nice to meet you."

Char laughed and clapped her hands. "So, let's get started and see how it goes. John, you do the singing part. Scott, get your guitar." She looked at Nicole. "Oh, do you need a minute to relax? That was quite a performance."

Nicole said, "Maybe a minute, long enough to use the ladies' room."

"That's fine, dear. I'll get the men ready and loosen up my own fingers. Take your time."

SCOTT NEARLY FELL over when he heard his mom tell Nicole

to take her time. His mom was a very precise woman and if worship practice was supposed to start at four o'clock it started at four o'clock and not one second later. When his mom had entered the room and Nicole was on the drums, he'd been surprised to watch his mother stop all forward motion and still, as she listened to Nicole. It was now fifteen minutes after when they were supposed to start, and she'd told Nicole to take her time.

He had to admit that everyone had stood in awe, and watched as Nicole had played. It was nearly a religious experience to have that pounding sound flow through him. His feet felt the vibration and it had travelled up through his body while the sound pounded in his ears and brain and heart. He couldn't really even explain it. He guessed a person would simply have to experience it to fully understand.

He tuned his guitar and waited for Nicole, his body still vibrating from the beat of the drums. He heard his mom running through some scales and his dad sorting through the music they would be singing. It didn't take Nicole long, but it looked like she splashed cold water on her face. Scott wondered how much energy she'd expended during that performance.

She'd looked magnificent with her eyes closed and her body moving in a natural grace he'd never thought of regarding the drums. Sunlight had shown into the room from the stained-glass windows, almost like a benediction on her routine. He knew he was being silly, but he couldn't shake the thoughts.

Nicole slid behind the drum set and picked up the sticks and a slight frown formed. "What's wrong?"

"You need better drum sticks. These are old, dried out, and awkward."

"We'll order some immediately."

She shook her head. "But what if I don't stay?"

"Then we'll have better sticks for the next guy... or woman. You'll have to show me what to get, I have no idea."

Char said, "All right now, let's get going. Let's start with the hymn."

They practiced all the songs through one time. Deciding how many verses they wanted to sing, what order they wanted the different bridges and things to go in. All their normal practices they did every Saturday.

Once they'd gone through all the songs. Char said to Nicole, "You've played very conservatively this round and I appreciate that, for the first go through, as we make all the decisions needed, but now I expect you to play with the talent you have. Don't waste that amazing gift by playing like any other person could do."

Scott looked from his mom back to Nicole then back to his mom. She was dead serious, he looked back at Nicole who gave his mother a slight nod.

He could have been knocked over with a feather as they started the song list again and Nicole let her gift of music have free reign. It completely changed the songs from boring and old-fashioned to exceptional. He had to pay attention to not play at the wrong time, by sticking to the sheet music.

When they had finished the first song, which was the hymn, he looked at his mom and dad and then back to Nicole. "I had no idea it could sound like that. It was like God was right here in the room clapping along with you."

Nicole gave him a small smile and his mother clapped her hands in glee. "That was exactly perfect, Nicole. Never let your light and talent hide. God has given you an amazing gift."

Nicole squeaked out, "Thanks."

Scott's dad said, "No, thank you, Nicole, for sharing it with us."

Char spoke up, "Now, let's try the next one."

Scott was totally blown away as they worked through all the songs. He learned to read Nicole and how to stay in sync with her. He knew beyond a shadow of a doubt that tomorrow would be the best worship time he'd ever experienced. If he could get Nicole to stick around, the church might need two hundred bulletins, she might just fill the house. He had to wonder if her brother had the same talent, if so the two of them might bring the house down.

He couldn't be happier with Nicole coming to their town. It might have cost them a couple of fires, but it had been worth it. At least in his opinion. God really did work in mysterious ways.

When practice was over, they all decided to get pizza for dinner.

When they walked in the door Sylvia barreled over to them and looked at Nicole. "I hear you have an amazing talent on the drums, young lady. You've been holding out on me."

Nicole laughed. "Not at all, I just hadn't gotten around to sitting down with a drum stick in a while."

Sylvia pointed at Scott. "You are going to have a full house tomorrow, boy. You better have a good sermon worked out, or this girl and her talent is going to outshine you."

Scott looked at Nicole and back to Sylvia. "There is no doubt about that at all, Sylvia. I think God himself could come in to preach and Nicole would outshine even him."

Nicole gave a horrified gasp. "Scott, that's a horrible thing to say."

He shrugged. "Not when it's true."

CHAPTER 20

It was Nicole's day off and she wasn't sure what she should do with it. She'd enjoyed having dinner with Scott and his parents Saturday night. She'd been very comfortable with the three of them. Char made her feel right at home from the worship practice right on through dinner. She'd not given Nicole an inquisition at all, but she had been interested in whatever Nicole wanted to share.

Then Sunday was an amazing day. Sylvia had not exaggerated when she'd said word had spread about the new member to the praise band and the place was packed. They'd needed nearly all the bulletins she had printed. Scott had been thrilled and so many people thanked her for being there.

Between her helping Mary Ann and her skill on the drums, she felt like a celebrity. She had to wonder what would happen when the word got out about her brother and his fire-starting antics. Would people be as welcoming then? She was rather surprised that word wasn't out already, she'd always thought that was the way small towns operated, that everyone knew everything within minutes of it happening.

Nicole decided that maybe she should go back to exploring the town like she'd started to do a few days ago. Surely no one else would need help in childbirth, if she tried again. The tourist town map had all the locations of shops and restaurants marked on it, so she looked that over as she finished eating breakfast. So much of it was within walking distance she decided to leave her car and get some exercise while she perused the shops.

It was a lovely late summer day with the sun shining and just a hint of crispness to the air, to indicate fall was on its way. Several people waved to her as they drove by. She didn't know who they were, but she waved back anyway, assuming she'd met them at some point.

The art gallery was still somewhere she wanted to explore but she wasn't sure if it would be open. Surely Mary Ann would not be back to work so soon, but they might have other people who worked there. Nicole decided she would go there first just to see if it was open.

She wanted to look around in the costume shop that was next door. Not because she needed a costume but because she was curious. She couldn't imagine how a costume shop could survive in a town this size, even if it was paired with a bridal store.

Happy to see the art gallery was open she went inside. There was a woman in her mid-forties setting out new soaps and lotions. She called out a happy good morning to Nicole and kept working.

Nicole started on the other side of the store where she found so many fun things. There were wood carvings that were incredibly detailed, she loved one that was of a bird in flight. It was not an eagle as most people would expect to find, but it was a simple finch, which made it even more unique due to its humble subject. A person could find an eagle in almost every tourist trap in the country, but a finch was completely unexpected.

There was another carving of the Statue of Liberty which also surprised her. In New York it would be a common thing to find, but here in a small town in eastern Washington it was a surprise. She looked around for other carvings and found some that were not as surprising, a fish leaping from a pond and a black bear. What made those two unique was that the fish had a splash around it that was also carved from wood, it was so detailed and realistic she expected to see the water fall and still. The bear was in the midst of bushes and had a handful of berries it was lifting to its mouth.

She moved on and found a whole section of leather goods that were lovely. There were belts and wallets and some of the traditional leather working you might normally find, but the patterns were nothing she'd ever seen before. And growing up in Colorado she'd seen a lot of leather. These had patterns of flowers and foliage she'd never seen depicted in leather. She had to assume they were hand drawn and probably from plants found in Washington.

Nicole traversed around the room, she was amazed at the quality and the variation in what was included. The handmade quilts made her drool, she wanted half of them, at least. The jewelry that Mary Ann and Kristen made spanned the spectrum from simple and fairly common to complex and extremely unique. The glass sculptures were amazing, but they were way out of her realm of budget, starting at over two hundred thousand and running up to a million dollars.

When she'd worked her way through the museum slash store and over to where the woman was working restocking one of the tables, she'd found a ton of things she would love to have, but refrained from picking anything up. She needed to get some paychecks under her belt before buying anything.

The woman restocking looked up. "Oh, it's you. I didn't realize when you came in. I saw you play the drums at church yesterday. I'm Tammy O'Conner, my son, Jeff, practically dragged the whole family to church because he'd heard about your drum playing. He's always liked the drums, but money is tight, so I couldn't buy him a set or lessons."

Nicole was surprised by the woman's enthusiasm and wondered about it. "Well I'm glad he enjoyed it. How old is he?"

"He's nearly twenty-one. He works for Greg and has since high school."

That was not at all what Nicole had been expecting. She wondered if Scott would mind if she let Jeff come in and use the drums. She would be happy to teach him a few things. Nicole didn't want to say anything until she'd talked to Scott, so she said, "Well I hope you all come back on Sunday."

Tammy laughed. "I can guarantee that. Jeff plans to go as long as you're here, and since we've never been church goers, and he feels uncomfortable alone, we'll come with him."

Nicole didn't have anything to add to that, so she asked Tammy about the soaps she'd been stocking.

Tammy said, "These are made by one of our residents here in town. We never knew she made them and used to have to travel to Stehekin to buy them. That's just further up the lake. But when Kristen and Mary Ann opened the place Iris brought them in to ask if they wanted to stock them." She laughed. "The way Mary Ann tells it, she wanted to slap Iris for making her go to Stehekin every year to stock up and then use them sparingly to make them last."

"I met Mary Ann, so I can imagine that."

"Oh yes, I did hear about that. Thanks for being here when you were, we'd all been telling Mary Ann she needed to stay home and take it easy, but would she listen? No, she would not."

Nicole smiled, she wasn't surprised that Mary Ann had insisted she work.

Tammy shook her head. "We were trying to keep the place covered with at least two of us, but I had to leave early that afternoon to take my little ones in for their school physicals and Tim hadn't made it in for his shift."

"It all turned out all right, so I guess that's what matters."

"Thanks to you."

"I imagine Mary Ann would have called someone if I hadn't been here. Kristen wasn't far."

Tammy pointed to the back door. "They have a studio out in the back, she was out there, and I imagine Barbara called her, since Chris is a fireman, they have a radio in the shop. Kristen won't have one in the place because they distract her. She's got a workshop at their house too, but she prefers this one. She was also trying to stay near when Mary Ann was here, not that it did much good."

Clearly Tammy liked to talk. Nicole picked up one of the soaps and smelled it. "Oh, I think I need this one. I'm on a tight budget until I get a few paychecks, but I can't resist."

Tammy nodded and then patted her on the hand. "You just take that as payment for being in the right place at the right time."

"Oh, I couldn't."

"Sure, you can. Next time you come in you can pay, I promise."

"Well, thank you. I'm going to keep wandering around the shops in town to see what all is here."

Tammy laughed. "You do that, we've only got a handful of them, but they are fun to browse."

"Thanks for the soap."

"Thanks for helping our Mary Ann. See you Sunday."

~

SCOTT PUT down the book he was reading. It wasn't holding his interest and it wasn't because he'd read it before. In fact, that was why he'd picked it, because it always kept him entertained. Today Harry and his antics weren't cutting it, he knew why, but was loathe to admit it. Nicole. He couldn't keep his mind off her.

She was exactly perfect for him. Her drum playing had brought in nearly the whole town for Sunday service. He'd been surprised and thrilled at all the new faces. There was no telling how many people would be back next week, but he'd gotten at least one shot at them and for that he was grateful.

Nicole's role as his admin was going great. She managed to decipher his handwriting and kept him fed and organized. The woman was fun to be around, and both his family and friends enjoyed her company. His mom had called to tell him what a fun time she'd had on Saturday and also how excited she was with the turnout on Sunday. Nicole was beautiful and so darn sexy he could barely keep his hands and lips off of her.

Scott was going to be severely disappointed if she left to go with her stupid brother, if they couldn't keep him in town. Now *that* was something he could do, find out how that was going. A visit to the police station was just the ticket. He pulled on some socks and shoes to go have a chat with Nolan.

Nolan was on the phone in his office when Scott arrived, he'd realized halfway to the station that Nolan could be out on a call or have a day off. So, to find him in his office was a relief, Nolan looked up and motioned Scott to come in, as he hung up the phone.

"Hi Nolan, do you have a minute?"

"I do, and I wanted to talk to you anyway. That call was from the sheriff department in Colorado. Seems Nicole's dumbass brother set fire to a building that the owners were trying to make a historical location. It was someone's homestead, a hand-built cabin from the eighteen-hundreds. The people who owned it are pissed, and want Colorado to extradite his ass back there to face charges."

"Shit."

"Shit is right. The only thing that might, and I mean might, save his ass is that the county he did it in is the county that Alyssa and Rachel moved to. So, we have a little tiny bit of sway with them. I talked my ass off trying to convince them to let us keep him here. The sheriff is going to attempt to convince the owners to do that. But we won't know for a day or two. The rest of the places he set fire to are giving him to us to prosecute, as they were old buildings that no one cared about, and they often had to chase teenagers or the drug addicts out of them."

"So, no loss on those."

Nolan nodded. "But Colorado is another story and since that's his home state, they would win if they pushed."

"How's Kent been treating you?"

"He's surly, but nothing I can't handle. Probably scared and hiding it with anger."

Scott agreed that might be true, but it was time to see what was up. "Mind if I have a chat with him?"

"Not at all, feel free."

Scott walked back to the cells and found Kent sitting on his bunk with a sports fishing magazine. He walked up to the bars and said, "Hello, Kent. I'm Scott Davidson, the pastor in town. I was thinking maybe we could chat."

Kent looked up and shrugged, he didn't look defiant, or happy to see a visitor.

"Your sister is working for me."

Kent's hackles rose at that. "I don't want to discuss her."

"You think she betrayed you."

"Not think. Know. I know she betrayed me."

"That's not the way anyone else sees it. She's trying to help you, before you ended up in jail for murder."

Kent folded his arms. "I wouldn't. I only burn old abandoned buildings."

"Except for the Howe's home."

"I didn't know they still lived there. No one had been around for weeks."

Scott nodded. "It's true they'd been down in Oregon looking for a new place to settle near their daughter and grandkids. But you could have killed them."

"I didn't know they were in there."

"Doesn't matter, if they hadn't gotten out and called the fire department that whole house could have burned down, and you'd be facing no less than two counts of manslaughter. Some people might have pushed for murder."

Kent frowned and said forcefully, "I didn't know."

"That's no excuse. You still started a fire that could have ended in death."

"I wasn't trying to hurt anyone."

Scott wasn't letting that fly. "But you could have and that's why Nicole was trying to find you and stop you. Before you ended up in prison for the rest of your life."

"Well I'm in jail now, so what difference does it make."

"There is a big difference between a few days in a city jail and the rest of your life in prison. Nolan is trying to talk the rest of the states into letting us try you, rather than being sent back."

Kent shrugged. "Doesn't seem to matter much where I spend my time. I'll still be in jail."

"Except *we* want to try to give you a work release program with a deferred sentence. If you do well, you won't spend much time in jail."

"Why would you do that?"

"Because Nicole went to bat for you, before she would give us any information. She said you were a good man and just needed help to control your fire issues. We thought we might have a solution for that."

"I didn't know."

Scott was getting tired of hearing that. "We don't know if it will work however because the place you burned down near Rocky Mountain National Park was in the process of being declared a historical location. The people that owned it want you brought back to stand trial. If that happens, we won't be able to get you that work release program."

Scott had finally gotten through to him. Kent said with anguish in his voice, "But I didn't know—"

Scott was over it. "I don't want to hear that again. Stop using 'I didn't know' as your excuse for everything and grow up. You didn't know the Howe's were home and you could have killed them. Killed them. You didn't know you were burning down a historic site. You didn't know your sister was trying to save your dumb ass. Well now you *do* know. So, what are you going to do about it?"

Kent started to open his mouth. Scott held up his hand. "No. I don't want to hear it. You think about it, think hard, and maybe even pray about it. You've got a chance to turn your life back to the right path, but the first step is to stop being the victim and become the man your sister thinks you are."

Scott turned to leave but stopped and looked back at the man in the cell. "And just in case you've forgotten, Nicole lost her parents too, and then you ran off to act out. You left her when she was grieving and gave her another worry on top of it. You just think about being in her shoes. You are not the only one hurting. She's prepared to follow you wherever you end up, so you're not alone and neither is she."

Scott stormed out of the police station and was glad no one saw him leave. He wanted to hit something he was so angry. Nicole deserved someone better than that guy.

CHAPTER 21

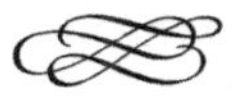

Scott wanted to talk to Nicole, he'd managed to calm down after seeing her idiot brother yesterday. He just wanted to see her. He made a couple of phone calls to see if he could arrange something he knew she would enjoy before he called her. He'd woken a couple of people up, but he didn't really care that much. They could handle it or pay him back later.

"Good morning, Nicole. Did I wake you?"

Her voice was soft and muffled. "Mmm, not quite, but close."

"I'm sorry it's so early, but morning is when the fish like to bite."

"What?"

Now he had her attention. "I thought maybe you'd like to go out on the lake this morning and see if we can catch a fish or two."

"Really? Yes, of course. I can be ready in five minutes."

He could hear her moving. "Great I'll be in the parking lot. It's cool on the lake in the morning, so dress in layers."

He was in the parking lot with a thermos of coffee and some

rolls from Samantha's, when Nicole rushed out of the rectory. She'd pulled her hair up into that high pony tail that had driven him wild a few days before. It exposed her neck and he wanted to nibble on it and run his tongue over the tattoo she had behind her ear. He'd not gotten close enough to see exactly what it was.

He shook his head to think of something else and noticed she was dressed like any other fisherman he'd ever seen, in flannel, jeans, and work boots. There was a turtleneck sweater under the flannel shirt, and she carried a warm jacket and a back pack.

She climbed in his vehicle, her eyes sleepy looking, her scent filling the interior, and Scott had to clench his fists on the steering wheel not to reach for her. Maybe this wasn't such a good idea.

Nicole beamed at him. "This is such a great idea, thanks for thinking of it. I spent yesterday exploring the town and shops, and had no idea what to do with today. I'm so glad you called."

All right if he could make her this happy then he would suck it up and enjoy her company, he just needed to stop lusting after her. Easier said than done.

"So, do you have your own boat?"

"No, but a friend has one and I took the chance that he didn't have it booked today, since tourist season has wound down." He stopped in front of Amber's restaurant. "Wait here, I'll be right back."

Amber was at the hostess stand and saw him come in. "I've got your picnic right here. But you owe me for getting it ready so quick. What's the rush?"

"Nicole likes to deep sea fish. So, I wanted to take her out on the lake when they might be biting."

"Oh, if it's for Nicole than I suppose it's for a good cause. She's already a favorite in town."

"She is, even Fred didn't complain when I told him I wanted to borrow his boat to take her out."

"Well, you better get going then. Have a fun day."

Scott picked up his lunch and hurried back to the SUV.

"What's that?"

"Lunch."

She gestured toward the backseat. "Then what's in the back?"

"Breakfast."

"Oh. I brought some snacks too, in my backpack."

"Clever girl. We might have enough food to stay out all day."

Nicole eyed the mounds of food and laughed. "Maybe two days. If we didn't have to work tomorrow."

Desire shot through Scott as he thought about spending the night on the boat with Nicole. It had a tiny sleeping cabin, but the thought of spending the night on deck, under the stars, was fascinating.

He shook off the idea as he pulled up to the dock to find Fred ready to let them board. Nicole and Scott carried the food and coffee onto the boat.

Fred chuckled. "You planning to stay on my boat for a week? Looks like you've got enough food for an army. You did say it was just the two of you going out, didn't you?"

"I did. We both had the idea to bring food. So yeah, we probably have more than we need. But more is better than not enough and starving."

Nicole nodded. "Plus, fishing is hard work and we'll need sustenance."

Fred chuckled again. "Yeah it can be, if you catch anything."

Nicole squared her shoulders. "Oh, we'll catch plenty. Of that, I have no doubt."

Scott watched Fred try not to contradict her and wondered who would be the victor in this little battle.

Fred looked at him. "You don't want me to drive?"

"Nope, we'll be fine."

Fred handed Scott the keys. "All righty then, have fun."

NICOLE WAS ACCUSTOMED to men who thought she didn't know what she was doing on a boat. So, she just ignored Scott's friend. She'd just prove it to him by bringing a nice catch back. She wasn't quite sure what kind of fish they would find on the lake, trout for certain including maybe mackinaw. Whitefish was also a probability, and being in Washington, salmon were a good bet, although they might not have started out here naturally, with the lake being so far inland.

They pushed off from the pier and she coiled up the ropes. Scott pulled the boat out into the lake. It was not a terribly wide lake, only about a mile wide, but it was long, over fifty miles and she'd heard it was very deep. She'd noticed some brochures when she'd stowed the food. She could read those later if she wanted to.

It was a pretty day with the sun just hitting the water, making it sparkle on the blue lake. Even if they didn't catch a thing, she was certain she would enjoy the day. Not that she had any intention of not catching anything, but still it was a great way to spend the day.

Nicole got them both a travel mug of coffee and a couple of the rolls from Samantha's bakery. She'd noticed Scott favored bear claws and she liked the palmiers Samantha made out of puff pastry. She took the food over to Scott as he picked up some speed. Her ponytail was blowing in the breeze and she was glad she'd put her jacket on as the cool air whipped around them. She laughed with pure joy of being on the water.

Scott looked over at her and grinned, her joy was obviously infectious. She handed him his mug of coffee, after he'd taken a sip and put it in the cup holder, she handed him a bear claw. He ate as he drove, he seemed to have a specific destination in mind. So, Nicole munched on her palmier and decided to enjoy the ride until he got where he was going.

Then they could talk about what they were looking to catch, she wondered about a license. She didn't have one, but maybe Scott did.

After a few minutes Scott cut the engines. "I usually have good luck in this area. We can drift a while here with no problems."

"What kind of fish do you have?"

"We have about ten indigenous species and then another half dozen that were introduced into the lake. Among them a half dozen types of trout, and a couple varieties of suckers, whitefish, and salmon."

Nicole nodded, "I wasn't far off then, in my guessing."

"Good for you. I've got a license, and I got you a one-day permit from Fred, since we're taking out his charter. If you stick around, you'll probably want to get your own permanent license."

His words brought back the reality of her situation and some of the joy drained from her.

He obviously realized what he'd said because he took her hand. "Don't give up yet, we've still got a way to go."

"I didn't hear back from my parent's lawyer yesterday. I'll have to call them again later today or tomorrow. I was kind of surprised that Samantha mentioned my brother when I stopped by her bakery yesterday. No one else in town has acted strange or said a word, but Samantha knew."

"Oh, everyone knows all right. But you helping Mary Ann

and playing in the worship band trumps your brother's idiocy."

She was completely surprised when he said everyone knew. Not one person had acted oddly toward her. How was that possible? "Seriously? Why? He's a criminal."

"But you aren't, and you helped a stranger. A stranger that we all love. So that business about your brother needing help to deal with his issues just fades to the back." He shrugged. "Plus, everyone who has met you sees what a nice person you are."

"My brother doesn't quite agree with that."

Scott looked away from her. "Oh, I think he will come around sooner or later. He's bound to want some family support. He just needs some time to think things over. Now let's see if we can catch a fish or two, shall we?"

Nicole pushed her worry about her brother aside and vowed that she was not going to brood about him when she was on the lake, and would soon have a fishing pole in her hands. "I'm ready when you are. Unless you want another roll or cup of coffee."

"I'll get you set up and then go grab another of each. Did you want another pastry?"

"No. I had a donut while I was getting the coffee into the mugs. I'm good for now."

Scott pulled out the tackle for two of them and hooked them into the downrigger. Once they were set, he let Nicole cast off and then attached a bell to the line. "Sometimes the salmon don't hit hard enough to pop the line loose so if the bell rings, grab it and jerk it hard."

"No, really?"

"Don't get sassy, these lake salmon are sneaky buggers, they can snatch the bait right off the hook without you even knowing. They aren't like their deep-sea cousins that hit harder. Check the bait often."

Nicole nodded and then grabbed her rod and yanked it free. She pulled on it and then let the fish play out for a moment before pulling it back in. She did that a few times to let the fish wear itself out a bit, clearly the hook was well set because it wasn't getting away. Scott grabbed the net as she started reeling it in continually.

When she got it out of the water, he scooped it up. "Great job, that's a nice-sized mackinaw."

"It is, we'll have trout for dinner."

"I didn't even see or hear it hit. Obviously, you don't need my two cents. I'll go get more coffee and breakfast, want more coffee?"

"Sure, that would be great," she said as she cast off again.

Before Scott got back, she had two more fish, a whitefish and another type of trout.

"Well for goodness sake, you're going to reach our limit before lunch at this rate. You've got a Mountain Whitefish and a Westslope cutthroat trout."

Nicole laughed at his expression. "I told you I was good at fishing."

"Yeah, but we're not trolling or anything we're sitting perfectly still and you're pulling them in like crazy."

She nodded happily. "I am, what is the limit?"

"Honestly, I'll have to look. I know it's ten mackinaw, fifteen whitefish and five trout not counting the mackinaw. If we catch anything else, we'll need to investigate, oh and we can only have between us four types of limited fish."

She saw Scott's pole bounce a tiny bit and hurried over to reel in another one, but it got loose when the hook didn't set well. She hated that when it happened, now there was an injured fish in the lake. Nicole knew it was all part of the experience, but she preferred to land them not just hurt them. She pulled the hook in and rebaited it and sent it back out into the water.

Scott grinned, “So how many of these came from my pole?”

“Just one and that one that I missed.”

“In that case I better finish my breakfast, so you don’t have to watch both of them.”

“I don’t mind I’ve manned more than one rod often.”

They fished in happy silence, trolling occasionally, until the sun had grown hot and was overhead.

Nicole pulled her hook in and secured it. “Let’s eat. I’m starving, and the fish are being lazy now.”

Scott nodded and reeled his line in. “Great plan, my bear claws wore off a while ago.”

After washing their hands, they worked together to get the food out. Rather than sit in the tiny kitchen they went up to sit on the deck. Scott looked at the number of fish they had and shook his head. “Too bad we weren’t in a competition. We’d have kicked butt.”

Nicole smirked. “Yeah, well, if I’m around next year we can do that.”

Scott pointed to her food. “Eat, miss smarty pants.”

CHAPTER 22

Scott was trying to decide if he should tell Nicole about the people in Colorado trying to extradite her brother to come back and stand trial. He was certain she would want to know. But she seemed to be having so much fun, he didn't want to ruin it.

This was the first time he'd seen her so relaxed. The tension from her shoulders was gone, as was the line in her forehead between her eyes. He'd not realized that little line was not permanent. Looking at her now he could see the hint of where it appeared, but it was not in evidence. So, he guessed it was a stress line.

She looked up and caught him staring. "What?"

He fabricated a little, "Oh nothing, just noticing your nose is a little pink. Not enough sunscreen."

"I would have to have pure zinc not to get some pink out here on the water. But the air is thinner in Colorado, so I have a pink nose anytime I'm outside for a while."

"Yeah we're only at about a thousand feet here. Not even close to the mile high you start at in Colorado." He dearly wanted to ask her if she liked it there better than here, but he didn't know if he wanted to hear the answer.

He ate a few more bites of food and then decided she should know what he knew, if he didn't tell her she'd be ticked off when she found out. He waited until she was nearly finished with the food on her plate.

"So, I wanted to tell you about my visit to the police department yesterday."

Her hand stilled with an orange slice on the way to her mouth. "What did they say?"

"I talked to Nolan and he said nearly all of the states were cooperating with the idea of trying him here in Washington."

Her face took on a glow that he was about to put out.

"All except for Colorado. As it happens the little cabin lean-to thing he burned down there, was in the process of being registered as a historic location. Apparently, it was someone's homestead from the early eighteen-hundreds, and they are not happy with him torching it. The owners are trying to convince the authorities to bring him back to face trial."

Her hand had dropped slowly back toward her plate, until it lay there, limp, still holding the orange slice. She looked down at it, let go and put her plate to the side. "Well, hell. I wasn't that excited about leaving Chedwick. I like it here, the people are so nice, and I like my job, and the cottage, and playing drums in the worship band, and being out here on the lake, and well... everything."

Scott wondered if he was part of that everything. She looked so defeated he hurried to tell her the rest. "Don't give up yet. The county your brother burned in, is a county where we have a tiny bit of influence. A couple of the girls who grew up here, went to Colorado and married into a family that has a decent amount of pull in those parts. So, Nolan talked to the sheriff and then called the head of the family and told them all what we want to try to do for Kent."

She didn't look convinced but there was a tiny bit of what he thought was hope in her expression. "That was nice of him, but will it help?"

"It might, the sheriff and the family have known these people a long time and although they are the stubborn sort, they might be able to convince them to let us keep and try your brother."

"How soon will we know?"

"Nolan said in a couple of days."

"So maybe tomorrow?"

"Maybe."

She nodded and picked back up the orange slice, then she dropped it back on her plate. "Is there anything we can do?"

"Not that I'm aware of, besides pray."

She sighed, and he noticed the little line was back on her forehead. He wished he'd kept his mouth shut. But he also knew that she deserved to know the truth. Sometimes it sucked doing the right thing.

Nicole stood and went over to the side of the boat. He stood and walked over to her. He slipped an arm around her shoulder and she leaned into him without turning to look. He drew her closer and wrapped his other arm around her too. He stood behind her now with her standing in front with her back to him, his arms wrapped around her holding her close.

He wanted to give her comfort and some of his strength. He wanted to heal what was broken and fearful. He wanted to help but he didn't really know how.

She let him hold her for a long time before she sighed again and pulled out of his arms. "Thanks for telling me. I need to think about this and maybe make some plans. I don't know. How can I make plans when we don't know what will happen?"

"I think you should hold off on any plan making. Just take it one day at a time until we hear back from Colorado. And your parents' lawyer. Just wait until you know what plans you need to make. In the meantime, just breathe."

"Yeah I guess you're right." She took a deep breath and then turned toward him and her face had a sly expression. "If I have to leave, you're going to have a lot of fish to eat," she said with a nod toward their catch.

He chuckled. "I'll have a church fish fry and make everyone bring side dishes for a potluck."

She looked a little wistful. "That sounds like fun."

Scott shrugged. "We can do that before you leave. We might need to catch a few more but there's no reason we can't have a potluck on Sunday and fry up those fish."

"Really?"

"Absolutely. We can call Sylvia right now and tell her to get it in the works." He looked at Nicole and she looked hopeful, so he pulled out his cell and called Sylvia.

Nicole beamed when he hung up from telling Sylvia his plan. "We better catch a few more fish then."

"We've got another dozen or so before we reach the limit, let's see what we can do."

NICOLE SET about catching more fish. A potluck and fish fry sounded like so much fun. She was surprised at how little effort it took to get it going. One simple phone call. They needed a lot more fish if everyone that had been at church was going to join in the fun. She wanted to make it special since it would probably be her one and only time to participate in a small-town potluck.

Returning to Colorado didn't hold a lot of excitement for her. She'd lived there her whole life and she would be fine, she had friends, she could get another job and an apartment. It simply did not have any allure, now. Whereas this place was completely new and different, living on the lake all by itself was an exciting idea, not counting the friendly people and the hottie pastor.

She sighed and put her mind on fishing, she wasn't going to think about what might have been. No flights of fancy for her, she was a straight forward thinker. A couple of weeks was probably all she had left here in this town, so she was going to make the best of it.

Scott took the boat out trolling for a bit after he'd gotten his line back out in the water. Since it was later in the day the fish weren't biting quite as much. When she got a hit, he stopped the boat and came over to help, just as his line hit, too. They both pulled in a good-sized fish, hers was a kokanee and his was a whitefish. They only had one more trout they could catch to fill both their limits, so they were avoiding the bait that they favored.

After Scott had sent his line winging back out into the lake, he came to stand by her. "You're kind of quiet and you don't look like you're having as much fun. Do you want to go back?"

"No not at all. I am having fun. I'm just more determined to catch us enough fish for a good fry."

"You know there will be other main dishes, for people that don't like fish, and also to make sure there is plenty of food for everyone."

"I've never been to a small-town potluck, so no, I don't really know what to expect."

"You've been to some kind of potluck, haven't you?"

"Well I've been to things where everyone brings food and shares like a tailgate party, or a holiday where we all help. But not a lot of regular potlucks, just for the heck of it."

"Well you're in for a treat then. On the other hand, I've never been to a tailgate party, we don't have enough kids for a football team, plus the remote location is a hinderance to competition."

"Well, then I'll have to compare the two and let you know how they vary."

She got another hit on her line and they worked together to bring it in. "I was going to say the major difference between the tailgate and the potluck was the location, with one being in a parking lot, but then I wasn't sure where you were going to be putting the grills."

Scott laughed. "Probably in the parking lot. But even if we eat outside it will be at tables with folding chairs, not off the back of pickups with lawn chairs."

She shrugged. "That's not a huge difference. Some of those tailgaters are pretty serious. Especially the ones for Bronco games."

"Yeah, I've seen some of them on TV, those fans are kind of rabid."

"They are, indeed."

His line hit so he went to reel his fish in, she watched the way the muscles in his arms worked as he pulled in a huge kokanee. She sure did like watching him, it was nearly mesmerizing as the sun highlighted him against the blue water surrounding them. She would be happy to watch all day.

He snapped her out of the trance with a request for her to grab the net. She felt her face heat realizing she should have already had the fish in it. It was kind of silly he had to ask. He didn't say anything as they got the fish on board.

Once the fish was safely stowed, he drew near her and

caught her gaze. "You seemed to be ogling me instead of helping just then."

"No. I was just..." she had no excuse at all, she couldn't think of a thing and a slow grin slid across his face, "... all right maybe I was ogling you, a little. Or maybe it was the huge fish."

He chuckled and drew in closer. "I want to kiss you, Nicole."

Oh yeah, she could be on board with that. He didn't kiss her though, he just looked in her eyes and his nearness made her pulse race. Then they were even closer, and she didn't know if he had moved, or she had. She lifted her face to him and still he didn't move. Was he waiting for permission? Maybe.

She whispered, "I'd like that, Scott."

He let out a breath he must have been holding. He slowly lowered his head and she went up on her toes to get closer. Quicker. She wanted to taste him. His lips touched hers in a barely-there kiss, a skim of his lips across hers. Tingles shot through her and she wanted more.

She put one hand up around his neck and pulled him closer as she raised up on her toes to strengthen the contact. He didn't hesitate to act on her hints, and their lips met firmer and more deliciously. Scott licked the seam of her mouth and she opened to him. His tongue delved in, to taste, to savor. He tasted like sunshine and the water, with hints of their lunch, but most of all she tasted him, and she loved it.

They kissed for long moments, his hands were on her hips, not pulling, not caressing, just resting there. She wanted them to move.

Scott pulled back, breaking the kiss. His breath was coming in harsh pants, just as hers was. Nicole didn't want to stop, although catching her breath would be fine, she wanted to pull him back in and start up again.

He panted out, "We need to stop."

"No, we don't. I see no reason to stop."

"Fish, we need to fish."

She looked at all the fish they'd caught. His latest catch was enough to feed half the town and added to the rest of the haul they probably had enough food. Nicole frowned and then shook her head. "No, I actually think with your last one we're good."

He groaned. "You're not making this any easier."

"I don't particularly want to make it easier. I vote for more kissing. And maybe more than kissing."

He ran a hand through his hair. "I'm trying to do the right thing, Nicole."

"Right for whom, exactly?"

"You. Me. The situation."

"The situation?"

"Yeah, not knowing what might happen in the future."

"Oh, my leaving." That did shine a different light on the subject. But she didn't necessarily see it as a reason to stop. In fact, if she was leaving wouldn't it be good to enjoy the man while she had the chance?

"Yeah, I don't think it's a good idea to go down that path until we know what might be at the end of it."

"But…"

"I don't do casual relationships. It's not a good role model."

A role model? He was worried about being a role model? Well wasn't that a fine kettle of fish? She supposed his being a pastor was a good reason to be careful about his relationships. But there wasn't anyone anywhere near them to be a role model to.

Well fine, if all she was to him was a detriment to him looking saintly, he could stuff it. Nicole turned away from him and went back over to start putting away the gear. She was ready to head back.

"Nicole, I didn't mean that the way it sounded. I just don't want us to get carried away and regret it later."

Carried away? The man was digging the hole he was in deeper by the word. She turned back to him. "Just drop it. I got it. Let's get back. I have some things I need to do."

Scott sighed but helped her clean up the tackle and then he started the boat off toward the town while she went down to the galley to get the food ready to take with them. *Dumb ass men, I don't need his rejection. In fact, I don't need him at all. He would just be a complication anyway.*

Nicole stayed in the galley, avoiding him, until they neared the shore. She started hauling up the food leftovers and put them on the benches. It would take several trips to get all the food and all the fish loaded into his truck.

When they neared the dock, she saw his friend Fred waiting for them. Even showing off their catch to the idiot did not lighten her mood. He was duly impressed, and Scott bragged about her fishing abilities and that he would love to have her on a competition next year.

She tried to look cheerful, but the looming thought that she would be far, far, away from this town and any fishing competitions put an even bigger damper on her enthusiasm than was already there.

It probably wasn't a good idea to get too involved with the people here anyway. So, she wouldn't miss them when she left. Of course, saying that might be easier than actually doing it.

CHAPTER 23

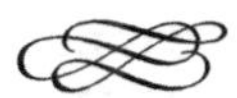

Scott knew he'd said something wrong. Nicole had lost her spark, and in fact, her motions were very jerky, like she was pissed. But he truly didn't know what he'd said or how to make it better. It clearly had something to do with kissing. Or not kissing.

She'd not even gloated at Fred, who totally deserved gloating after the way he'd acted earlier that morning. Fred had even noticed Nicole's quiet and had sent Scott a puzzled look. He'd just shrugged because he only had a vague notion of what was eating at her.

The three of them loaded up the SUV with the left-over food and the fish they had caught. Scott had brought a cooler along to keep them in. The fishing boat had its own with a handy net that allowed them to scoop up their catch and transfer them easily.

They both thanked Fred for letting them use the boat and Scott told his friend about the fish fry pot luck after Sunday service.

"As long as I don't get a charter before then, I'll be there to eat some of Nicole's fish."

Nicole gave him a weak smile. "I hope you can make it, Fred. We wouldn't have all of these without your boat."

Fred rocked back on his heels. "And your expertise."

Scott noticed her smile warmed a little at Fred's praise, but it was not nearly as bright as it had been this morning. After they had clambered into the vehicle Scott paused before starting it. "What's wrong, Nicole? What did I do to dim your enjoyment of the day?"

"Nothing really. It's mostly the fact that I probably will be leaving soon. I'm not particularly looking forward to that."

Scott wasn't looking forward to that at all and in fact was going to do his best to make sure she didn't leave. "I'm planning for the best outcome. If anyone can convince the sheriff to not extradite it's Alyssa."

"What's so special about Alyssa?"

"First, she's the sister in law to one of the deputy sheriffs and she married into one of the oldest families from that area. They have a lot of pull and hopefully can talk the homestead owners out of pursuing. But more than that Alyssa has always been very persuasive."

As they drove to the church Scott told the story about how Alyssa had campaigned hard to get her father to marry his second wife, Ellen, who had been Alyssa's third grade teacher at the time. By the time they parked, and he finished the story Nicole was laughing at the antics of the small girl and her eyes had the sparkle back in them.

Scott was thrilled that he'd managed to get Nicole out of the doldrums. He'd been entering high school when Alyssa had pulled her shenanigans, but he'd still heard all about them. It was a favorite story in the town.

They took the fish into the church kitchen. It was a professional setup, so definitely the best place to prepare the fish. They had cleaned them as they had fished and used the insides as bait, so nothing was wasted.

Since they weren't going to eat the catch for five days, they needed to freeze it. Some of the fish they cut into steaks and then wrapped them in butcher paper to freeze. The smaller fish they left whole to be fried. With the two of them working it didn't take too long to process all the fish and get them into the freezer.

When they were finished Scott was ready for a shower. Nicole looked tired, too. He said, "I don't know about you, but I need a shower and a nap and maybe dinner."

Nicole nodded. "I hear you. So, I'll see you tomorrow. I am going to take one tiny one home for my dinner tonight if that's okay with you."

"Absolutely. You can't fish all day and then not have even a bite of your catch. I plan to take one too. See you tomorrow."

Nicole looked at him for a long minute then she took her backpack and her fish and left the room. He wasn't sure what she'd been thinking as she looked at him, but he couldn't help wanting to pull her back into his arms for more kissing. He'd refrained, and now he wished he hadn't, but he was dirty and smelly, so maybe it was for the better. Although she was probably dirty and smelly too, just in a prettier way.

He rolled his eyes at himself. *Go shower, idiot.* He grabbed one of the fish packets they'd made and turned off the lights as he walked through the empty building.

NICOLE TURNED off the water in the shower, she was clean again. She loved to fish but it was hot sweaty work and then processing all the catch made everything smell like fish. She'd thrown her clothes in the washer on the way to the shower.

She wrapped her hair in a towel and dried off before

applying moisturizer to her whole body, especially the areas that had been exposed to the sun. She didn't burn easily, so she wasn't worried about that. But the wind and the sun could dry everything out, so a little extra caution wouldn't go amiss.

Her nose and cheeks were a little pink, but she'd kept sunscreen on them all day, so she didn't think they were burned, it was just a little added color. She put on some clean, old, comfortable sweats and thick socks. Her hair was as dry as she was going to get it without a hair dryer, so she brushed it back out of her face to let it air dry.

She decided to call Kent's girlfriend, Tracy, and let her know they had found him and were waiting to see what would happen next.

It wasn't a fun conversation to have, but she was glad she'd done it. Tracy needed to decide what she wanted to do with her life. Kent wasn't going to be in Denver again regardless of what happened.

Nicole was ready to eat after that conversation. She was one of those people that ate to alleviate stress, she had a high metabolism, so she had not yet had to worry about eating too much.

Plus, even though she was a stress eater she always tried to make good food choices. Carrots instead of chips was one of her best ones, she liked carrots even better than chips, most of the time. If she wanted chocolate she went for the high-end variety where a little would satisfy rather than eating a whole bag of a lesser brand.

She was ready to cook her fish, fortunately she loved to fish, and she also liked to eat them. Unlike some people who enjoyed the sport, but then didn't eat what they caught. That was a big fat waste in her book.

There were plenty of spices in the cupboard, so she fried up her fish in butter, dill and a few more seasonings, and made some rice to go with it, along with steamed vegetables. It was a meal fit for a king, or at least a happy fisherwoman.

Her phone rang, and she saw it was Scott. She pushed answer. "Hello?"

There was a moment's pause and then he said, "Hi Nicole. This is Scott, which you probably already know. Anyway, I was wondering if you needed any spices. I didn't want your fish to be too bland."

Spices? He was calling about spices? She supposed that was nice of him but totally unnecessary. Hadn't she told him the kitchen was well stocked? She thought she had. "No, I'm fine, there are plenty of seasonings here in the cottage. Maureen must have left them."

"Oh good. I was willing to bring some over if you needed them."

"No, need in fact I just finished eating. It was delicious."

"Oh good. I just put mine on to fry and then thought about you. Um, cooking your fish, I mean."

Nicole couldn't figure out what was going on. Scott was sounding very odd.

"Oh darn, hold on a sec."

Nicole frowned at the phone. This was getting weirder by the minute.

Scott came back on the phone panting, which reminded her of his panting earlier in the day when he'd kissed her boneless and then pushed her away. "Sorry. I nearly burned my fish. I had to flip it."

"Well then you should probably go, fish doesn't need too much cooking, you'll dry it out." Why was he still talking to her?

He muttered, "I suppose you're right. I'll see you tomorrow."

Before she could say goodbye, the line went dead. She looked at the display and shook her head. She had no idea why he'd called. For spices he was going to bring over while his fish burnt into a piece of charcoal? The man was definitely odd.

Rather than worrying about Scott and what he was thinking, she cleaned up her little kitchen and decided she would spend the evening reading. She felt like re-reading Harry Potter. She'd read it many times, but it was always worth another round, and since the stories were all on her phone, she could enjoy them anytime. The question was, should she start from the beginning or with her favorite?

She decided to start at the beginning. She found a quilt, wrapped herself in it and delved into the world of magic and muggles.

Before she'd gotten through the first chapter the phone rang again, with a number she didn't recognize. A Colorado number.

She answered it rather than letting it go to voicemail. She normally didn't answer numbers she didn't have stored in her phone. They were too often telephone solicitations and no she didn't want a vacation package, and her credit cards were just fine as they were, thank you very much. But she did answer this one.

A business-like voice said, "Nicole Roman?"

"Yes."

"Hello, this is Marilyn Ramsey. I'm sorry for calling so late but I'm just back from vacation and got your message about your parents' estate."

Nicole was glad she was sitting down. She cleared her throat which had gone suspiciously dry. "Yes."

"I'm sorry to inform you that the estate is not yet settled. The house has not sold. We've had some interest and one person almost went through with it, but backed out at the last minute."

Her shoulders slumped at the bad news. She needed some

way to pay for a lawyer. "Oh well, thanks for letting me know."

"The real estate company was wondering if you would want to come down a bit in price. Maybe five thousand dollars? That would still leave you and your brother with a nice profit and might instigate a quicker sale."

Nicole had no idea what a lawyer might cost so was reluctant to lose out on an extra five grand, but some money was a lot better than no money. She said, "Yes, that would be acceptable."

"Very well I will inform the agent. I'll call back as soon as I have more news."

She muttered a thanks, as the line went dead. She laid her head back and stared at the ceiling. She needed help. Any kind of help at this point. She tried to think of a way to pay a lawyer but there was nothing, no thoughts besides despair.

She looked back at her phone and the struggles Harry was having with his muggle aunt and uncle. She wasn't in nearly as bad of straits, but then again this was real life, not fantasy.

CHAPTER 24

Scott was feeling a little sheepish when he went into the church the next morning. He'd acted like an idiot last night calling Nicole to see if she needed spices for her fish. He'd tried to play it off as a friend helping, but he knew better. Maureen always kept a lot of spices and she hadn't taken things like that with her. So of course, Nicole didn't need seasonings for the fish.

He'd just wanted to talk to her, mainly to see if she was back to being aloof. But she'd seemed fine. Not talkative, but that could mean anything, like she was busy. What an idiot he was sometimes.

When Nicole got to work, he would just ignore his idiocy and do his job and let her do hers. If he could simply stop thinking about her, that might actually work. He was so relieved when his phone rang, he didn't even look to see who was calling.

"This is Scott."

"I know it's you, Scott. You're supposed to say hello. Or even, hi Maureen."

Scott laughed. "I didn't look to see who it was, I just answered."

"Well that's odd. So how are you doing in my absence?"

"Not too bad. I hired a woman who came in last week and she's been managing to keep me sane. She said something about you leaving a very detailed document."

"Well, yes I did. I didn't want some poor soul to have to fumble around in the dark. Did you check references or anything or just hire her right off the street?"

"Right off the street. Never even thought to ask for references let alone check them."

Maureen sighed, and he could envision her look of exasperation. "I suppose I shouldn't be surprised. Anyway, you called and left me a rather cryptic message. Which is why I'm calling you from sunny Florida, instead of sunbathing."

Scott could not imagine Maureen sunbathing, so he stayed away from that idea. "Yes. I need to know if there are organizations that we are affiliated with or know about, that help people with lawyer expenses."

Maureen gasped. "Is your new secretary a criminal?"

"No, not at all." He didn't want to get into the whole story on the phone when Nicole could walk in any minute, so he didn't elaborate. "So, are there places?"

"Yes, of course. Some of them take a while and others have very severe restrictions. Let me make you a list. Since we're stateside for another three days, I'll email you. We haven't quite figured out technology, computers or phones, when we're on a cruise ship or in a foreign country. So, it's better to do it while we're here. But we did have a fantastic time in Brazil."

"Brazil was your first trip, that's wild."

"It's always been a dream of mine. I had a friend who was from there, so it makes sense in a weird kind of way."

"Anyway, I'll get you a list of organizations to start looking at."

"That would be great. Thanks, so much, Maureen. Where are you going next?"

"Tahiti is next on the agenda, it's somewhere Dennis has always wanted to go."

"Wow, that's quite a difference."

"Which is why we're spending some time in Florida to toughen up my skin, so hopefully I don't burn like a lobster. Washington dwellers do not move easily to tropical climates without burning."

Scott laughed. "Yeah, you've got that right. We have very pale skin from having no sun, although we're not quite as bad over here as it is in Seattle."

"No, we do have a lot more sun days than Seattle, that's for sure. But still not like Tahiti. Well, Dennis is here to drag me out into the sun. It won't help being here if I spend the day indoors. I'll send you a list tonight. Oh, I have one suggestion you can start with today."

Scott jotted down the name and said goodbye. He'd just heard Nicole enter her office. He didn't want to say anything to her about looking for possible help until he had at least done the preliminary work to see what was required. So, he slid the note into a desk drawer, not that she would probably know what it was about, but he didn't want to chance it.

Nicole knocked, and he called out for her to come in. She did, but she didn't look especially happy today. She said, "Good morning, Scott. What do you need me to do today?"

He tried to decide if he should simply ask her. It was hard to say. Sometimes people wanted to be asked and sometimes they did not. Of course, she could tell him to butt out if she didn't want to talk. And if he didn't ask, she might want to talk but not feel comfortable to bring it up.

Rather than letting his mind go round and round he just

asked, "Are you all right? You look a little down. Is it from yesterday when I did whatever it was I did to irritate you?"

She huffed out a laugh. "No, I'm over that, it's your loss. I heard from my parents' lawyer and the house hasn't sold yet, so I'm kind of bummed about that. They suggested we lower the price another five thousand to see if we could get it to sell."

His loss? What was his loss? He needed to think about that later. "Oh well yes, I suppose that would be disheartening news. But not hopeless yet. We still need to hear what Greg has found out and what the people in Colorado have said about the extradition. So, we're not at the place that you need money quite yet."

"I know but it takes time to close on a house and then get the money. Unless someone walks in with cash and wants to close immediately it could be weeks. I don't want my brother to have a crappy lawyer if he can have a good one."

He didn't want to sound like he was ignoring her concerns by there-there-ing her. Nothing was more irritating in his opinion than someone who didn't really listen and simply said everything would work out. Sometimes pastors took that easy route and it didn't help. Yes, praying about it was an excellent thing to do, but being open to God's leading was just as important, He often led people to the right answer and what steps they needed to take.

"I'll be praying for a quick sale. But we also need to do our due diligence to make sure there aren't other options we might be missing, than to simply look to the sale of the house as the way to finance it. So, keep thinking and leave no stone unturned."

"Thanks for that, Scott. That actually makes me feel better. There might be another way that I haven't thought of." She smiled at him and he felt his heart stutter at the radiance on her face. She was so beautiful and not just an outer beauty, but her joy at the simple idea he'd given her shown from within. It took her normal prettiness and enhanced it to stunning.

He sat there staring, his mind gone blank, or had evaporated in the glow. Nicole started talking and he attempted to get his mind to engage so he could at the very least listen to what she was saying. He might not be able to speak yet, but he needed to at least hear her.

"I'll go start on the mail and bills and stuff. If you need me to do something different just holler." She stood and took the mail and offering to her desk to get it ready.

He was both relieved and regretful when she closed his door. He could breathe again and think. Which was a good thing. But the warmth and glow left with her, and he felt cold and alone.

Which was ridiculous, he couldn't sit around all day mooning after the woman. He had a job to do.

He had no idea at the moment what that job was, but he was quite certain he had things he needed to do.

NICOLE PUT the items she carried on her desk. She felt lighter than she had felt since she got the phone call from the lawyer last night. She'd laid awake half the night worrying about her brother and the house selling and her moving and every dreadful scenario that could possibly happen. Then she'd spent no more than ten minutes with Scott and saw it all in a whole new perspective.

He'd not poo-pooed her concerns but had opened her eyes to a new way to think about the situation. She had pinned all her hopes on the house selling. So, what were some other options. Maybe a loan? A fundraiser? A fishing competition prize? Maybe she should go to work on a fishing boat, they probably had some operating out of Seattle, fishing in Alaska. But that might take a while. She jotted those ideas on a piece of paper. What else? She would think about other options while at the same time hoping the house would sell. But first she needed to do her job.

Nicole paid bills and logged them into the accounting software. She tallied up the tithe which was much larger than last week. Oh, some kind of drum competition? She jotted that down.

And she needed to ask Scott about drum lessons for that boy whose mother worked at the art gallery. It's too bad her brother hadn't been learning about the glass, selling one of those sculptures would make all of their money problems look ridiculous. Of course, it would take him some time before he got good enough to sell them for that kind of money.

Maybe she could do a fundraiser with her performing on the drums. Like a show. She jotted that down too. When she got off work or ran out of things to do, she was going to look on the internet and see if there were any kinds of competitions for her particular skills.

Lots of things to think about, none of them might come to fruition, but at least she wasn't sitting around depressed. She finished up the work she knew to do and noticed that it was about eleven. By the time she went to the bank and the post office she could pick up lunch for Scott.

She knocked on his door. When he bid her to enter, she said, "While you sign the checks, I have a question."

Scott nodded and began scrawling his signature on the three checks she had for him. "A lady at the art gallery said her son is very interested in playing the drums. I was wondering if I could show him a few things."

Scott's gaze whipped to her. It was penetrating and more intense than she'd ever seen. It was almost scary. "Jeff? Really?" Nicole could practically see his mind whirling. "If he's interested, I wonder how many other teens and young adults would be. I've been trying to get an older youth or young adult group going for ages. We've got a significant amount of money set aside to do things for that age group. What if we bought some of those practice drum set things and you taught them lessons? Would you be interested in that?"

She nodded as she thought it over. "That might be fun. Those tabletop drum sets run from fifty to a hundred dollars each."

Scott clicked on his computer. She sat in the chair across from him while his eyes searched the information. "We've got several thousand in both age groups. So more than enough money to buy practice kits. I should probably run it by the governing board for a vote. And we could announce it at the service on Sunday and see how many kids would be interested. We could do one night for both groups or two nights if there is enough interest. We would need to pay you differently for that work."

"Oh, you don't need to do that. I'm happy to show them."

"No. You need to be paid for your expertise. I'll do some research and see what drum instructors are paid. But I can't imagine they don't make at least forty dollars an hour and that would be for a single student. You teaching a whole roomful would be more."

Nicole laughed. "Are you joking? Forty would be more than enough. How long of a session are you thinking?"

"My motivation is to get them in the door, so I can influence their lives or at least be a listening ear. So, what if we did forty-five minutes, took a break for snacks and a little discussion about life in general, and then did another forty-five minutes. That way they get a solid hour and a half, and I can bend their ear for a half hour, while they refuel."

Nicole nodded, thinking that another sixty dollars per week would be awesome.

"I'll get started on talking to the board."

She remembered she also wanted to ask him about lunch. "I was going to go to the bank and post office, what do you want for lunch?"

Clearly his mind was in a whole other universe because he nodded at her and finally said, "Anything is fine."

She chuckled as she left him with his out-of-this-world thoughts, glad he'd finished signing the checks.

CHAPTER 25

Scott was thrilled with the ideas for a youth group. He wondered if he could expand on the idea. He could teach guitar. If Nicole's brother got to stay in town, maybe he could teach bass guitar. Why had he never thought of this before? He'd told Nicole to think outside the box, but he'd not done it himself.

This was a new generation, he needed to get out of his father's mindset about how to bring people into the church. He'd been shocked when the place was packed last weekend and all they'd done was have Nicole on drums. But it really added depth to the worship and he'd loved it.

He realized he'd gotten complacent. Yes, their town was small, but there were still a thousand people and in his youth, there had been two churches, one had closed when the economic downturn had happened, when he was in his teens.

In the summer the population swelled with both the seasonal workers at the park and hotels, but also the tourists. He'd never really made a play for the tourists and that was just wrong. He hadn't even advertised the church in the visitor's brochure. He just assumed that people on vacation weren't interested in attending church.

A few people had dropped in over the years. And now that he was thinking about it one man had said something to him about having trouble finding a church to attend. He hadn't thought a thing about it at the time, but now he saw the comment in a whole different light. It wasn't the location they'd had trouble with, it was knowing there was one to find.

He shook his head. Time to rectify that. A call to Trey would fix him right up. Trey could make up a website and also get him an ad in the visitors' brochure the next time they printed some. He'd have to wait a day or two since Trey was busy with Mary Ann and the new baby.

Scott was exhilarated about these new ideas. Maybe he should apply it to all areas of the church. Writing down areas he wanted to think about he decided that maybe brainstorming with Nicole would be even better. She had a fresh perspective of the town and church.

He needed to get the first phase of the drum lessons started and that meant a call to Sylvia, she could get the ball rolling. He wanted to spend a chunk of the money they had set aside for the teen programs and that took running it by the governing board. He still had the ability to make it happen, but the board of directors was there for just that, to direct. They could mention any concerns they had and if they really wanted to, they could veto the idea, but he didn't think they would do that.

Sylvia didn't answer her cell, which meant she was probably at work. He dialed the pizza place and she answered the phone. "Hi Sylvia, this is Scott."

"Hi Scott. Are you calling for lunch?"

"No, I was wondering if you could set up a board meeting. Nicole was asked about drum lessons and I thought maybe we could use that as a way to draw in the teens to a youth group."

Sylvia hummed. "Interesting idea. Tell me more."

Scott quickly told her what he was thinking. When he finished talking, Sylvia said, "I'll be happy to set up a meeting. I'll try for tomorrow morning."

"Great thanks."

"You sure you don't want lunch?"

"Nicole is going to pick something up on her way back from the post office and bank. I have no idea what."

"Good enough. I'll let you know when the meeting is set for. Later."

She hung up and Scott grinned. She'd not shot his idea down and wasn't stalling on the meeting, which he took to mean she liked the idea. He really needed to work on his sermon and hoped he'd be able to concentrate on it instead of all the ideas whizzing through his brain.

Then again, he could preach on thinking outside the box and letting God lead you down new paths. If the church board didn't shoot the youth group idea down, he could end his sermon with the announcement of when it would be starting.

With that idea in mind he started jotting down notes. He had two whole pages when he began to run out of steam.

Scott only remembered about Maureen's phone call when he found the note, he'd jotted down the information on. Looking at the clock he decided he had enough time to start the search.

NICOLE THOUGHT about her brother as she drove by the police department. She'd finished with the bank and post office and only needed to get some food before heading back to the church. Her heart wanted to stop and see her brother, but her head warned her he'd not been pleasant the last time. The tug of war was intense as she parked on the street in front of the station, debating whether to go in or not.

She jumped when someone knocked on her window. Nolan was looking in at her through the glass. The car was still running, so she powered down the barrier. "Hi, Nolan."

"Morning, Nicole, are you coming in to see your brother?"

"I was trying to decide. He wasn't very nice to me last time I was here."

"Yeah, but I think you'll find his attitude much improved since Scott came in and had a talk with him."

"Scott came in and talked with him? Why?"

Nolan lifted one shoulder in a half shrug. "He was just making it clear your brother understood the circumstances and the reasons you helped us find him."

"Oh."

"Come on in. I think you'll be glad you did. If he gets surly, we'll only give him bread and water for a few days. That will knock some sense into him."

"I'm not sure that would help my case."

Nolan rocked back on his heels, grinning. "You might have a point. Come on, trust me."

Nicole sighed, she did want to see Kent, even if he was cranky. "All right, you win." Nolan waited while she powered her window back up, turned off the car, and got out.

"I can't stay too long. I need to get lunch for Scott. Although I haven't decided what yet."

"I can take care of that." He pulled out his phone and called a number. "Hey Amber, Nolan here, can you add something for Nicole and Scott? Thanks." He put his phone back in his pocket. "We've got lunch ordered and one of the deputy's is picking it up in forty-five minutes, plenty of time for you to chat with your brother. That's why I saw you, I was getting the dispatcher's order and there you were."

"Dithering."

Nolan barked out a laugh. "I haven't heard that word since my grandmother died. I would have said contemplating your actions."

Nicole grinned at him. "Very diplomatic of you, police chief."

He shrugged. "Part of the job description."

He walked with her to the back of the building where the cells were. Her brother was sitting on his bed reading a book, several more were stacked on a table or on the bed. There was also a notepad Kent had clearly been taking notes in, the pen was clamped between his teeth.

"Kent, you have a visitor."

Kent looked up and saw Nicole, she watched as emotions flit through his eyes, love, anger, resignation, finally settling on excitement, which she had not expected.

Nolan had also been watching closely and turned to leave when the excitement had appeared on Kent's face. "Holler if you need anything."

Kent put the book down on the bed with the notepad keeping his place and set the pen on the table.

Nicole said, "Are you still mad at me?"

Kent looked chagrined, then shook his head. "No, I understand why you needed to do it. And you were right, I wasn't getting better. The house I set on fire, at first, I was thrilled, it was the largest by far and would burn for a long time. But then I saw the old people and all their animals coming from the back and I was horrified that they were in the house. I'd not had any idea."

"I know."

"No, but that was just the start of the realization of what I'd done foolishly. They brought in a backhoe and started digging up the grass and small trees between the house and the forest. One of the trucks didn't even start on the house, just started spraying down all the foliage and closest trees. That's when I realized they were more worried about a forest fire than they were the house."

Nicole felt all the blood drain from her face and her hands started shaking. She sat on a chair next to the wall. "Oh my god. What if…" She paused, she couldn't even say it out loud.

Kent shook his head. "Yeah, your dumbass brother could have started one of those horrible out-of-control forest fires. The guy on the tractor was ordering around about half the firefighters, who were working with him to create a fire break."

"Half?"

"Yeah, shit Nicole, I almost had heart failure when I saw them tearing up the ground and pouring water on the trees and bushes. The fricking house was burning and the old people were losing everything and they had to concentrate on keeping it from getting into the trees, because some idiot hadn't thought about the consequences to his actions."

Nicole closed her eyes, thinking about all the horrible fire disasters that had been on the news the last few years.

"That's when I got a job at the park and decided to stop burning. I did good for a couple of months. But then some little kid got lost in the park and it took the whole staff hours to find him. He'd curled up in the Noah's ark building in a corner behind some plastic sheep and had fallen asleep. His poor parents." Kent shook his head.

"The stress."

"Yeah, I couldn't handle it and needed to burn something. But this time I made sure there were no trees around and it was an abandoned shack with no one living in it. But I still felt bad about it and called my old therapist. He set me up with a doctor in Chelan, but I haven't been able to go yet, because the cops started patrolling the dock and the upper road."

Nicole didn't know what to say about that. Kent getting professional help was a step in the right direction but was it enough?

"Nolan told me what they are trying to do about the trial and maybe a work release program. He brought me in all these books to start reading. I really hope it works out. Your boss said they were having trouble because one of the things I burned down is a historical monument or something."

Nicole nodded. "Yeah, I heard about that, too."

"Nolan said not to give up hope and Scott suggested I start praying. So that's what I've been doing, reading and praying. So even though I was pissed at you to start with, this was the best possible place to get caught. I'm sorry I was a douche. Can you forgive me?"

"Of course. I love you, silly. I'm glad you contacted your old doctor. Did you tell Nolan about the psychiatrist in Chelan?"

"Yeah he's coming in to see me tomorrow on his day off. He said he could do that every other week until I either get extradited back to Colorado or can come into Chelan. He's also got an acquaintance in Colorado he can hook me up with."

Nicole felt her stomach drop at that idea but kept the smile on her face. "So, you're learning to work with glass by reading?"

"Yeah, Nolan says reading about the basics can't hurt."

"Do you think you'd like it? If you get to do it."

"I do. I've always been fascinated by the process. And maybe working with fire will be enough to keep me on the straight and narrow. That and the doc, and you, of course."

He ducked his head. "Thanks, sis. I'd give you a hug, but the bars are kind of in the way."

Nolan walked up just then, and Nicole wondered if he'd been listening to their conversation or had just come to get her because their lunch had arrived. "I can open your cell for you to give your sister a hug."

She was thrilled to walk into her brother's arms and he about squeezed her breathless. They rocked together for several moments before reluctantly leaving the other's arms. Nicole kissed her brother on the cheek and hurried out of the cell before she started blubbering. One of the deputies brought Kent's lunch back, so she used that as her excuse to leave. Saying a watery goodbye and that she'd be back soon.

Nolan followed her out and handed her the lunches. He told her to come back anytime. She fled as the tears threatened to overflow. She sat in her car for a few minutes letting herself cry and settle.

It had been the best visit she could have hoped for. Kent was ready for help and excited about the idea of working with glass. Now all she needed was money to pay lawyers and one or two tiny miracles. Easy peasy.

CHAPTER 26

Scott's head was spinning, at least that's what it felt like. He'd spent over an hour looking at organizations that helped people financially. The problem was that most of them helped with emergency housing or food or clothing.

The one Maureen had suggested did help with lawyer expenses, but it was such a lengthy process, he wasn't sure it would work for them. It was designed for people who had been discriminated against, whether at a job or for medical care. It was a long-term group, which he was very glad to know existed, but it wasn't what would help in this case.

Then he'd started his own internet search. But the organizations that helped with law cases were more about finding a cheap lawyer, or a pro bono one, or some even taught people how to defend themselves. Again, not what they needed.

He was feeling defeated, but still held out a glimmer of hope that Maureen would come through. Maybe he should have been more specific when he'd talked to her. But rather than call her back he would wait and see what she sent.

Still, he'd wanted to have good news for Nicole when she got back, and he didn't. Darn it.

There was a knock on his door which was probably the woman herself, back with lunch so he called out and stood to go with her to the kitchen. She opened the door and walked right up to him, grabbed his shirt and dragged him down for a firm smacking kiss.

When she drew back, he managed to sputter, "Not that I'm complaining, but what was that for?"

"You, talking to Kent."

He'd been a little worried that she would be ticked off at his interference when she found out about it. Apparently, that wasn't the case at all. "So, it helped?"

"Oh, yes. He was wonderful. Come let's eat and I'll tell you the story." She hooked her arm through his and they went together. She didn't wait until she got to the lunch room but started jabbering right away.

He could barely keep up with the story she was talking so fast, and she seemed to be using some sort of sibling code that he knew nothing about, but her enthusiasm and joy was all he really needed to see. The rest was just icing on the cake.

"Nolan gave him books to read about glass blowing?"

"Yes, and he was taking notes. I've not seen him this excited about learning in, well, ever. He was an okay student and got good grades but there was never anything that really thrilled him to learn about. That's exactly what I saw today, a hunger to learn."

She laughed her silvery laugh that shimmered through him and set his blood on fire. She didn't notice and kept right on talking as she took sandwiches out of the bag and opened them, like she had no idea what they were.

She didn't ask him what he preferred, but just kept one and slid the second one over to him, as the non-stop stream of words continued to pour out of her. She waved a hand full of napkins at him before her eyes filled and she told him about Kent wanting to give her a hug and the bars being in the way.

He said, "But Nolan would have—"

She didn't let him finish. "Oh yes, Nolan was right around the corner and immediately opened the door, so we could hug each other, but it still made me sad to think of Kent behind bars. It's going to kill me if he has to stay in jail, especially if he has to go to Colorado."

Scott took her hand and squeezed it. "Don't give up hope. Think about the best possible outcome, not the worst. It's always best to dwell on the positive not the negative. I choose to believe God is on our side."

Her laugh had a watery sound to it this time which didn't send fire into his veins, but it did send a fierce need to be her champion.

He didn't know how to do that, so he tried to think of a distraction. "So, while you were out running errands and seeing your brother, I was thinking about the drum lessons."

Nicole looked up from the sandwich she was picking at. "What about them?"

"Well, not so much that in particular, but I think I've gotten into a rut in my thinking. I just follow the same practices as my father and grandfather. The idea of a drummer's group got me wondering where else I am blind about the church. I thought maybe you could give me your insights, now while the place is new to you and you haven't become accustomed to the 'way it's done'."

~

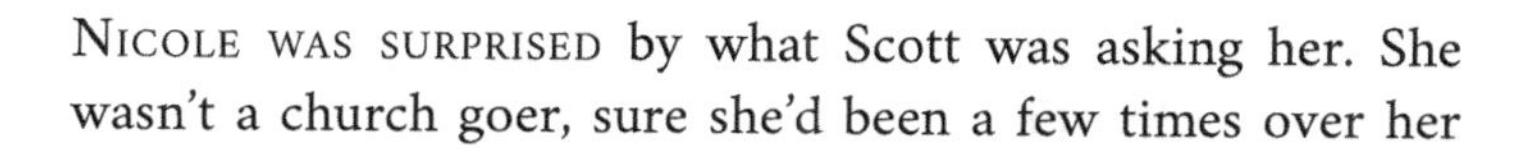

NICOLE WAS SURPRISED by what Scott was asking her. She wasn't a church goer, sure she'd been a few times over her lifetime, but not enough to know anything about how things worked in a church. She had definitely seen some things her that she thought were old-fashioned and weird, but she didn't want to hurt his feelings or what was the term, sacrifice the holy cows?

"Gee Scott, I don't have a lot of advice on church. I haven't been to many and certainly not faithfully."

"Perfect. That's the perspective I want. Think back to your first few moments here. What struck you as odd or old-fashioned?"

"Well the hottie carpenter hanging the bulletin board being the pastor definitely surprised me."

Scott guffawed. "Well, thank you kindly for the compliment, but let's move past that one."

She was frantically trying to think of something she could say that wouldn't hurt his feelings. To stall she said, "Let me think." Then took a big bite of her sandwich.

He laughed clearly seeing through her stalling technique and took a bite of his own.

As she slowly chewed her sandwich, she thought through her first days here. The place could use some modernization for sure. The colors were from the sixties, the flowers they set out were boring. The Sunday brochures had nothing to recommend them. The people filed in and out on Sunday like there was no talking allowed. She'd seen several people frown at the kids when they clapped at the end of the songs. Scott was welcoming and so were Sylvia and Carol Anderson, but the rest, not so much. She didn't want to heap too much on him at once. Where could she start?

The drapes! The ugly shit-brown drapes that made her want to vomit and rip them off the walls to have Kent set fire to them. Perfect, she was certain he'd not picked those out. The looked like they'd been hanging there at the back of the stage for a millennium.

"Well there is one thing that I think needs to go..."

Scott's gaze snapped to hers. "What? Tell me."

"The drapes."

Scott frowned like she was speaking Greek. "What drapes?"

"Those ugly brown drapes, at the back of the stage, in the sanctuary."

She could see him thinking. "There are ugly brown drapes in the sanctuary? Really?"

Scott got up, leaving his lunch on the table and marched down the hall and into the worship hall. Nicole followed him, was he kidding? He walked in and stopped dead still and stared at the stage.

"I've never even noticed them. Those things are hideous."

She couldn't believe her ears. "Seriously, how could you not notice them?"

He rubbed his hand on the back of his neck. "They've just always been there. Like the walls. Or the... dear God, are those carnations? We have carnations on the altar? Aren't there any pretty flowers this time of year?"

"You seriously didn't notice the drapes or the carnations?"

"Not until just now. This place looks like something out of the fifties."

She grinned at him, she wouldn't have to say much at all, now that his eyes were opened as a young man and not a stodgy old fart. "Yes, it does."

"Well, no wonder no one my age or younger wants to come here. It sucks."

Nicole laughed as he looked around the room in horror. He picked up one of the Sunday bulletins and flipped through it and groaned. "Well, hell." He ripped it in half and in half again and again until it was the size of confetti and threw it in the air. "This whole place needs a major overhaul, starting with me and my expectations."

He looked around like he didn't know where to start and then headed toward the stage. He grabbed one of the drapes with both hands, he wasn't really just going to yank them down, was he?

"Wait. You can't just pull them down it will make a mess and possibly tear holes in the wall. Plus, you have to make sure what's behind them isn't worse."

Scott turned toward her. "Worse? Is that possible?"

"Just look behind them."

He pulled back a corner and groaned. "It's dirty teal and gold print wallpaper. Who in the heck thought that was a good idea? Do you suppose they had gold shag carpeting too?" He shuddered dramatically.

She took him by the arm. "Sounds like a sixties thing. Come on, we need to strategize this. Baby steps, not mass destruction."

They went back toward the kitchen, but as they walked Scott continued to look around and groan like he was in pain. He detoured to the church foyer and marched over to the table that sat there covered in a tablecloth that had seen better days. He lifted up a corner and moaned. Nicole walked over to see what it was, as Scott took everything off the top of the table and yanked the cloth off. Under that was a pad like what is used on a dining room table to keep hot dishes from damaging the wood. He pulled that off too and Nicole was shocked to see a gorgeous cherry wood buffet.

Scott pointed to it. "Do you see this? It is clearly a hand-crafted piece of fine furniture from maybe the thirties and has been covered by this ugly tablecloth my whole life."

"It's beautiful." She ran her hands over the top, the finish was still perfect.

Scott gripped his hair with both hands and pulled. "What were they thinking?"

Nicole took him by the arm and led him toward the kitchen. "I'm sure they were simply trying to protect it."

"But what good is it to have, if no one ever gets to enjoy it?"

He sank down in his chair and Nicole pushed his sandwich toward him. "Eat. You can't do anything right now but assess what can be done. Plus, you will have to run it by the board and make sure you have the money to make changes. We can start with a list and ideas."

He picked up his sandwich and waived it at her. "I don't care if they like it or not, we will be modernizing. If it's only taking the stupid tablecloth off that buffet and updating the Sunday bulletins from that ugly tri-fold thing. I imagine there are better programs out there to produce them."

Nicole said, "I think the program your using is probably fine, but maybe a newer version of it. I looked at the version and it is from 1998."

His head snapped up and he swallowed. "Seriously?"

CHAPTER 27

Scott was ready. He and Nicole had talked for hours yesterday about changes that would liven up the church. They'd made lists of everything, from simple things like changing the Sunday bulletins to major overhauls like the ugly curtains and outdated colors. New technology for the Chapel and Sunday school rooms would bring them out of the flannel graph era. They'd found several great teaching series that could be watched on large screen TVs if they had them in the rooms, for little kids to adults. A real projector installed into the ceiling of the sanctuary, instead of the overhead projector and pull-down screen for the popular worship songs would be great.

By the time they'd finished it was late and they were starving so Nicole had invited him over to the rectory for what she called kitchen sink casserole. She'd explained that it wasn't the traditional kitchen sink casserole, he hadn't even known there was such a thing. Her take on the food dish was to assemble leftover ingredients to make something tasty, she'd had chicken, which she shredded and had added leftover corn, from late season locally grown fresh corn. She'd fried up some bacon and added a white sauce and topped it with cheese and French-fried onions. He'd been skeptical, but it was delicious, served with premade dinner rolls from a can and salad.

He'd enjoyed the entire evening and had managed to keep his attraction for her on the back burner, so they could simply have fun and enjoy a meal without any sexual undertones creeping in.

The board members would be arriving any minute. Nicole had made coffee and had gotten an assortment of baked goods from Samantha's bakery. She said she could have just heated up some of the baked goods from her freezer, but didn't want to cause any trouble if some of the women's auxiliary was also on the board of directors. Better to go with something no one had brought her as a gift.

Clearly the board had already been talking about the idea of drum lessons. He'd just barely introduced Nicole to the ones she hadn't met yet, when they all started talking about their ideas for the drum lessons. A drum corps or drum line was suggested, and did she know how to teach them to march and play at the same time?

Nicole flushed at the barrage of questions. "No, I have never taught drum lessons, other than to the kids of my parent's friends. No, I've never marched with a drum, and that would take purchasing a different type of drum. We were talking about some practice pads to start with, not real drums."

Sylvia nodded. "Yes, that does make sense. But we want to encourage them. Too bad we missed the parade they had for the town fundraiser."

Mrs. Tisdale said, "Plus, we've got money set aside for youth groups and haven't used it in forever."

Carol Anderson frowned, "Now Ruth, don't look sideways at the boy. He's had some big shoes to fill and he's starting to make this his congregation. Anyway, I move we buy two dozen practice drum sets, sticks and headphones and one more full drum set, and that we pay Nicole sixty dollars per hour for the two-hour youth drum lessons. Unless there is enough interest and then it will be two two-hour sessions, one for younger kids and one for older."

Nicole looked flustered and Scott felt the same. He said, "But I don't think we'll need two dozen, or another full set."

Carol said, "If we get enough, the kids can take them home to practice. Which means they will also come back each week. The extra set of real drums is to let one of them play with Nicole during worship, when they're ready. Do I have a second?"

The decision was taken right out of his hands and he just sat there and watched while they voted in the drum lessons. Nicole looked extremely nervous and he figured she was worried about all the expense if she had to follow her brother.

He was much more worried about the next item he wanted to bring up and that was the redecorating and modernization of the church. People had strange ideas about making changes.

When Sylvia was finished with the vote, she asked him if he had any other items of new business he wanted to address. He felt his palms grow wet and wiped them on his jeans.

"Yes, I do. The drum lessons got me to thinking about other ways we could be more welcoming." His mouth was dry, so he took a sip of his coffee. Everyone else sat there watching him and Nicole gave him an encouraging nod. "Well I noticed that some of our décor is, well, is a little on the old-fashioned side of things."

Ruth asked, "Spit it out boy, what are you thinking about?"

Carol rolled her eyes. "Ruth, stop. Let the man speak."

Scott swallowed. "Well the curtains in the chapel are old and outdated. I looked behind those and there is some, um, wallpaper that has seen better days."

They all just sat there watching, so he sucked it up and went on. "We could use a couple of large screen TV's in the classrooms and maybe a real projector mounted to the ceiling that we could get hooked up to a computer for the modern songs and maybe announcements."

Ruth looked at the other board members. "Anything else, Diamond Jim?"

Shit, they didn't like his ideas, should he continue? He didn't know, but decided in for a penny in for a pound. He cleared his throat. "The foyer and carpeting could be updated too. And maybe the bathrooms. But we don't have to do it all at the same time. We could do it little by little."

Ruth looked at Sylvia. "It's a start."

Sylvia nodded. "It is."

Frank Miller, who owned the garage in town said to Ruth, "Stop giving him a hard time, you old bat."

Ruth chuckled and nodded to Frank to continue.

"I say thank God, he is finally seeing the need to modernize and isn't still stuck in his parents and grandparents' ways." He pointed at Scott with the tire gauge he always had in his hands during these meetings. "We've been waiting for you to realize it's your church now and you need to do things your way. And that starts with modernizing. That god-awful wallpaper was your grandparent's idea back when wallpaper was 'the thing'."

Carol laughed. "Scott, your parents couldn't stand it any longer after they'd taken over the church for about nine-months and covered the paper with curtains. Believe me, at the time the dirt brown curtains were soothing."

Ruth cackled and rubbed her boney hands together. "We

have plenty of money set aside for redecorating and even the electronics you want."

Sylvia grinned at the rest of the board and then looked at Scott. "You get started with quotes on exactly what you want. Bring us back a list and a budget and a time line. It's your church now Scott, give it your personal touch. And don't worry we won't let you do anything stupid."

George who was the school's janitor nodded. "We're proud of you, Scott, and glad to be using the transition fund again. Anything else, or are we done here, I'm sure that someone's made a mess at the school by now, so I need to be getting back."

Scott was too shell-shocked to say anything but. "I'm good."

Sylvia adjourned the meeting after saying everything was ready for the fish fry on Sunday. Then they all left chuckling and excited by the idea of Scott making the church his, and not his parents'.

Nicole said, "What just happened? Two dozen practice sets, another full set. Are they crazy? Sixty dollars an hour for an untrained teacher? Have they lost their minds?"

Scott wasn't listening to her, when he finally looked up at her, he narrowed his eyes. "I have a very sneaky board."

"What do you mean?"

"They've been putting money into that fund all along for this. I think they've wanted to make changes for a long time, and I wasn't ready. I don't know how much money is in it because I never could figure out what it was for. They called it the 'transition fund', and every time I've questioned the amount of money going into it, the entire board stiffened up and demanded that we keep putting money into it. Make the church my own? I had no idea, they were just waiting for me."

Nicole laughed. "Guess you better get to work on prices

and what you really want, and maybe take a look at the fund and see how much is in there."

Scott nodded and then clunked his head on the desk. "I guess I better, and you need to order drums and sticks and headphones."

"But Scott, what if I can't stay? They will have spent all that money on drums and have no one to teach the kids?"

Scott shrugged, it hurt to think of her leaving, but he couldn't put that burden on her. "Don't worry about that. We'll cross that bridge when we come to it. Maybe we could advertise for a teacher. Some old rock band hippie from the sixties, we could save the hideous wallpaper for him. Now let's go find things to make all this happen."

NICOLE WAS FLABBERGASTED about what had taken place during the board meeting. She'd primarily been there to take notes. But they'd grilled her on the drum idea and then planned to pay her an astronomical hourly wage to teach a bunch of kids the drums. But the scariest part of all was them spending nearly two thousand dollars on practice sets for the kids when they didn't even know that she would be staying. Scott had shrugged it off, but she just couldn't do that.

Could she find a way to stay even if her brother got extradited back to Colorado? That was too sad to think about, leaving him all alone in jail and not even being near enough to visit. Leaving this town and the church and the exciting idea of teaching drum lessons was sad to think about, too. She was not going to think about leaving Scott. She was not going to think about Scott at all. In fact, she wasn't going to think about any of it, she was going to do what the church board had told her to do, and that was order drum sets.

As Nicole researched where to by twenty-four practice

drum sets and headphones and drumsticks and tape, she didn't allow herself to think about the future. When it started to creep into her thoughts, she felt panic edging closer, so she clamped down on those thoughts. The future was not here, she was going to stay in the present, period.

When she finished with her research, she set it aside and focused on her work chores for the day. When Scott was ready, she would show him what she found to get his opinion. There were a couple of options. One was cheaper, but slower and the other more expensive, but she would have the equipment next week if she ordered by tomorrow. She suspected Scott would vote for the faster option to get things rolling, but the discount from the other company was significant.

Nicole also wanted to look up the program they used for making the bulletins and see how much an upgrade to the newest version and what the newer software offered. She was thrilled to see it offered a thirty-day free trial period, so she downloaded it and did a few mockups for Scott to look at. When she got back from the printer with her ideas in hand, she saw that Scott's door was open, so she went to see if he'd been looking for her.

"Oh good, Nicole, I was looking for you. I need some input on things."

She laughed at his befuddled expression, his hair was standing on end where he had clearly run his hands through it. "Perfect, because I need your feedback too."

"Two heads are better than one," he said and then waved toward the papers in her hand. "What's that?"

"The software you have for the church bulletins has a thirty-day free trial on the upgrade, so I downloaded it and tried out a few options."

Nicole quickly folded the sheets in half and handed them to him.

"Are you serious? This is the same software we've been using? Are you sure?"

She shrugged. "Well it's a dozen upgrades later than the version we have, but yes, it is the same software."

"Well glory be, I never would have guessed. Is it expensive?"

"Not really, a couple hundred dollars."

He frowned. "Is it hard to use?"

"Not at all. I did these in about a half hour."

Scott looked so disgusted with himself. "Don't hesitate, buy it. I've got a three-hundred-dollar discretionary allowance that I don't have to get approval for. Why didn't I do this earlier?"

Nicole felt bad for him he was so irritated with himself for going along with the status quo. "Well maybe Maureen was happy with the older program."

Scott smirked. "Great excuse, let's go with that one, rather than me being an idiot."

"Don't be so hard on yourself. It was comfortable, like an old friend. You didn't realize things needed to change and were probably worried about doing too much and having people complain. There are a lot of people who might have fought you over even a little difference. I remember something like that happening at a church our family went to when I was little. There was a blow up about moving the piano to the other side of the stage. It was nearly a fist fight, my parents never went back to church after that, saying they didn't want that kind of influence in our lives."

"I suppose you're right but still, we have carnations as the altar flowers. I mean sure carnations in the dead of winter when nothing else grows is great, they are pretty enough, but in the spring and summer and fall, let's at least use seasonal flowers."

"I'll call the florist later and let them know that is your preference."

Scott suddenly looked like a light bulb had gone on. "You know what? I think we started having carnations when the economy was so bad, and half the town left for greener pastures. They were probably the cheapest flower."

Nicole nodded. "And they do last a long time."

"Exactly. I feel better. I took over for my dad at what was probably the lowest point in the economic downturn."

Nicole was happy to see he was moving away from self-flagellation. "Good now let's share our thoughts. Should I order us a pizza or something for lunch, so we can work on all of this?"

Scott grinned. "I'll do the honors. I've got them on speed dial."

While Scott ordered delivery, Nicole went to get her information on the drum sets and a pad of paper to take notes, just in case.

They spent the rest of the afternoon talking about ideas and making plans.

As she'd assumed, Scott wanted the drum sets ordered as quickly as possible, even at the higher expense. It was probably for the best, if she did end up moving, they would have them in time to do a few weeks of lessons.

They concentrated on the sanctuary first. Looking at different decorating ideas for the stage, tile, wood, paint. No curtains and no wallpaper.

Scott had stated emphatically that he didn't care if it was coming back in style, no wall paper. Nicole had laughed at his outraged face when she'd suggested the idea. She'd really done it simply to torment him, it had worked too.

They found an app that would allow them to simulate the different ideas. And had spent at least an hour trying out different decor.

He mentioned that they had a contractor in town who could do the work.

Nicole nodded. "That's good, otherwise you would have to wait to get someone in here. You know that contractor might have some good concepts, too."

"He just might. I'll call him and see when he can come in to chat about it."

While Scott called the contractor named Marc, Nicole ran to the bathroom and then decided a little pick-me-up snack might be good. She snagged the left-over sweets from the morning board meeting and went back to Scott's office just as he hung up the phone.

Scott looked up with a bewildered expression. "He said he could stop by tomorrow morning. He also said he would bring by the sketches he had ready for me."

She didn't know what to say, with so many people confirming they'd just been waiting for him she could imagine he felt like an idiot. Nicole set the snacks on the desk. "Don't worry about it. He probably has all kinds of sketches sitting around that he hopes someday someone will need. It's not a very big town, I don't imagine he has a ton of business, so why not doodle ideas? Have a bite we've been at this a long time; the pizza has worn off with all this thinking."

He absently reached for a sweet roll, totally missing his favorite bear claw. "It's just kind of disconcerting…" He took a bite and then looked down at the pastry. "Oh, I thought…"

Poor guy he was quite discombobulated. "I wondered why you didn't take the bear claw."

He shrugged and took another bite of the cheese Danish. "I thought I did take it. These are good too."

"But not your favorite."

He nodded. "But not my favorite."

She hated to bring it up, but it had to be done. "So, do you want me to send those screen shots we made to the board or do you want to wait to see what the contractor says tomorrow."

"Might as well wait and see what Marc suggests. I wonder if he's already bought the materials."

Nicole giggled nervously, she wouldn't put it past the guy. "Don't be silly I'm sure he hasn't done that."

Scott lifted one eyebrow at her, and she giggled again. "Well, I hope not anyway."

CHAPTER 28

Nicole woke early Sunday morning, she was ridiculously excited about the fish fry and church potluck. When she'd left work last night the whole parking lot was filled with barbeque grills on one side and huge lines of tables on the other. When she'd questioned Scott about what all they were going to be cooking on all those grills he'd laughed and slung his arm around her shoulder.

Pointing with his other hand he said, "We'll cook the fish on those three. Hank Jefferson and his family will probably bring nearly a side of beef that will be grilled on those over there. And then there will be corn on the cob and various vegetables for the last ones."

"Do we have folding chairs for the tables?"

"Those aren't the eating tables. Those are for the side dishes."

"What! That's enough tables to feed the whole town and they're only for the food? No way."

"Yes, way. People will bring tables, chairs, blankets and

whatever, to eat over in that grassy area. Some will take it inside to the cafeteria."

Nicole looked at the grills and the tables and the grassy area, it was an enormous setup. She whispered, "So, is the whole town coming?"

"Yep, whether they come to church or not, nearly everyone in the town will be by at one time or another. Some will come on lunch breaks, others after work."

"So, this is an all-day affair?" She was totally mystified by the entire idea.

"Yes, not everyone comes to church on Sunday, but it's still the local gathering place for the town. Everyone that can be here, will be here."

She shook her head still not quite grasping the concept. "I had no clue, I thought it was just for the church people."

"Nope, welcome to small town life."

Remembering the phone call from earlier she said, "Carol Anderson called and told me to bring whatever I had frozen from the auxiliary women's offerings. She said they never really expect the recipient to eat everything they bring."

Scott grinned. "I'll bet they were surprised that you didn't bring some of them the other day to the board meeting."

"I didn't want to offend anyone."

He squeezed her shoulder. "You'll find very little offends people here, contrary to most other places."

So here she was bringing a good two-thirds of what had been frozen over to put in the kitchen for later. She'd set it out last night to start thawing. They'd done the same with the fish taking them from the freezer and putting them in the gigantic refrigerators to defrost.

She still didn't know quite what to expect but she was excited, it was kind of sad her brother couldn't be there to join in the fun. She wondered if she could get a plateful to take to him at some point.

When the service started, the room filled up, Scott had set up extra chairs saying some people would come out of obligation for attending the barbeque and since she was drawing a larger crowd, they might need them.

When they got to the announcements and Scott told the gathering that they would start having a drum group on Thursday nights, people cheered. Nicole was glad she was in the front row ready to go up on stage, so not too many people could see her red face. She'd never experienced so much enthusiasm for her talent, it was kind of embarrassing.

When she got up to sit behind the drums, she was shocked to see that every seat was taken, and people were standing around the back. As the transition for worship took place the children were invited up to sit on the floor. Even with their vacated spaces filled up, there were still people standing. She looked at Scott who just shrugged and grinned.

Nicole looked around the room absently, noticing some people she'd never seen before. Until her gaze stopped abruptly on the one person she never expected to see in the crowd. Her brother. Kent was sitting in the church service, Nolan was on one side and Greg was on the other.

Kent had a huge smile on his face as their eyes met and held. She stared at her brother in wonder and tears filled her eyes. His smile got bigger and he winked at her.

Nicole was glad she didn't need to see her music for the first song, because it was going to take her a minute to compose herself. Fortunately, her hands and feet were ready to play, so she blinked away the tears.

As they played the songs, more and more people filtered into the room, the place was packed to the gills. The sound of singing nearly drowned out the music, until someone at the back turned up the sound.

When the worship ended Scott walked up to the podium. "Since there is no way to walk up and down the aisles, we'll just pass the offering plates around, give what you want or if you can't, take what you need. Someone at the back, please put the plates by the sound system."

Nicole and Scott's mom stayed seated at their instruments because their seats had been taken by others.

Scott said, "Hopefully we won't get in trouble with the police or fire department for packing this place past capacity, but since I see Nolan and Greg in the crowd, I'm not too worried."

Everyone laughed but didn't move or leave.

Scott preached a short sermon and Nicole was surprised that some people didn't slip away during it. But no one did, and everyone listened respectfully, even laughing at the right times.

When the service was complete, he called out. "Let's get the grills going and the food on."

Everyone laughed and started to make their way outside. Scott's mom took the offering upstairs, from what Nicole could see the plates were overflowing. The teens were clustered around the sign-up sheets for the drum lessons and clutching the information flyers in their hands.

Nicole didn't see where her brother had gone, and she was disappointed not to be able to give him a hug. She supposed they had to take him back to jail.

When she was grabbed from behind and swung around into a hug, she knew it was Kent and her heart soared with joy. "You got to stay!"

"I did and I'm staying for the picnic. They put one of those ankle bracelets on me, but I have no intention of running. I'm ready to face the consequences of my actions, just like Scott talked about today."

Nicole didn't remember Scott saying anything like that, but maybe that's the way God worked, that a person heard what they were supposed to hear.

Kent continued, "Besides if things go well, I've got the best chance to make something of myself, right here in this town."

Nicole hoped that would be the outcome, but doubts crept in and she decided to heed what Scott had said about trusting God and concentrating on what was good, not bad.

~

SCOTT WAS beside himself at the number of people attending church this morning. He knew everyone would come to eat but he'd never had so many attend church before a potluck, a few yes, but not that many.

He was thrilled to see all the teenagers and young adults clustered around the signup sheets for the youth groups and drum lessons. Both boys and girls. He wondered if they would have enough practice sets to go around.

When his mom whispered in his ear the offering total, he nearly fainted. Well that would certainly buy more practice drums if they needed them. Not that they didn't have more in the youth fund, because they did.

Old man Peterson walked up to him and he felt his mood sink, the guy never liked his sermons and always criticized them. Scott vowed to smile and take it, it was all part of being a preacher.

The old guy shook his hand and said, "Mighty fine sermon today, Scott."

Scott was shocked beyond words but managed to choke out. "Well thank you, sir."

"You're welcome. I can see you're doing a good work here, boy."

Had he stepped into the Twilight Zone, Scott was mystified. "I'm doing my best, sir."

Old man Peterson cleared his throat. "Still, I'll send you a few tips and mention the things that you could have done better."

All right, life on the planet had not gone completely haywire. Scott was nearly relieved. "I'll look forward to it, sir."

When he shuffled off Scott's dad came from behind him. "I've never seen that man complement anyone. Good job, son."

"I was afraid I'd tumbled into an alternative universe."

John chuckled and slapped his son on the back. "Let's get out there and supervise the cooking."

"I'm sure Sylvia has that handled."

"I'm sure she does too, but we should at least pretend we're in charge."

They made their way through the crowds bustling about to get things ready.

"You know if the girl stays you might need to build a larger building."

Scott barely kept walking he was so surprised at his father's statement. "Don't you think this is an anomaly that will go away?"

"Nope, I don't. With Nicole bringing in droves to hear her drums and you preaching like you did today, I think it could very well be a sign of the future. Plus, I heard through the grapevine that you're planning to spruce things up."

Shit, he should have called his dad and told him. "Oh, well, um I just thought..."

John chuckled. "You thought right. Your mother and I changed things when we took over from your grandfather. It's time for you to put your own stamp on things. Darn proud of you, son."

Relief filled Scott and he hadn't realized he'd been worried about hurting his parent's feelings. "Thanks, dad."

CHAPTER 29

Nicole was completely happy with her brother by her side at the potluck. She started to introduce him to some of the people she knew. They hadn't gone far before Kent had grabbed her arm to halt their progress.

"What is it?"

"The people whose house I burned down. I need to go apologize."

Kent turned and walked off toward an older couple, Nicole hurried to catch up with him. He stopped and said, "No wait here. I need to do this alone. If they don't punch me, you can come meet them."

Nicole didn't want to let him go alone but decided that his desire to do so showed he was maturing, and she knew she needed to let him. She couldn't mother-hen him his whole life. She hung back and watched her brother approach the couple and felt Scott draw near to her.

Many people in the crowd also turned to watch and the noisy crowd became hushed as all eyes followed her brother up to the couple. He spoke in a normal tone of voice not loudly to show off but not too quiet to hide what he said. "I'm Kent Roman, I'm the one that torched your house."

He rubbed a hand around the back of his neck but didn't back down. "I didn't know anyone was in the house, I thought it was abandoned. But that's no excuse, I was wrong, and I destroyed your belongings and scared you. I hope in time you'll forgive me. I mostly just wanted to tell you I wasn't trying to harm or kill you, or your animals. I was disgusted with myself when I saw you come around from the back of the house."

Ray Howe said, "Not disgusted enough to come help us put it out."

"I was just about to do that when the truck roared into the drive. I don't really know anything about putting out a fire, but I would have tried."

Ray said, "Fair enough. If you decide to stay in our town, I think you'd better join the department and learn."

Kent shuffled from foot to foot. "I totally would, but I don't think they allow convicted arsonists to join the fire department."

Mr. Howe said, "I think you'd be surprised who they let join the department."

Mrs. Howe had her arms folded and wasn't looking happy. "Well that's all fine and dandy, but we are now moving to Oregon without all our treasures and keepsakes and I, for one, am not too pleased with you, young man."

Kent nodded. "I understand that ma'am, I am really sorry. Can I do anything to make it up to you?"

"Well we still have to go through everything and toss what's ruined, and see if anything is salvageable. It's a big job for Ray and me."

"If Nolan will let me, I'll come out and help you with that." He lifted his pant leg. "I've got a monitor, so I can't go far."

Scott whispered in Nicole's ear, "Might do him good to see the damage he wreaked on them."

Nicole nodded her eyes still fastened on the confrontation.

Betty still looked fierce, but Ray said, "I think that would be a great idea. It's going to be a lot of work and none of it fun."

"Yes, sir, but it's a lot less than what I deserve, and you don't deserve to have to do it at all. I'll ask Nolan."

"Ask Nolan what?" The man himself had walked up behind Kent.

"If I can spend my days out at their house cleaning up the mess I made and helping them to salvage what's left."

Nolan rubbed his chin. "I think that would be doable. It'd give you something to do and a first-hand look at what the consequences of your actions are. You can start tomorrow." He looked at the Howe's. "I'm thinking you two would like to get to Oregon as soon as possible"

"We would but there's so much work to do."

Betty said, "Even just in the back of the house where the bedrooms are, everything has to be washed down before we can load it into a van to haul it down there. It makes me tired just to think about it."

Greg walked up. "We'll all give you a hand, Betty." He looked at Kent with a hard stare. "But we'll save the really nasty jobs for you."

Kent swallowed. "Yes, sir."

"And then if you stay, you'll be the most overworked probie the station has ever had."

"You'd really let me on the department?"

"If you work hard and pass probation, yes. But it's not going to be easy. You'll have to prove your dedication to our town and to protect the citizens in it."

Kent turned and saw nearly everyone watching with avid

concentration. He raised his voice. "I am truly sorry for all the trouble I've caused, and I promise to go to counseling, and work hard to show all of you that you can trust me, If I'm allowed to stay here in this town."

Nicole saw several people nodding, many of which she knew were on the department.

~

SCOTT WATCHED the young man admit to his mistakes and not back down from paying his penance by helping with the cleanup and then pledge to join the department. He had to admit he was kind of proud of the guy and wondered if Nicole felt the same way.

He hardly resembled the man they had arrested only a few days ago, the sullen victim was gone.

After Ray and Betty had left to go sit with friends, Scott saw Chris approaching Nolan and Kent who had their heads together presumably making plans for Monday.

Chris said to Kent, "Do you know who I am?"

Kent nodded. "Yes, sir, you are the amusement park owner where I've been working this summer."

Chris scowled at him. "Correct. Now do you also know whose barn you burned down?"

Scott could see Kent swallow as the truth hit him. "I'll bet it's yours, isn't it?"

"It was. When you're finished with the Howe's clean up, you'll be tearing down and cleaning up the barn."

"Yes, sir. I'm sorry for burning your barn."

Chris shrugged. "I don't much care that it was burned, except now it's unsafe and it needs to be taken down and disposed of."

Terry walked up then looking fierce. "I'll keep some of the

wood to make tables and stuff out of. I'll be happy to supervise the fire bug."

Chris nodded, "Excellent idea. I think maybe he should be on your squad, and I'll be his partner."

"I think that would be perfect, we'll keep the kid in line." Kent had turned a slight green color as the men glared at him.

Scott had to turn his back on the discussion before he burst out laughing. Terry and Chris were two of the most jovial, laid back and friendly men in town. The two of them playing the hard-ass card was more than Scott could bear to watch.

Nicole looked over at him and asked, "What's so funny?"

Scott could barely get out a low, "I'll tell you later."

When Terry and Chris marched Kent over to talk with Greg about their plans, Scott took Nicole's arm and dragged her over to meet some people. He knew she was confused but he didn't want to ruin Terry and Chris's fun, and if he started to explain he would ruin it with laughter.

Nicole didn't complain as he started introducing her around, but she did seem to keep her eye on her brother. He couldn't blame her for wanting to be with him. But it might be good for Kent to be a little intimidated. If things went the way they all hoped, he didn't want Kent to get the idea that what he'd done was condoned by anyone. So, having the guys on the department give him a little bit of a hard time couldn't hurt.

Nicole was welcoming and warm to everyone she met. Some of the mothers of older kids asked her questions about the drum lessons she was planning and if they needed to supply anything.

"No, the church is taking care of all the supplies needed for the class."

Tammy O'Connor whom Nicole had met at the art

gallery asked, "Could we bring some snacks for the break you mentioned?"

Nicole smiled sweetly at Tammy. "I think that would be lovely, but not everyone at the same time. Would you like to set up a rotation?"

Tammy beamed at the position of trust and authority. "I would be delighted. If anyone asks you about it tell them the first week is covered and that I'll be calling them."

Nicole didn't know it, of course, but Tammy and her son had gone through a difficult period a few years back. Letting Tammy run the snack rotation had given the woman something to be proud of, that wasn't linked to that time of difficulty. Scott's heart clenched at the look of happiness that spread over Tammy's face. Nicole had just given Tammy a gift of great value, respect.

Scott noticed that at every encounter Nicole seemed to do or say exactly the right thing, he was surprised but also humbled by her insight. He felt himself grow more in love with Nicole with each person she spoke with.

Some of the townspeople expressed the desire to help with lawyer costs. Nicole had been moved to tears by that, and had thanked the people profusely, saying that if it came down to them needing that, she would let them know. He could tell she was taking their offers seriously and carefully remembering who had volunteered.

After a few minutes Kent joined them, and Scott continued the introductions of both of them. Kent was completely respectful at all times. Scott was proud of him for being willing to face each person in the town. He asked each one to forgive him for bringing fear to the town, and he promised not to do it again.

When the food was ready, Scott said the blessing and invited everyone to eat.

Mabel Erickson marched up to Kent. "You can escort me, young man."

Kent threw his sister a look, but replied, "I would be happy to do so, ma'am."

"Don't you go ma'aming me. You may call me Mrs. Erickson or Mabel. No one calls me Mabel though, because I was almost everyone's third grade teacher and changing the way you speak to a former teacher never quite changes."

The two of them went off to the tables with Mrs. Erickson hanging on Kent's arm and chattering a mile a minute.

Scott chuckled. "If your brother makes it through this picnic, I think he'll be able to handle anything that comes his way. Mrs. Erickson is going to take him in and sit him down with all her old cronies and they are going to grill him much more than anything that will happen in court."

Nicole grinned. "It will be good for him. Speaking of which what were Chris and Terry doing? From what I've observed the two of them are the most easy-going people in town. Were they putting on an act?"

"Oh, I think they have every intention of putting your brother through the wringer. But it does go against their personality, so we'll see how long it lasts before they end up taking him under their wing."

Nicole nodded. "I don't see one thing wrong with that idea."

"Nope, me neither. Let's get some food I don't think we'll be seeing your brother for a while, unless you want to eat in the kitchen too."

"Not really. Can we go over and sit with Barbara and Mary Ann? I still haven't gotten to see the new babies. I'm kind of surprised they're here, those babies aren't very old yet."

"Great idea. The baby daddies are on point for fetching

and carrying, makes it easier on the mothers. And Kristen is entertaining Chris and Barbara's older ones."

Nicole followed his gaze to where Kristen sat surrounded by little kids. "Based on the few minutes I was with her I'm kind of surprised to see her surrounded by children."

A chuckle burst forth as he remembered back and said, "Yep when it first happened it surprised all of us, and several people hovered to make sure she didn't kill them. She'd told everyone to back the hell off, she was fine. They'd done that, and we all discovered that Kristen had a gift with children, it's adults she isn't that fond of."

CHAPTER 30

Scott was hanging out at home Monday morning thinking back over the potluck, it had been great. At the very end when Nicole had gone into the rectory and he'd driven home, he'd had a self-realization that had rocked his world. He'd felt bereft of her company as soon as she'd opened the door to her place. As he'd gotten in his truck, he'd asked himself what the deal was and had come to realize that he'd fallen in love with the woman.

Head over heels, ass over elbows in love.

He'd wanted to drive back, pound on her door and tell her. But he'd managed to talk himself off that ledge. He needed to think about everything, what he wanted, what he was willing to do, what her response might be about what he did.

He'd thought a lot about it in the night and then when he'd woken it was the first thought that crossed his mind. He had a peace about being in love with her and a joy that knew no bounds. It might seem too soon for most people, but he knew what he knew, and he didn't really care that she'd only been in town a couple of weeks.

However, he couldn't go running off half-cocked when they still had no idea what Colorado was going to do. If Kent could stay here Scott felt like the guy would have a good future. The town would keep him on his toes and make sure he didn't stray. They would make him work off his crimes instead of slapping him in a jail cell.

As if he'd conjured it with his thoughts his phone rang with Nolan's number and a cold chill raced through him as he answered.

His worst fears were realized when Nolan said in a low voice, "I've got bad news Scott. Colorado wants to extradite Kent back there to stand trial."

Scott's heart sank as all his ideas and plans went up in smoke. "Darn it. Any chance they'll change their mind?"

"The sheriff would be happy to, but the people who owned the homestead are pushing hard."

"How soon?"

"I told them the plans we have for Kent helping the Howe's and Chris with the structures he burnt. The sheriff agreed to let us keep him here for three weeks to work out his penance. Two for the Howe's and one for Chris."

"Gives us a little time."

"Not much. If you want that girl to stay you better get on your knees, Scott. Want me to call Nicole?"

Scott sighed. He didn't want to tell her, but it was his place to do so. "No, I'll tell her. Have you told Kent yet?"

"No, he's out at the Howe's. I figured I could tell him when he gets back from that. No need to hurry to ruin his day."

"Gives me time to tell Nicole first."

Nolan said, "Sorry to be the bearer of bad news."

Scott could hear the regret in Nolan's voice. "Wouldn't want to be in your shoes."

Nolan laughed. "I was thinking the same thing about yours."

After he hung up from talking to Nolan he did as the man had suggested. He had a long chat with God, asking, pleading, begging God to change the minds of the homestead owners in Colorado. Finally, he asked God to give him the strength to talk to Nicole.

After he talked to Nicole, he would call the starting person on the prayer chain, couldn't hurt to get more prayers going. He firmly believed God was still in the miracle working business. He would have called them first, but he didn't want Nicole to hear the news through the grapevine and that would be a very likely scenario, so he waited.

Nicole was surprised to find Scott at her door when she opened it. Happy to see him, she welcomed him in and noticed he looked grim. Dread filled her, and she knew she didn't want to hear what he'd come to say.

Her voice shook when she said, "I don't think I want to know why you're here."

He sighed. "You probably don't. But I wanted you to hear it from me. Colorado wants to extradite. Not the sheriff, but the people who had the fire."

Nicole slumped down on to the couch as her heart plummeted. She hadn't realized how much she was counting on staying in this little town, with all the people who'd been so nice to her. She wanted to be Scott's admin. She wanted to teach drum lessons. She wanted to play drums on Sunday during the church service. She wanted to be with Scott. And now it was all ruined.

She croaked out, "How soon?"

"They agreed to let him stay and work with the Howe's to

clean out the house, and with Chris to tear down the barn. Three weeks."

Three weeks, she only had three weeks. Three weeks wasn't long enough. But then again, she wasn't sure a life time would be long enough. It wasn't fair. She wanted to lay on the floor and kick her feet and scream.

But childish behavior is what had gotten them in this mess to begin with, so she stuffed down her feelings and plastered a smile on her face. "I guess you better start advertising for that old hippy drummer we talked about."

Scott flinched like she'd slapped him. "Do you have to go? I really want you to stay."

"He's my only family."

"I want to be your family."

Nicole couldn't bear to hear it, so she put her hand over his mouth before he said anything more. "No. Shh, don't say any more, it will be too hard. I have to go with my brother."

"Dammit, Nicole, you can't just abandon us. The kids in this town are so excited to learn what you can teach them. People are coming in droves to hear you play and I..."

"Stop, Scott. I can't bear it. I want to stay more than anything in the world, but I cannot abandon my brother. I will not abandon him. I can't do it. Please don't ask me to."

His expression turned to ice and he stood. "All right, if you're decided. I'll go, so I don't say something we'll both regret."

"Thanks for coming to tell me."

He softened just a little. "Of course. I wouldn't leave you to hear it from anyone else. Nolan said he would come by, but I wanted to be the one. You're too important..."

He didn't finish, and Nicole was grateful. She could tell he wanted to say more, and she was torn between wanting to hear what he would say and protecting herself from his words. She'd already made up her mind, she would go with her brother regardless of where he ended up. They were family and family stuck together. For good or bad.

She didn't encourage him to continue and his face hardened again, she wondered if his heart was hardening at the same time.

Scott walked out, and she knew he was angry. She understood, she was angry too. Not at Scott, but at the universe for giving her a glimpse into something wonderful and then yanking it all away. What had she ever done to deserve this?

CHAPTER 31

Scott was furious, not at Nicole, but at the circumstances. Well maybe a little at Nicole, why couldn't she see that they had a chance for a great life? He'd nearly told her he loved her and wanted to marry her. But she hadn't let him.

Did she know he was going to? Did that mean she wasn't interested in him? She said she couldn't hear anymore because it would be too hard. Too hard to leave them? Or too hard to know how they felt and not hurt their feelings?

Dammit, he didn't know what to do. He was tempted to go to Greg's bar and get falling down drunk, so he couldn't feel the pain. But Greg would know something was up and would pester him about it. He always did his pestering in a low-key fashion but those piercing blue eyes didn't let up until he got the whole story. He'd seen Greg bring more than one man down.

Scott could admit that Greg often had good advice for the guy or gal, but he wasn't sure he was up for it. He could also talk to his dad, but that wouldn't be a whole lot better.

He was kind of ticked off at God for letting him down.

Why did he bring Nicole into his life and then tear her away? It wasn't fair. He knew life wasn't fair, he'd told more than one person that life wasn't fair.

But the shoe was on the other foot now and he didn't like it one bit. No, he did not, and if this was another lesson about how he'd been superior and less than compassionate to his congregation, well, he was tired of that also. He knew he wasn't perfect, but didn't he ever do any damn thing right?

He clearly heard God say, "Melodramatic much? Quit whining and do something."

Do something? What could he do? It wasn't like he could change the mind of those people in Colorado.

Could he?

As the idea took hold he drove toward his home. He could be in Spokane by two if he caught the early barge. A flight to Colorado would only be a couple of hours. He could be in Spirit Lake by dinner time or maybe a little later.

The Rockin' K had plenty of space, he was pretty sure he'd heard that Alyssa and Beau's house was built and maybe even Rachel and Adam's. That would free up a couple of rooms in the family home.

He found himself packing before he'd even finished thinking it through. He'd have to take a couple of days off work. But first he needed to get down to the landing the barge would be leaving any time.

He drove up just as they were starting to pull the loading ramp away. He honked and drove up to it. "Sorry, but can I get on board?"

"You're kinda late for that."

"I know, but it's an emergency."

"I wouldn't do this for just anybody, pastor Scott, so don't let it get around that I let you on late."

"My lips are sealed."

He breathed a sigh of relief as he drove his car onto the

barge. He didn't get out to chat with the operators as he normally would have. Instead he sat in his car and made calls to nearly everyone in two states. When the barge docked, he had airline tickets purchased and a rental car on reserve. He'd asked his dad to cover for him and he'd called the prayer chain to ask them to pray and pray hard that he'd have success.

As he drove the three hours to the Spokane airport he went over and over what he wanted to say to them. When he thought it was perfect, he recorded it into his voice mail. This was quite possibly the most important speech of his life.

NICOLE SPENT the rest of the day wallowing in her disappointment. She couldn't settle on anything but drifted, she'd had plans before Scott had come over. Nothing important but a day of activity. Now she just wanted to go back to bed and hide under the covers.

But she only had three weeks left, she really should make a list of things she wanted to do before she left. Every time she sat down to make that list, the tears formed and blurred her vision, so she gave up.

Nicole thought about going to the jail to visit her brother, but she needed to get beyond the crushing disappointment before she faced him. She was certain Kent was disappointed too, so she didn't want to add to that. She would need to be positive about the move before she saw him. Or if she couldn't bring herself all the way to positive at least she needed to be beyond the devastated feelings she had at the moment.

She wanted to go say good bye to some people that had been especially nice to her but again not in her current state of mind. Blubbering all over them is not what she had in mind. Nicole wanted to give Mary Ann's baby something special, since she wouldn't be around to see little Nicole Scotti grow up. That just sucked.

Nicole had to force herself not to rail at God. That's what she wanted to do, but didn't he get ticked off at that kind of attitude? It's not like God was the one that forced her brother to burn down the place in Colorado.

Late in the afternoon there was another knock on the door. She almost didn't want to answer it in case it was more bad news. Not answering the door wouldn't make bad news go away however so she opened the door to find Scott's mother on the doorstep.

"I thought you might want some company," Char said.

"I'm not very good company right now, but I am kind of tired of wallowing."

Char nodded and bustled into the house. "I would have come earlier, but I decided you needed some time to process. Have you eaten today?"

"I had breakfast. Since then, no. I didn't want to bother."

Char took Nicole's arm. "Come into the kitchen with me then and I'll make you a little something."

"I'm not sure I feel up to eating it."

"I know, but maybe a couple of bites." After Char guided her into a chair, she looked into the fridge and then into the pantry. "Good, you've got everything. How about grilled cheese and tomato soup?"

Nicole gave Char a watery smile. Comfort food, exactly what her mother would have made. That or mac and cheese. "Thanks, that would be nice."

Char bustled around the kitchen heating the soup and making grilled cheese and chattering away about inconsequential things. Nicole watched and could almost feel her own mother right there in the kitchen with them. It was the closest she'd felt to her mother since that horrible day nine months ago. It soothed her, it didn't fix anything, but she felt a tiny bit better.

Char slid the plate and bowl in front of her and sat across the table. Nicole picked up her spoon and took a taste. It tasted like love and home and comfort. She nibbled on the sandwich and as the cheesy buttery goodness slid across her tongue, she realized she was starving. Starving for both the food and the well-being it brought.

Char didn't say much until Nicole had eaten over half the meal. "Scott called and told us that Colorado wants to extradite Kent and have him face trial there."

Nicole nodded as the pain hit her again.

"I know how much that disappoints me, so I imagine it feels like the end to you."

Nicole swallowed the bite of grilled cheese in her mouth and washed it down with the Arnold Palmer Char had made her. She didn't know how Char knew she liked them. When they'd gone out for dinner, she hadn't ordered one.

"It doesn't have to be the end."

"I have to go with my brother."

Char nodded. "I understand that. Scott doesn't, but he's never had a sibling, so he doesn't understand the bond. I have two sisters, so I do. We don't live near each other anymore, but we talk on the phone every week or two. Sometimes we all get on at the same time and facetime."

"Scott wants me to stay," Nicole said softly.

Char patter her hand. "Nicole, dear, we all want you to stay. But you have to do what's best for you."

Nicole's throat closed up as tears threatened.

"However, I still don't think it has to be the end. You could go with Kent and be near him during his incarceration and when he's finished the two of you could come back. I don't think he would be in jail that long, I looked on the internet and it looked to me like the sentence would be one to three years. With probation and possible restitution following that."

Nicole's heart sank, three years would be a long time, even a year seemed like forever. Considering that he had started multiple fires if they really wanted to, they could tack on additional years for the others.

Char kept talking. "I know it seems like a long time, but you've been following him for almost a year."

"Everything will have changed in that length of time. Scott will have a new admin and someone else to teach drum lessons. Nolan might not want to work with Kent anymore, or the firefighters either."

"It's possible, but that is not definite. We're a small town. It might take Scott time to find an admin, everyone in town is gainfully employed. No one else around here has the skills you do on the drums."

Nicole shrugged. "But that's a long time."

"It can be or maybe not. You could move near Kent but come back every so often to do drum lessons. Once a month maybe. Colorado isn't that far."

Nicole felt an ache in her chest, a longing of intense desire that it might still work out. But she had to be sensible, she couldn't just come back here every month. She would have to find a job in Colorado, and no one was going to let her take off for a week every month.

"I can't see how that would work."

Char nodded. "It would take some doing, but God could work it out."

Nicole tensed. God didn't seem to be on her side at the moment. She didn't want to say anything to Char but she didn't believe God wanted to help her.

Char smiled gently. "I can see you're not feeling very favorable toward God at the moment. That's to be expected.

It's often how we feel when something happens that makes it seem like God has abandoned us."

Nicole tried to smile but she didn't have it in her.

Char stood. "I'll leave you alone, now that I've got some food in you. I would be happy to chat with you any time. Just let me know if you want company."

Nicole walked Char to the door. "Thank you for coming to see me."

"You're part of this town now, we'll take you whenever we can have you."

Char pulled her into a hug. Nicole hung on tight, Char wasn't the size or shape of her own mother, but it was still a mother's hug and she missed those.

When they pulled apart Char took Nicole by the chin to look her in the eye. "Don't give up on God, he can handle your anger. Don't hold it in and stew about it, tell him how you feel."

Nicole didn't know what to say about that, so she just nodded.

Char took one step out the door and then turned back. "Scott will be out of town for a few days." Char looked away for a moment and then turned back. "On church business."

Nicole was shocked and saddened that he was going to be gone. That was less days to be with the man she had fallen in love with. "Thanks for telling me."

As Nicole shut the door, she realized what she'd just thought. In love? With Scott? Really? But as she pondered it, she realized it was true, she was in love with a man she would only see for a few more weeks. And that just sucked.

CHAPTER 32

Nicole struggled through the next days, with Scott out of town the church was so quiet. John Davidson stopped by for a little while each day to see if she had any questions or to sign checks. He didn't stay long but he did let her know that he would be the one joining her for the first youth group and drum lessons.

Nicole was both surprised and disappointed that Scott was going to be gone so long. She missed him, which was silly and futile since she would only be here for a few more weeks at best, but it didn't change the facts.

The best part of Wednesday was the delivery of the drum sets. They arrived Wednesday afternoon and the guy delivering them offered to take them into wherever she really wanted them rather than just dumping them in the church foyer.

She and Scott had decided on a large upstairs room for the lessons, so she directed the delivery guy there and went to her office to get some money to tip him well.

When everything was in the room it took up a lot of space. She decided that she would open the boxes and set the drum sets up on tables she and Scott had assembled. Getting the boxcutter she'd seen in her desk drawer she started in on the first box. By the time she'd gotten through the first three boxes she'd broken a sweat and the room was considerably messier.

When a man spoke from the door, she nearly sliced herself with the sharp blade when she startled. She turned to find Jeremy Scott, the author and fire investigator.

"I'm sorry I didn't mean to scare you. Did you cut yourself?"

"No. I didn't think anyone was in the building." She laid the boxcutter down, pushed her hair out of her face, and swiped at the sweat on her forehead. "Can I help you with something?"

"Actually, I came to help you. I got a load of books a little while ago and the delivery guy was telling me about the large load of boxes he'd left at the church. I'd heard Scott was out of town, so decided maybe you could use a hand." He looked around the room. "If only to have someone drag the empty boxes and three tons of Styrofoam out to give you more room."

She looked at the pile of shipping materials she'd already made from only three of the twenty-four boxes she had to go through and decided she would be thrilled for some help. "That would be amazing. Thank you."

Jeremy went and found a large trash bag and was filling it full of the Styrofoam when Greg walked in. "I heard you got a huge delivery and might need some help."

"Absolutely, Jeremy is on trash detail. These boxes are pretty sturdy and I'm having a little trouble slicing them open, they used staples not tape so I have to cut the cardboard. Would you like to do the honors?"

Greg nodded. "How about we both work on them? I have

my own boxcutter." He pulled a heavy duty one out of a back pocket. "Liquor boxes."

Before Greg got the first box slit open, Terry walked in. "Heard we were having a box opening party. Here let me take that boxcutter, little lady. You can work on the accessories."

Nicole happily handed Terry the box cutter, her arm was already sore from hacking through the thick cardboard. "That delivery guy is quite the town crier."

Terry grinned. "That he is. He said you were his first stop and it was going to take you a week to get all these boxes open. I must have been his fourth delivery."

Nicole shook her head. "How many more do you think he'll have? And will they all come to help?"

Terry shrugged. "Not all, some people can't just leave their jobs like the three of us."

"Four," Trey said as he walked in and started hauling cardboard.

Nicole put her hands on her hips. "Shouldn't you be home with your wife and new baby?"

"Mary Ann said if I didn't come to help you, she was going to put me on dirty diaper duty for the rest of my life, or at least until we didn't have any little kids. Since little Nicole is only our first, I hustled out the door."

Nicole laughed when she felt like crying. How could she leave this place, these people?

With the four men and herself it didn't take long at all to have all the practice drum sets unboxed and set out on the tables with drumsticks, tape, headphones, and music books. She also had a stack of cheap duffle bags that each student could use to transport their practice sets. If she'd been alone it would have taken two days to get them unboxed and the room cleaned up.

When the work was done all four men looked around the room, kissed her on the cheek and marched out of the building. She'd wanted to thank them in some way, but they'd said it was just small town living and the way they operated in Chedwick.

The next day when the youth started streaming into the building an hour before the meeting was supposed to start, she was glad they'd gotten the room ready the day before. The snacks had been delivered by Tammy, for the break, earlier in the afternoon and were ready in the kitchen. Even Pastor John had come early which she was grateful for, because he quickly checked off everyone who had signed up, and said they might as well start, because everyone had arrived.

So, they began the first youth and young adult group, forty minutes before it was supposed to begin.

With sixteen boys and eight girls ages twelve to twenty, she expected a rowdy group. But it wasn't that way at all. Everyone was respectful and quiet as she started the group by pointing out the different pads on their drum sets and what they were for. Then she taught them how to carefully wrap the tape around the drum sticks and why it was important to do so.

Only three students had trouble with the tape. She worked with each one individually until they got it correct. Next, she showed them the correct ways to hold the sticks and explained the reasoning behind it.

Before they got restless, she let them practice a simple beat. The joy on their faces was a sight to behold, it made her thankful she was there to see it and hoped they would be able to find a drum instructor to carry on the lessons.

After the break they would look at the music books and she would show them what the symbols meant. After an hour and a half, the kids were starting to wilt so she called for the break. As the youth bustled out of the door, heading for the kitchen, many stopped to thank her.

The rest of the evening went just as smoothly. The kids listened to what Pastor John had to say while they ate their snacks and then they hurried back to the practice room, ready to learn more.

The reading music portion of the night was more technical, and she wasn't sure if they all understood it. But then she selected a simple piece that they could all do together and let them practice it a few times. By the fourth time through the piece she was hearing very few wrong hits.

Each of them enthusiastically took their practice kits home with them saying they were excited to practice. When the last student was picked up, Nicole went into the kitchen to see if it needed cleaning. She was ecstatic to see that Pastor John had it all tidy, she was exhausted and collapsed into a chair.

Pastor John called out, "There's still some coffee if you want. It's decaf or I can grab you a soda if you need a boost."

"I could definitely use a boost but I'm not a big soda fan."

"The ladies started stocking cans of Arnold Palmers for you. Would you like one?"

"Oh, I didn't know, that's so sweet of them, yes please." Nicole felt like blubbering, everyone was so nice to her, they even started stocking her favorite drink. She sniffed and blinked back her tears as John brought her the drink.

He sat across the table from her. "Want to talk about it?"

She really didn't, but the words poured out before she could stop them. "Everyone has been so nice to both Kent and me. We are complete strangers and all of you have taken us in and made us feel so welcome."

"You and your brother are easy people to care for."

"Kent started two fires and could have killed the Howe's, that's not exactly easy."

Pastor John chuckled. "I guess that's true, but he's apologized for that and I hear he's been working hard cleaning up the mess he made. He digs right in and does the work, comes back to the jail filthy and exhausted but is ready to go the next morning with no complaining."

Nicole was glad to hear that, she hadn't been by to see him because she knew he was working all day. She needed to fix that, they needed to talk about the future. "That's good to know."

"And you've certainly done your fair share of helping around town. Everyone likes you, and you fit in. Not everyone does, you know."

He wasn't making this easier. She whispered, "But we have to leave, and I feel so at home here and it sucks. I don't want to go. I like it here. And you just bought all those drums and I won't be able to teach them more than just the rudimentary skills before they come to get my brother. It's not fair."

He patted her hand. "Life never is fair. Have you talked to your brother since we heard from Colorado?"

Nicole was surprised at the abrupt change of subject but also relieved. "No, I was thinking I need to get over there, so we can make plans."

Pastor John stood. "I think you should go now. Tell him about your first drum lesson. You did a fine job, by the way. It's kind of a big group though."

"Yes, it is. I was thinking it would be better to divide it into two groups maybe by age. Eventually it would be more practical to divide them by skill, but to start with the ages would be fine."

"I agree, once you have the chance to determine their skill level you could have a beginner and an advanced class."

She followed him out the door, thinking it would be someone else to determine that, she would be long gone by then.

~

SCOTT SAID goodbye to Alyssa and Rachael and slid into his rental car, for the two hour drive back to the Denver airport. It had been an utterly exhausting trip. He'd never talked and wheedled and coerced so much in his life, even as a kid—an only kid—who'd got away with a lot, using those tactics.

Before he'd met with Gordon and Martha Wall, he'd done his homework on them and what the property had looked like. He'd been surprised to hear that most people thought they'd been having illusions of grandeur.

Since he'd stayed with the Kipling's he'd talked to them first. The twins Cade and Chase had been in the house and had shown him where he was bunking. So, he'd started with them. Cade had about laughed his head off, when he'd asked about the Wall's structure becoming a National Historic site.

"Not likely, it was four sticks and a tarp." Cade had said between bouts of laughter.

Chase had rolled his eyes at his twin and explained. "It really wasn't much of anything. There were four walls and the ceiling was a tarp, not even animal skins, which is probably what they'd used when they homesteaded it. The door was another tarp, again probably originally a bear skin or something."

Scott had asked, "So, you don't think they would have gotten it approved as a historic site?"

Cade had burst into laughter again and Chase had shaken his head. "No. I really don't. But maybe you should ask mom or dad or Grandpa K. They might know something we don't."

So, that's what he'd done. He'd asked the three elder Kipling's who had concurred with the twins' opinion. After Grandpa K had given his opinion he headed off to his room and Travis had called up his buddy Sheriff Drake. Sheriff

Drake had rolled in at the same time as Drew was coming home from his shift on the department, so they both sat to have a confab around the kitchen table.

Meg Kipling had served everyone pie as they talked. It had been delicious. Once they'd settled down to talk, Sheriff Drake had rubbed a hand on the back of his neck. "I really don't want to extradite the guy back here. It's expensive, it takes one of my deputies away for at least a couple days, and the Wall's are not going to have much of a case anyway. Yes, Kent burned down their shed. But it's not like they'd ever kept it in pristine condition to make it a historical site. They'd used it for all kinds of random crap over the years. Plus, kids had gone in there and partied."

Scott had asked, "So, what can I do to persuade them?"

They'd all talked and brainstormed and had come up with some ideas. But Martha and Gordon Wall were no pushovers. Even after he and the couple had come up with a decent idea of compensation, they'd wanted to think about it overnight. So, he'd had to go back the next day and start all over again.

Fortunately, he'd had a longer chat with Grandpa K and he'd given him a few tips that had finally slanted the negotiations to Scott's favor. But the Wall's had still insisted that it be drawn up legally so on the third day they'd all gone into Granby to see a lawyer, and have legal documents drawn up.

Even then the Wall's had pushed for more, but Scott had taken Sheriff Drake with him to go to the lawyer, since it was his day off, and he'd been willing to do so to keep everything legal. So, when the Wall's had brought up their new idea, Drake had gently— but effectively—shut them down.

So, Scott was on his way to Seattle, to implement the second part of his plan.

CHAPTER 33

Nicole had spent the last two days thinking about what her brother had said when she went to talk to him Thursday night. The police department had been locked and she wasn't sure if anyone would let her in to see him. But then the door had buzzed, so she'd walked in.

The dispatcher had hollered out. "Go on back, Nicole."

Had she even met the night dispatcher? She didn't remember meeting her, but she'd met so many people she could have forgotten one, or a dozen.

Nicole had gone back to find Kent on his bunk studying the glass sculpting books. Her stomach dropped at the sight, had no one told him he was being extradited?

He looked up when he heard her approach and a huge smile covered his face. "Well, hello sister of mine. I was beginning to think you'd forgotten about me with all your activities. You had the drum session, tonight, didn't you? How did it go?"

She told him all about it and how it was almost eerie the way the kids had been so quiet and attentive.

"They are eager to learn. I feel the same way about the glass blowing classes Nolan is going to give me."

She swallowed and rubbed her palms down her jeans, as she gathered her strength. "Kent you are being extradited back to Colorado, did no one tell you that."

"Oh yes, they told me, but Nolan doesn't think I'll be incarcerated more than a couple of years, five at most. Then I'll come back, and he'll teach me. I was hoping for the deferred sentence, but I can wait. I can do a lot of book learning while I'm in jail. There's a lot to learn about how to make the different colors and shapes."

Nicole was surprised to hear him talk about being in jail like it was going to be some extended classroom. "You're planning to come back?"

"Well of course, you'll be here, and Nolan said he would teach me whenever I was able to work with him."

"What do you mean I'll be here? I was planning to come with you."

"That's ridiculous. Come with me? So, I can sit in jail and you can visit me once a week? No, you need to stay here and teach the kids the drums and work at the church. And I'll eat my hat if you aren't married to Scott by the time I get back. I've seen the way you look at him, like he's a giant popsicle and you want to lick him. He looks at you the same way, in case you haven't noticed."

Nicole's face heated at her brother's description. But she was still confused by his other statements. "But I can't just abandon you. You're my brother."

"Oh, for cripes sake, you aren't abandoning me. I fucked up and need to pay for my crimes. That doesn't mean you have to, too. You've made some good friends here and carved out a nice niche for yourself. You stay here, and I'll be back as soon as I can be. Thinking of you here in this place will be a lot easier on my mind, than thinking about you finding a place and job and everything, near whatever facility I end up in."

She had just blinked at him as her mind whirled with all he'd said. "I need to think about that. I'd planned to come with you."

"You think about it. But I'll be just fine and will jet-set it back here as soon as I can, and I expect you to be here, not in Colorado. Now you go on back to the rectory. I have about half a chapter to go in this book, and then I need to hit the hay. Working with the Howe's is kicking my butt. But I'm glad to be doing it. Sure gives me a fresh perspective about burning places. God, what an awful mess it is."

Nicole had stood to leave still stunned by her brother's attitude, and she'd been thinking about it ever since. He'd had some valid points, but she still waffled with her feelings about leaving him. She wanted very much to stay here, but how could she live with her conscience if she did?

She'd finally gotten sick and tired of thinking about it late Saturday afternoon, and had gone over to the church to pound on the drums. As the rhythm had poured out of her in a tribal beat, her mind had slowly cleared, and her decision became clear. By the time her arms were aching from the exertion and the last sound faded she knew exactly what her course would be.

She laid the drumsticks down and wiped the sweat from her forehead with the hem of her shirt. Nicole looked up when she heard a strangled sound come from the back of the church. Scott was seated in the very back row. It was dark back there and she could barely see him. She hadn't turned all the lights and night had fallen as she'd played.

Their eyes met, heat and electricity flowed back and forth between them. "You're back."

"I am. I came to talk to you and felt the vibration of the drums from the parking lot. So, I came in to watch. You are magnificent on those things." As he spoke, he walked slowly up the aisle toward her and she couldn't move. She was mesmerized by his look, by his voice, trapped in his gaze.

He stepped on the stage and held his hand out to her. She took it and felt her whole body sigh in contentment.

Scott drew her close and ran his hands down her arms. "Let's lock up, then I want to go somewhere we can talk."

"To the rectory? I've got a roast in the oven."

"Perfect."

As they walked through the darkened evening, she couldn't hold it in any longer. "I can't do it you know."

"Can't do what?"

"Leave this place. The town. The church." She paused and then gathered her courage. "You."

He took her hand and squeezed it, but didn't say a word.

SCOTT DIDN'T KNOW whether to laugh or cheer. He'd just spent the better part of a week trying to ensure she wouldn't have to leave, and she'd decided not to, while he was gone. His heart soared, that she wanted to stay, even if it meant leaving her brother. He didn't know what to say and when he did figure it out, he wanted to see her face when they talked about it.

Outside in the dark wasn't the right place, so he waited until they got into the house and she'd turned some lights on. He noticed her movements were a little jerky, was she embarrassed?

Once he could see her face, he took her by the arms and looked into her warm brown eyes. "I'm so glad you feel that way, Nicole. I just spent the last six days working to keep you here."

She looked into his face scrutinizing his expression. Apparently, she read sincerity because she softened, and joy filled her expression. "You did?"

"I did. It's kind of a long story. Do you want to hear it now or while we eat?"

Her stomach rumbled, and his answered in like. She laughed. "I guess our stomachs have voted. You make drinks while I pull the roast out."

"Deal."

"There's a bag of salad, maybe make us each a small one to start with."

He whined, "Do we have to?"

She laughed at his silliness. "Yes. The roast needs to sit for just a couple of minutes before we cut it up. You can eat the salad and then wash the nasty vegetable taste out of your mouth with the roast and potatoes."

He sighed dramatically. He really didn't mind salad at all, but it was fun to tease her about it, she seemed to like salad with everything. "If I must."

He chopped up a couple of tomatoes and a baby cucumber he found and added those to her salad from a bag.

When they sat down with their salads he asked, "So what made you change your mind? You were dead set on leaving the last time I saw you."

"A few things actually. I talked to my brother and he said he fully intended to return and study under Nolan the first chance he got, and he wanted me here waiting for him rather than finding a new job and living near whatever jail or prison he ended up in. He said one visit a week wasn't worth it, in his opinion."

Scott nodded. "That makes sense. What else?"

"The drum lessons, they were so much fun, and the kids were excited, but extremely obedient and respectful. There was no discontent at all, and they were all here an hour early. We ended up starting forty minutes before it was scheduled, because everyone was already here."

"I'm glad to hear that. I suppose we shouldn't be surprised by their enthusiasm. Our town is not really a hot bed of activity. They all like the amusement park but even with the local discount, it gets expensive."

"We'll need to make two groups. All of them in one, is too large and it doesn't allow the older or more talented kids to move along quicker."

Scott had thought all along one group would be too hard to manage. "Fine with me. Did my dad talk during the break?"

"Yes, and the kids were attentive there. Of course, I'd worn them out with over an hour of lesson." She grinned at him and his heart skittered, she was so beautiful.

He didn't want to push, but she'd mentioned not wanting to leave him, so he prompted her. "Anything else?"

She said, "And I missed you." Then she got up to carve the roast.

He followed her and pulled her into his arms. Their bodies meshing like two puzzle pieces. "I missed you, too. I couldn't stand the thought of you leaving, so I went off to Colorado to talk to the property owners there."

She gasped. "You did?"

"I did. I made a deal with them that will allow your brother to stay here to be tried."

She squeezed him so tight he could barely breathe. "That's wonderful. Tell me the whole story, every tiny detail."

He chuckled. "I was there for two days. Let's put the rest of the meal on the table and I'll tell you all about it."

"Fine, you cut the roast and I'll make the gravy."

While they ate, he told her about dealing with the Wall's and how they'd tried to push for more, and stall, and basically be a pain. She'd laughed at how hilarious Cade had felt the whole thing was and how he'd made fun of the structure saying it was four sticks and a tarp.

Nicole asked, "You said you made them a deal. What was it?"

Scott wasn't sure how everyone would feel about this, but it had swung the decision, so he'd thought it was worth it. "Well they wanted compensation for the shed and the fact they thought they could make a bunch of money off of it as a historic site. So, I promised them that they could have one of your brother's sculptures after he'd worked with Nolan for a year."

Nicole frowned. "But what if he never gets any good?"

"They've heard of Lucille and even Nolan's work, so they thought Kent had a very good chance of getting good enough to make it worth their while. One of his sculptures could end up going for six figures."

"Do you really think so?"

"He'll be learning from one of the foremost glass artists in the world. It's entirely possible." He shrugged.

"So, they're willing to gamble on that?"

"According to everyone in Spirit Lake, there is a much higher probability of that, than them getting the shed declared a historical site, even before it burned."

She laughed, and the sound shimmered through him. God, he loved her laugh.

"You had a productive time then."

"I did, but that's just the first half of the story."

"It is? Really? Well tell me the rest."

He'd had a long day and wanted to relax so he said, "Let's tidy up the kitchen and go sit on the couch while I tell you *the rest of the story*."

"Okay, Paul Harvey."

It thrilled him that she'd picked up on the reference, they were so made for each other. "Thanks for the meal, it was delicious."

"My pleasure, and well worth it for your good news."

Scott wagged his eyebrows at her. "The good news is just beginning."

She clapped her hands together. "Goody, let's get this cleaned up then. Do you want some coffee while we continue?"

"No, I think water would be better. I've had a lot of caffeine today." He needed to get some sleep and he already knew his thoughts about Nicole would keep him awake, he certainly didn't need another stimulant.

When they were comfortably seated on the couch, he said, "So the rest of the story took place in Seattle. I went to talk to a friend of mine and Greg's."

"A lawyer?"

"Yes. David Williams kind of grew up here in Chedwick."

"How can you kind of grow up here?"

"His parents lived here for the first twelve years of his life and then they got a divorce. His dad moved to Seattle and his mom stayed here. So, David spent part of the time in Seattle with his father and part of the time in Chedwick with his mom. His father being a lawyer you can guess who got the better deal."

"The father."

"Yeah. Anyway, when I got to Seattle, David and I had lunch. Apparently when Greg called, he had talked to David's dad, Henry, who thought Greg's request was highly amusing and ridiculous. He'd not told Greg that, but said he would ask around in their firm to see if anyone was interested in defending Kent. Come to find out he did no such thing."

"I don't think I like that guy."

"You have very discerning tastes then. David said his father had yucked it up saying something like 'they didn't have anyone in their firm stupid enough to want to take a pro bono case for an arsonist who deserves to spend time in prison.' It had kind of pissed David off, but since he didn't have any other information, he hadn't pursued it."

"Now I really don't like this Henry guy. And no one ever said it had to be pro bono."

"I totally agree. Anyway, I told David what it was all about, and he said he would gladly take the case. Not only did it interest him, but he'd like to do it just to defy his father."

"Not exactly a stellar reason for taking it."

"Defying his dad is just the side benefit. David thinks he has a reasonable chance of winning the case and he's willing to do it pro bono. He said if the people of Chedwick were invested in you and Kent it would make him happy to fulfill their desire. Plus, the pro bono would irritate his father even more, which made David grin."

Nicole laughed. "If you think he's the man for the job, I'll go with your assessment."

"Good. David has a case he has to finish so he will come out the end of next week to talk to your brother. Then he can see when the court date can be set." Scott pulled out his phone to look at the time, his mind was starting to shut down.

He stood and said, "I think I better get home and get some sleep, all this traveling has my system confused and we do have church in the morning. So, I'll leave you now and see you tomorrow."

Nicole walked him to the door and gave him a warm hug that had his body springing back to life. She whispered, "Thanks Scott. I really didn't want to leave, and I also didn't want to abandon Kent, regardless of what he said. Now, maybe I won't have to."

"The battle is not over but we're in a better position now." He kissed her on the forehead and left, before he was tempted to do more.

CHAPTER 34

Nicole was walking on air all the next day. Everything was turning out amazingly. She was going to get to stay in Chedwick, in her job and comfortable house. Running the office and teaching drum lessons. Hopefully her brother's court case would be in his favor, but even if it didn't go as she hoped it would, he would be staying in Washington state, which means once he was out of jail, he could come back to Chedwick to finish his probation. It was the best news.

The only thing that wasn't stellar was that Scott kept dashing off. He'd worked so hard to keep her in town, so she knew he didn't think of her as a casual relationship. So why was he still holding her at arm's length? It was frustrating her to no end. Why would he go to all that trouble and then... She had to stop thinking about it. She'd barely slept last night with the thoughts and questions running through her mind on a non-stop loop.

Nicole was happy to see her brother in church again this Sunday. She could hardly wait to tell him the news, that he wouldn't be extradited and could stand trial right here, and would even have a good lawyer with ties to the town.

As she sat at the drums to play the worship music, she felt her joy pour out of her through her hands. It was like she really was worshiping God for answering her thoughts. She'd not exactly put her hopes and desires into the form of a formal prayer, but it seemed to her like God answered them anyway.

The church was packed again and there wasn't even a potluck afterward. She wondered if they would need to find a way to expand. If people kept filling the place, they might have to think about that. But maybe it was simply the newness of everything, and it would eventually mellow out and go back to previous numbers. Well, previous numbers, plus the drum students and their families. Scott announced that they would have two drum nights starting this week on Wednesday and Thursday, so the class size wouldn't be so large.

After the service was over Nicole sought out her brother. "I have great news."

Kent gave her a small smile. "I could use some."

"Why? What's wrong. Nothing's wrong, it's just that helping the Howe's clean up the mess I made is rough. I never even considered that what I was burning was someone's property. Mrs. Howe tries to put on a good face, but I can see her heart is broken by so many of her things burned. Sometimes she leaves the room and when she comes back her eyes are red and puffy, and I know she's been crying."

"That must be hard."

Kent shook his head. "It is. She's only a few years older than our mom, and I keep thinking how mom would have felt if all of her special things had been burned up by some dumbass who was acting out. I wish I could have foreseen this, because it would have stopped me cold."

"At least you know now and won't be doing it again."

"Yeah, that's for sure. Even if I can't work with Nolan and learn to use fire appropriately, I don't think I could ever go back to torching property. Not after watching the pain I caused those nice people."

Nicole felt bad for her brother but at the same time she saw it as a major turning point in his life. She was glad he'd been assigned to help the Howe's with the clean-up. It was painful for him, but it would also change his life for the better.

He sighed. "So, what's your good news?"

"Scott went to Colorado and talked the people there into letting you be tried here. He had to promise them one of your art projects after you work with Nolan for a year."

"Really? But what if I suck at it?"

"You won't. Just listen to what Nolan has to say and work hard."

A small smile slid onto his face. "You always have had too much faith in me. But I will do my best, and I don't mean that lightly, I will work hard. I'm glad I can stay in Washington."

"Me too, even if you have to go to prison it will be close enough for me to come see you. But there's even more good news."

"Tell me."

"Scott got you a good lawyer who is willing to work on your case for free."

Kent frowned. "Why would he do it for free?"

"He grew up here and wants to do something for the town, but it's mostly about thwarting his father, I think. His dad sounds like kind of a jerk."

"Not the greatest reason for taking the case, but I'll take it. So, I was thinking about something. When the house in

Colorado sells. I'd like to take my share of it and put a down payment on the Howe's house."

That surprised her. "Why would you want to buy a half-burned house?"

"I'm the one who burned it, so it seems like the right thing to do. Plus, what is left is solid and I like it. It would take me a long time to fix it back up, but I just feel like it's the right plan."

"Okay. If it is still on the market when we sell you can do whatever you want with your half. I don't have any idea how much it will be though, or if you can get a loan for the rest."

"No, I don't either, but I want to try."

Nicole nodded. "Fair enough. You might want to talk to Kyle, the real estate guy."

"I will, but part of it will depend on the outcome of my trial."

"True. Your lawyer is supposed to be coming in the end of next week."

"Thanks, sis." He kissed her on the forehead.

"Don't thank me, thank Scott."

"Thank me for what?" said a voice from behind her.

Kent looked at Scott as he walked up to stand by Nicole. "For going to bat for me, both in Colorado and Seattle. I owe you."

"Just keeping my admin and drummer close at hand. Nicole tells me you play the base."

"I do. If I don't get carted off to prison, I'll join the band."

Scott grinned. "Excellent, totally worth the work I did this last week. I might stop by to see you one of these days."

"That would be great. I'm at the Howe's from eight am to seven pm, Monday through Saturday. Anytime other than that would be fine."

Scott laughed. "They're keeping you busy then."

"Yes, and it's nothing less than I deserve."

Nicole's heart swelled as she realized her younger brother had turned into a man who was taking responsibility for his actions. Her mom and dad would be proud of him, and she was too.

Kent nodded toward someone across the room. "I gotta go. I'll talk to you guys later."

She and Scott watched him walk away.

Scott said, "Quite the change in him from when I first met him."

"I was thinking the same thing. He's growing into a fine man, right before our very eyes."

"Yes, he is. So not to change the subject, but I was wondering if you'd like to go fishing tomorrow."

Nicole thought that sounded like a great idea. "Absolutely. I need to get a real license now that I know I'm staying."

"You will, but we'll get you another tourist license for tomorrow."

"Yay."

SCOTT HOPED he didn't throw up. His stomach was in knots and his hands were cold. He hadn't thought he would be this nervous, but he was. Everything was ready, he'd even gone by and talked with Kent last night. Her brother had been totally on board with the idea and had wished him luck. He hoped he didn't need it.

He'd just barely pulled into the parking lot of the church when Nicole came racing out with her backpack and climbed into his SUV.

"I'm ready. Let's get going before the sun comes up."

He chuckled at her enthusiasm and some of the nerves settled. Not all of them, but a few.

It was a short drive to the landing where they parked and

pulled the supplies they'd both brought out of the vehicle and walked down to where the boat was moored. He was surprised to see Fred on the dock with his hands on his hips staring at the boat.

Fred said, "I don't know what to do. It won't leave. He's never once been on my boat before."

Nicole gasped, and Scott broke out in a huge grin. There on the highest point of the boat was the town peacock, with its feathers fully arrayed.

Scott clapped Fred on the back as nearly all the rest of his nervousness faded. He couldn't have been more thrilled to see that darn peacock in his life. "Don't worry. I'm perfectly happy to see that peacock, giving his approval to this adventure."

Fred slid his gaze from the peacock to Scott, Scott could see the light bulb come on as his friend put two and two together.

Scott grabbed Nicole's hand and drew her up to step onto the boat. He called out to the peacock. "Thanks, for the stamp of approval." The peacock shivered, and his feathers settled as he jumped down from his perch and left the boat.

Nicole watched the bird go. "That was very odd."

Scott cut her off before she could ask any more questions. "Can you store the gear, I'll get us moving, we don't want to miss the sunrise."

"Oh sure. Good idea."

Scott pulled the boat out of the harbor and was heading toward his favorite fishing spot when Nicole came up with the coffee and rolls, he'd bought for breakfast. It was nearly an exact repeat of the first time they'd gone fishing. So far, anyway.

When they got to his favorite spot, she went to start pulling the gear out to fish. His nerves amped up slightly so he didn't hesitate. He didn't want them out of control.

"Nicole, before we set the rods, I wanted to talk to you about something." He took her by the hand and led her over to where they could see the sunrise.

She didn't argue, but she did look longingly toward the equipment, and the rapidly lighting sky. "What did you want to talk about?"

"Us."

"Us?"

"Yes. Nicole, from the first moment you came charging into my church I was hooked. You caught me so quickly I didn't even feel the hook slide in and I never want to be released. I want to come out fishing with you. I want to play worship music with you. I want you to be my admin, but also my partner. I want you by my side for the rest of our lives. I know we haven't known each other long, but for me, it only took a moment to know that you are the one for me."

He got down on one knee and pulled the ring out of his pocket. "Nicole will you marry me and be my partner in this life?"

Nicole looked like she might faint, so he waited patiently, well mostly patiently, for her to process. "Are you serious? We really haven't known each other long."

His heart sank, but he was willing to wait for this woman for however long it took. He realized that he'd known Nicole about as long as Maureen had known her tourist before running off with him. Once again God was showing him his cockiness and judgmental attitude. He said, "I am serious and if you want some more time I can wait."

"Oh, I didn't say that. It's just all rather sudden and… no that's ridiculous. I was willing to stay here to be near you, and you worked hard to allow me to stay. Yes, of course, I'll marry you." She pulled him up and snuggled into his arms.

She lifted her head up to his and whispered, "Kiss me."

Their mouths met in an explosion. Hunger and happiness

fighting for supremacy. She tasted like coffee and pastries and warm woman. He couldn't get enough of her, and she seemed to feel the same way as she plastered her body against his.

When they needed to breathe, he pulled her in even closer and she was tucked right beneath his chin, their hearts beating in a furious tandem. When he had enough breath to speak, he said, "I talked to your brother last night and he was happy to accept me as his possible future brother-in-law."

"You talked to Kent?"

"I wanted his blessing."

"Aw."

He pulled back. "I got a ring in Seattle, but since I didn't know your size or anything it's fully customizable." He opened the box to show her what he'd picked out.

"Oh, it's gorgeous." She took it out of the box and slipped it on her finger. The fit was close, maybe a half size too large.

"We can get that fixed right here in town. Kristen can do it."

"Oh, goody I don't want to have to go to Seattle. I like it here and don't want to leave. All that time I thought I might have to, was enough for me. I was dreading it every day, every hour."

He lifted her chin and kissed her softly. "So was I. It made me sick to think about."

She got a sly look on her face. "So now that we're engaged and it's not a casual relationship anymore. Do you think you could relax your standards enough to, what do they say in the vows? Oh yes, worship me with your body?"

He chuckled, "Well not exactly, but if I'm taking your meaning correctly, I believe I could be persuaded. After all we did get the blessing of the town peacock." He took her hand to lead her below deck.

"Is that what it was doing?"

"Yes, he appears at times when something significant is going on and most of us believe he's giving his approval to the event. You heard Fred say he's never been on his boat."

They spent most of the day in each other's arms learning about the delights of the flesh. When they had worshipped each other, to the point of exhaustion, they finally did a little fishing. They caught enough for several meals, but nothing like the first day.

Neither of them complained about that.

EPILOGUE

The courtroom was packed, it seemed to Nicole that every single person who lived in Chedwick was in the room. The lawyer Scott had secured for Kent, David Williams, had made a compelling argument for Kent.

He'd come into town a few weeks ago and had talked to nearly every person in town. He'd surprisingly talked to Kent last. She wasn't quite sure why he'd done that, but she had to hope he'd done it for a good reason.

As Mr. Williams had brought many people up to testify, she'd started to see the logic behind what he'd done. It seemed to her that he'd wanted their take before he was influenced by his client. He'd gotten statements from the other jurisdictions where Kent had started fires and they were all in favor of rehabilitation and restitution rather than jail time.

All the testimony had been geared toward that outcome, but the judge didn't look convinced. Nicole's hands were ice cold even the one that Scott was holding. His warmth didn't make up for the fear coursing through her.

The judge said, "Well, Mr. Roman, it seems like everyone is convinced that you should be rehabilitated rather than spending time in jail. Why do you think that you deserve that kind of preferential treatment?"

Kent cleared his throat. "Begging your pardon, your honor, but I believe I do deserve jail time."

Nicole's breath hitched, what was he doing. She wanted to jump up and shush him, but Scott squeezed her hand, so she didn't move, she barely breathed.

"The people in this town are very forgiving, but I've learned some powerful lessons being here. The first was that my insensitivity caused great heartache to some very kind people who did not deserve it. Not only that but if they hadn't been in such good health both mentally and physically, I could have killed them. And if the fire department hadn't been so quick to respond with the knowledge of this area, I could have started a major wild fire."

Kent shook his head and looked down in shame. "So, no, your honor, I don't deserve preferential treatment. I deserve jail time."

Then he stood tall and squared his shoulders. "However, I feel like this town and the people I've wronged would be better compensated by me being out of jail. Mr. Thompson has offered me an excellent way to learn how to use fire for good, instead of destruction, and I would like the opportunity to pursue that."

The judge said, "Go on."

"If I am any good at the craft, I plan to send everyone whose property I torched a sculpture. Not only the people in Colorado but all the others. I also want to buy the house the Howe's own, at full market value, before I burned it. My parent's home sold recently, and I plan to put my half of the proceeds in, as a down payment." He waved his hand toward the Howe's, who had tears in their eyes.

"Lastly, I plan to join the fire department. The guys have told me they intend to work me hard to teach me to be a man instead of a little boy acting out. I have every intention of becoming that man."

Nicole was so proud of her brother.

He continued, "So, your honor, I am prepared to go to jail and serve my time if you deem that the best course of action. If you do, it will simply slow down my ability to pay back the people I've wronged, but make no mistake, I will pay them back."

The judge sat back in his chair and narrowed his eyes as he watched Kent. Her brother didn't squirm under the glare or look nervous in any way. He stood tall and firm in his commitment and conviction.

Finally, after what seemed like hours the judge leaned forward. "Very well. Sentence deferred, as outlined by Sheriff Thompson. Court is adjourned."

Nicole hugged her brother as did many others, the men slapping him on the back. The whole town proceeded out of the courtroom. When they got to the parking lot they stopped in shock. Kent's car was in the parking lot and was buried under stress balls in the shape of flames, fire hydrants, fire extinguishers, and fire trucks. The town peacock stood on top of the car with his feathers flared out and one of the stress balls in his mouth.

Nicole laughed at the sight, then looked at her brother. "Welcome to Chedwick, Kent."

The End

If you enjoyed this story, please leave a review on Amazon, Bookbub, or Goodreads.
Thanks so much!

ALSO BY SHIRLEY PENICK

LAKE CHELAN SERIES

The Rancher's Lady: A Lake Chelan novella

Hank and Ellen's story

Sawdust and Satin: Lake Chelan #1

Chris and Barbara's story

Designs on Her: Lake Chelan #2

Nolan and Kristen's story

Smokin': Lake Chelan #3

Jeremy and Amber's story

Fire on the Mountain: Lake Chelan #4

Trey and Mary Ann's story

The Fire Chief's Desire: Lake Chelan #5

Greg and Sandy's story

Mysterious Ways: Lake Chelan #6

Scott and Nicole's story

BURLAP AND BARBED WIRE SERIES

A Cowboy for Alyssa: Burlap and Barbed Wire #1

Beau and Alyssa's story

Taming Adam: Burlap and Barbed Wire #2

Adam and Rachel's story

Tempting Chase: Burlap and Barbed Wire #3

Chase and Katie's story

Roping Cade: Burlap and Barbed Wire #4

Cade and Summer's story

ABOUT THE AUTHOR

What does a geeky math nerd know about writing romance?

That's a darn good question. As a former techy I've done everything from computer programming to international trainer. Prior to college I had lots of different jobs and activities that were so diverse, I was an anomaly.

None of that qualifies me for writing novels. But I have some darn good stories to tell and a lot of imagination.

I have lived in Colorado, Hawaii and currently reside in Washington. Going from two states with 340 days of sun to a state with 340 days of clouds, I had to do something to perk me up. And that's when I started this new adventure called author. Joining the Romance Writers of America and two local chapters, helped me learn the craft quickly and has been a ton of fun.

My family consists of two grown children, their spouses, two adorable grand-daughters, and one grand dog. My favorite activity is playing with my grand-daughters!

When the girls can't play with their amazing grandmother, my interests are reading and writing, yay! I started reading at a young age with the Nancy Drew mysteries and have continued to be an avid reader my whole life. My favorite reading material is romance, but occasionally if other stories creep into my to-be-read pile, I don't kick them out.

Some of the strange jobs I have held are a carnation grower's worker, a trap club puller, a pizza hut waitress, a software engineer, an international trainer, and a business program manager. I took welding, drafting and upholstery in high school, a long time ago, when girls didn't take those classes, so I have an eclectic bunch of knowledge and experience.

And for something really unusual… I once had a raccoon as a pet.

Join with me as I tell my stories, weaving real tidbits from my life in with imaginary ones. You'll have to guess which is which. It will be a hoot!